I0761823

SCALES AND SENSIBILITY

STEPHANIE BURGIS

FIVE FATHOMS PRESS

For Tricia and Tiffany, who never let me forget this story. Thank you! - xo

NOTE TO READERS

This book uses British rather than American spellings...as its characters would consider only proper. ;)

CHAPTER 1

It was a truth universally acknowledged that any young lady without a dragon was doomed to social failure. But it was becoming increasingly obvious to everyone in Hathergill Hall that for Penelope Hathergill, actually having a dragon would *guarantee* disaster.

"Mother!" Penelope's piercing shriek rattled the glass in the chandelier above her. "He's done it again!"

"Oh, dear..." Lady Hathergill closed her eyes and sank back in her chair, waving a limp handkerchief in the general direction of her niece. "Do see to that, won't you, Elinor?"

"Yes, Aunt." Sighing, Elinor folded the mending she'd been working on and rose to help her cousin.

It was a servant's job to clean most messes, but the maids had mutinied several days earlier, and the dour housekeeper, Mrs. Braithwaite—who intimidated even Penelope—

had announced that she, too, would give her notice if any of her girls were asked to touch 'that foul creature's mess' again.

And as Penelope herself could never be expected to clean up any of the messes that she caused...

Well, that left Elinor. As usual.

"Please stand still, Penelope," she said, as she wiped at her cousin's back with a handkerchief. "If you want me to get it all off—"

"It's disgusting!" Penelope wriggled impatiently and glared at the brightly-coloured dragon perched on her shoulder. "And it's all your fault. Horrid creature!" With a sudden, impatient gesture she reached up and pushed him off her shoulder.

"Rawk!" His tiny, cobalt-blue wings fluttered uselessly; he tumbled snout over tail, heading straight for the ground.

"Penelope!" Elinor dropped her slime-covered handkerchief and dived for the falling dragon. She grabbed him just in time and gathered him up to her chest, stroking his hot skin consolingly. "What were you thinking? You know his wings were clipped by the breeder. He could have been hurt!"

"He deserves it." Penelope crossed her arms and glared down at him. "He knows perfectly well what he's doing, I can tell. Just before he let it out this time, I heard him laugh out loud."

It hadn't been a laugh; that chortling sound was a sign of fear in dragons. Elinor had read about it when she'd first learned that the family was buying a dragon for Penelope's social début.

But she bit her lip to hold back the angry remark that wanted to escape. There was only so much that a poor relation was allowed to say in this household, especially when it came to her cousin Penelope...and if she let Penelope see the look on her face right now, she would be in real trouble. So instead, she looked down at the dragon who was shivering in her arms.

From the tip of his snout to the end of his tail, Sir Jessamyn Carnavoran Artos was only two feet long, and when he curled up like this against her, he formed a big ball of warmth that felt nearly the same as her old tomcat back home. But his worried golden eyes blinked up at her from a face that glittered such a deep blue and green, his scales looked like precious jewels.

Given her choice of dragon, Penelope had of course chosen the prettiest one she had seen...not the cleverest nor the calmest, which would have been far more useful. It would take a dragon with nerves of pure steel to ride calmly on Penelope's slim shoulder as she alternately shrieked with laughter or with fury and smacked him every time he accidentally slid an inch or let his claws dig into her skin. Elinor's jaw clenched at the thought of it.

If either of Elinor's younger sisters had been there, matters would have gone very differently. Rose would have stood nose-to-nose with Penelope and shrieked directly back at her about her intolerable cruelty to an innocent beast;

Harriet would have come up with a mathematically perfect plan to exact revenge.

When their parents had died, though, one year earlier, a flurry of panicked letter-writing had erupted in the extended family. After six months of heated wrangling about whose responsibility they really were, the three Tregarth girls had been scattered to the far corners of Britain to join different sets of relatives. Family or not, no one was willing to take on all three sisters at once.

So that left only Elinor to face their cousin Penelope now, alone and all-too-miserably aware of the practicalities of the situation...as always. It was her lifelong curse.

Rose and Harry wouldn't have let practicalities hold them back; Rose was too romantic and high-minded to care, and as for Harry—well, Elinor was certain that anyone who spent her life mastering higher mathematics simply for her own amusement was incapable of feeling intimidated by Penelope.

Elinor, though, couldn't stop thinking about exactly what would happen if she let loose all the outrage that had been building inside her for the last six months. As hard as she tried, she couldn't imagine any good result.

All that she could imagine was the mundane reality of disaster: she would be tossed out of Hathergill Hall in disgrace, leaving no one who even tried to moderate Penelope's behavior to the servants, the poor little dragon, or anyone else who ever got in her cousin's way. And with less than five shillings in Elinor's purse—Uncle John, of course, saw no need to give her an allowance, as she was already living off his generosity—leaving Hathergill Hall wouldn't bring her freedom.

It would only mean utter ruin.

So she took a deep breath and unclenched her jaw. She set Sir Jessamyn gently down onto the ballroom floor and said, as quietly and as humbly as possible, "Perhaps you would like to take a rest, Penelope. Your nerves—"

"A rest? A *rest*?!" Penelope's voice built up in volume until Elinor's ears rang and Sir Jessamyn scuttled behind her legs, wrapping his tail tightly around her ankles. "You want me to take a rest *now*, when I am only six days away from making my social début with a dragon who cannot even contain himself in company?"

Be humble, Elinor told herself. *Be calm*. "Perhaps, if you could try to control your temper just a bit while he is riding on your shoulder—"

"Control my temper?" Penelope stared at Elinor with as much outraged disbelief as if her cousin had claimed to see a single spot on Penelope's perfect skin. "Are you actually claiming this dragon's malfunctions are *my fault*?"

"I'm sure that isn't what your cousin meant, dearest." Lady Hathergill must have recognized the warning signs of a true Penelope tantrum; she opened her eyes and put herself to the almost-unheard-of trouble of straightening in her seat. "No one would ever think of criticizing you, my love."

I would, Elinor thought. But she forced herself to nod submissively, lowering her eyes.

It wasn't enough.

"After everything I've been through..." Penelope's voice thickened with oncoming tears; her blue eyes glistened. "After all the trials I've been forced to put up with..."

The tears were real, Elinor knew. That was the worst part of life with her cousin. Penelope sincerely believed that she was oppressed by terrible injustice at every turn.

"Losing the best seamstress in Kent, just before I could come out in Society—"

"Mrs. Hunt was terribly irresponsible, dear, we understand." Lady Hathergill's voice had flattened with what Elinor hoped was a lack of conviction, but it might just as easily have been mere exhaustion. "She should certainly have waited until after your début to give up her business."

"Penelope, you must remember that her leg was badly broken," said Elinor. "The physician did tell her she needed rest."

"She could still use her hands perfectly well!" Penelope glared at Elinor. "No, that was only an excuse. The truth is, she simply didn't care about my début. She didn't even care that I would have to appear at my very first ball looking like an ugly, fashion-blind country bumpkin!"

"Now, dear..." Lady Hathergill was already sinking inexorably back into her chair. It certainly wasn't the first time that everyone in Hathergill Hall had heard the full litany of Penelope's misfortunes.

"And that wasn't even the worst of it." Tears were streaming down Penelope's pink cheeks now, making her look like an angry china shepherdess. "First Papa wouldn't let me début in London..."

...*Until September*, Elinor finished silently. She wasn't rash enough to remind Penelope out loud that her tragically denied London visit had only been postponed until the Little Season officially began in one month's time...or that her début ball at Hathergill Hall next week was designed to be the largest, most impressive, and by far the most expensive event ever to be hosted in the county.

...Or, for that matter, that Elinor's own social début, planned for her eighteenth birthday twelve months ago, would never happen at all.

"Then Mrs. De Lacey blatantly snubbed us, despite all of Mama's promises..."

Lady Hathergill's eyes fluttered shut, avoiding confrontation as usual. It was up to Elinor to draw a deep breath and say, as calmly and as reasonably as she could, "The only reason Mrs. De Lacey had to cancel her visit was that she had a putrid sore throat. That could hardly be deemed an insult to anyone, surely."

"A putrid sore throat? In August? Who takes ill in August? No, she obviously invented it as an excuse not to come. And it's all Mama's fault for arguing with her all those years ago, Papa said so." Penelope whirled to face her somnolent mother accusingly. "How could you have been so stupid as to offend her? Didn't you even think of how important she was to become?"

The real question, as far as Elinor was concerned, was:

how had Lady Hathergill ever managed to argue with anybody? From the moment Elinor had first entered Hathergill Hall six months ago, she had never once seen her aunt contradict either her daughter or her husband, no matter how unreasonable either of them became. It was as if she had given up on even possessing any real opinions of her own.

It was utterly maddening—especially when compared to Elinor's own mother, Lady Hathergill's younger sister, whose fierce, protective fire still burned like a beacon in Elinor's memory.

But Penelope was still ranting. "What is the use of Mama having an old friend at the pinnacle of London fashion if she won't even attend my début ball?"

Elinor gritted her teeth. "I'm sure you'll meet Mrs. De Lacey in September, and"—*be humble, be submissive*—"you may impress her then."

After all, Mrs. De Lacey was in the gossip columns of the national newspapers nearly every week with some witty new saying, radical house redesign, or astonishing new purchase that had set all the *ton* alight. The balls and soirées that she hostessed were discussed all across the length and breadth of Britain, and her husband's early death had left her one of the wealthiest widows in the country. Even her invention of a scandalous new private club for women, which had been preached against in outraged pulpits across the nation, had only led to even more public invitations from the smitten royal family.

In other words, Mrs. De Lacey never let anything or anyone stop her from doing what she wanted. That meant that she and Elinor couldn't have been more different—so why should they agree on Penelope?

"And then Papa fobbed me off with this worthless excuse for a *non-functioning dragon*!" Penelope pointed at Sir Jessamyn with a trembling finger. His glittering green ears flattened in panic against his head. His tail tightened around Elinor's ankles until she teetered on her feet and had to hold out her arms to keep her balance.

"Penelope, please," she said, "if you could just try to be a little more patient with him—"

"You're doing it again!" Penelope stared at her. "Listen to her, Mama! She really is pretending that it's all my fault!"

"I only meant—" Elinor began.

"After everything I've done for you!" Penelope choked on a sob. "How could you, Elinor?"

Elinor stared at her cousin open-mouthed. She couldn't even think of a response.

"*I* allowed Mama and Papa to take you in, despite all the horrid inconvenience. I allowed one of my maids to do your hair! I even told my friends it wasn't kind to mock you for being so grim and sour-faced all the time. I told them you couldn't help being plain and tedious. And Mama promised me—she promised!—that you would give me so much help with my début that it would all be worth it in the end."

Elinor swallowed. Her mouth felt dry. There was a distant ringing in her ears, like the whistle of a steam engine charging towards her, something loud and angry and dangerous that she had never, ever given into before.

Penelope didn't seem to hear it.

"I even let you be fitted for new gowns from *my* seamstress! Mama asked if I would mind it too terribly, but I said no, because I was tired of you looking like a crow all the time in all those terrible black gowns."

Elinor heard her own voice as if it came from very far away, beyond the ringing in her ears. "Those black gowns were mourning dress, Penelope. For my year of mourning. For my *parents*."

"Well, I don't know why you bothered to change into brighter clothing once the year was up," Penelope said. "It's all wasted on you anyway—it's not as if you're ever going to find a husband, are you? You're not even a Hathergill, only a poor relation who couldn't find anyone else to take you on. Your only *purpose* is to help me with my début, and instead you're always nittering and moaning at me, 'but Penelope' this and 'but Penelope' that. I could go mad from the endless sound of your voice. Faugh!"

She narrowed her eyes and pointed at the dragon who had wound himself around Elinor's ankles. "You're exactly the same as him. Non-functional!"

Sir Jessamyn let out a low, trilling chuckle of fear.

...And the steam engine finally arrived.

"That is it." Elinor's ears were ringing so loudly now that she could barely hear her own voice even as it rose to a yell so dangerous and war-like, she would never have suspected herself capable of creating such a sound. "That. Is. *It*!"

"What? What? I beg your pardon?" Lady Hathergill's head jerked up as she woke from her snooze. "Did someone say it was time for tea? Penelope?"

Penelope had scooted back a step at Elinor's yell, but her shoulders stiffened at the sound of her mother's voice. "It is *not* time for tea, Mama," she said. "It is time for someone to explain to my cousin exactly what her place is in this household, for once and for all!"

"Thank you, Penelope," Elinor said. "But actually, there isn't the slightest need for that."

She knelt down and scooped up Sir Jessamyn with unaccustomed, fluid grace. With the steam engine's whistle still ringing in her ears, she could have easily smashed through the windows of the elegant drawing room or picked up the piano in the corner and thrown it straight at her cousin's pretty blonde head. It posed no difficulty at all to scoop up one trembling, chuckling dragon and set him securely on her shoulder.

"You have made yourself perfectly clear," said Elinor. "So I shall do you the favor of removing both my non-functioning self and your non-functioning dragon from your life. Unlike you, this dragon is not a wild animal, so *he,* at least, deserves some courtesy!"

"Ohhh!" Penelope shrieked. "Ohhh! *Mother*, did you hear what she just said to me?!"

"Oh, dear," Lady Hathergill moaned, and put one hand over her eyes.

Perched on Elinor's shoulder, Sir Jessamyn let out one last chuckle of terror...and through her ringing ears and haze of fury, Elinor finally remembered what that sound always signified when it came from this particular dragon.

"Oh, no," she breathed. Hastily, she began to stroke his back. "Please, Sir Jessamyn—please don't, not now—"

But she was too late.

Hot, steaming dragon slime exploded down the back of her gown, soaking through to her skin as Penelope's shrieks of outrage rattled the chandelier overhead.

It wasn't quite the exit that Elinor had hoped for, but she held her chin high as she marched out of the room, with Sir Jessamyn shivering on her shoulder and her wet, slimy skirts sticking to her legs at every step.

CHAPTER 2

The road to Elinor's personal ruin began just outside Hathergill Hall.

Unfortunately, she had to pack first.

It would have been infinitely more satisfying to march directly from the drawing room to the front door without looking back. But even in the grip of the most towering rage she had ever experienced, Elinor found that she was incapable of abandoning practicality so entirely.

All of her clean clothing was still folded neatly in her bedroom, as were her precious letters from her sisters...and, of course, her four shillings and sixpence. If she abandoned them, she would have nothing at all.

Unfortunately, by the time she finished folding her clothes into her valise and slipped her few coins into her reticule, her lovely, warm haze of fury began to slip away. She tried hard to cling to it, but it was too late. Like it or not, her mind had begun to work again.

And the practical, sensible conclusions that it drew, when it looked back at the last half hour...

Elinor's fingers trembled uncontrollably as she set the last of Harry's letters into the valise. She drew a deep, gasping breath. It sounded like a death rattle.

Sir Jessamyn was sitting on her bed—or rather, what had been her bed, for the last six months—gazing up at her with inquisitive golden eyes. She put out one trembling hand to touch the hot, smooth scales on his head.

"Oh, Sir Jessamyn," she whispered. "What have I done?"

Downstairs, she heard the all-too-familiar sound of Penelope's voice rising in a furious lecture. It was far closer than it had been the last time she'd heard it; her cousin must have left the drawing room by now. From the sounds of it, she was near the front door—probably demanding that the poor footmen apprehend Sir Jessamyn, and quite possibly Elinor, too, depending on exactly how angry she was and how much revenge she planned to exact once her father returned.

Elinor looked at Sir Jessamyn, and he looked back at her. "I think we'd better take the servants' stairs," she said. "Don't you?"

They left through the tradesmen's entrance at the back of the house. It felt horribly like skulking away in defeat, but it was definitely the practical thing to do. Penelope didn't care to keep her toys once she had lost interest in them...but she never wanted anyone else to have them.

Elinor didn't like to think what would have happened to the little dragon the first time he lost control on Penelope's shoulder during a society ball.

"At least there's one consolation, Sir Jessamyn," she said, as she set off down the long and dusty road that led through the fields and away from Hathergill Hall. "You'll never have to enter Society, now."

Sir Jessamyn chirped softly and rested his small, warm head against her hair. The weight of him on her shoulder felt oddly reassuring. As she felt his hot breath brush against her ear, the tight band of panic around Elinor's chest finally began to loosen its grip, until she could breathe properly again.

It was true that Elinor had lost her parents to death and her sisters to the far ends of Britain. Even if she could afford the travel costs to reach either Rose or Harry, it would be a wasted trip; their host relatives had made it perfectly clear that each of them could cope with one Tregarth girl and no more.

But at least she wasn't alone anymore.

"The question is, Sir Jessamyn, what are we to do?"

Sir Jessamyn, unsurprisingly, refrained from comment. So it was left to Elinor to think for both of them as she walked down the endless road, kicking up dust with every step.

It was an ordinary, bumpy and narrow country road much like the ones back home, lined by a wall of thick hedgerows on one side and a murky, water-filled ditch on the other, dug to carry away the run-off from the farm fields. The sun was still shining overhead quite as cheerfully as if she hadn't tossed away her entire future. As she walked along, she could almost believe that she was safely home again, on her way back to her younger sisters and their parents after a long morning's walk for pleasure.

Almost...but not quite. Two crows perched on top of the hedgerow ahead; when their beady eyes alighted on Elinor and her companion, the bigger one let out a hoarse caw, and Sir Jessamyn stiffened nervously, his long, curving claws clenching tightly around Elinor's shoulder.

"Shh." Elinor reached up a hand to stroke him. "Shh. I won't let anyone hurt you ever again, I promise."

The crows took off in a flutter of black wings, beating their way into the sky. As Elinor watched them fly away, she heard her cousin's words again. *"I was tired of you looking like a crow all the time..."*

Her fingers clenched instinctively. Sir Jessamyn made a sound of protest.

"Oh, I am sorry! Poor Sir Jessamyn." Elinor loosened her grip on him and leaned her head against his apologetically. "I'm not doing very well so far, am I? But I will find a safe home for both of us. Somehow."

Harry would have thought of some bizarre but brilliant scheme by now, she was certain. It was due to Harry's inventiveness, combined with Elinor's stubborn practicality and Rose's overflowing charm, that the three girls had survived six months of abject penury—and managed to cling to the safety of their father's vicarage, despite all of the parish council's attempts to reclaim it—before their relatives had finally claimed them.

But Harry wasn't here now. And Elinor...

Crows, she thought, and sighed. Perhaps Penelope had been right about her. Elinor certainly couldn't dream of winning a wealthy husband to rescue her from poverty now; she had neither the looks nor the charm for that fantasy, and besides, she was sensible enough to know that wealthy gentlemen weren't naturally prone to marrying penniless girls. In fact, she was lucky not to be as startlingly beautiful as her sister Rose, right now; a beautiful girl on her own, without any protection, would be in serious danger from any gentlemen she met.

But being plain and tedious—yes, even crow-like—could have some benefits. One of her aunt's friends had complained again and again over the past few months of the difficulty of finding any governesses for her younger children who wouldn't attract her horrible older sons' attentions. Why shouldn't Elinor be the answer to that sort of plea?

She might not be as clever as Harry, but she was perfectly adept at sums and at French, she had read voraciously throughout her life, and now, she had one more dazzling qualification. A mere housemaid might not be allowed to bring her own dragon into a house, but a *governess* could claim a dragon of her own as a real advantage: she could teach her wealthy students how to properly handle Society's most fashionable new accessory.

It was the perfect solution for both of them.

Elinor was so pleased that she stopped walking to grin at Sir Jessamyn on her shoulder. "There!" she said. "I *have* thought of something. We will be all right, after all!"

And then four snorting carriage horses swept up around the curve of the road behind her and the leader's shoulder knocked her off her feet, straight into the watery ditch.

IF THERE WAS anything worse for a lady of dignity than being sent head-first into a ditch, it was, of course, being *witnessed* flying head-first into a ditch. Even as Elinor jerked her head up out of the dirty water, panting and spitting out dark-coloured liquid that tasted appallingly like manure, she was horrified to hear the carriage pulling to a halt close by with a jangle of reins and a clatter of horses' hooves. Worse yet, she heard a man's worried voice—and then the unmistakable thump of feet landing on the ground.

She groaned, and wished she *couldn't* glimpse her own reflection in the murky water.

Her bonnet had come off in her fall, and at least half of her hair pins had escaped. Her face and gown were both hopelessly streaked with mud—not to mention her arms, which were still planted elbow-deep in the disgusting water, a foot or so beneath the road, while the lower half of her body clung tenaciously to the dirt above. Her skirts had thereby slid well above her ankles, and the only way she could imagine to return to safety would be to wriggle backwards ignominiously, like a worm.

If only this ditch were a few helpful feet deeper, Elinor would have let herself fall all the rest of the way in so that she could swim away from the social embarrassment.

The little dragon, who had hopped off her shoulder just in time, nosed anxiously at her exposed ankles, squeaking.

"It's all right, Sir Jessamyn." Elinor sighed and braced herself to start wriggling. After the last six months with Penelope, she ought to have been hardened to humiliation. "I'll just—oh!" Her voice came out as a squeak of surprise as two big, warm hands closed with shocking intimacy around her waist.

"I do beg your pardon." It was the same voice she'd heard calling out directions to the coachman. Now the speaker lifted her up and set her on her feet with apparent ease, while Sir Jessamyn skittered back nervously. The moment that Elinor's feet touched the ground, the hands that held her dropped away, and the man behind her cleared his throat. "I didn't mean to presume, but it seemed the only way to save you."

Elinor turned around...and had to stifle a groan of pure horror.

The gentleman who'd saved her was tall and broad-shouldered and only a few years older than her, with rumpled brown hair, warm hazel eyes, and a ruefully appealing smile. Even worse, he was dressed in the sort of close-fitting, forest-green coat and embroidered silver waistcoat that positively shrieked of money and taste—just like the elegant traveling carriage that had pulled up behind him.

Of course he was a romantic ideal come to life! What else could possibly make this moment more painful?

In any one of the sentimental novels that Rose had always devoured and that Elinor had always mocked, this would have been precisely the moment when the wealthy hero fell head over heels in love with the innocent young heroine and swept her away to a life of ease and romance as his bride...barring, of course, all the necessary misadventures with wicked cousins and leering highwaymen along the way.

Rose would have swooned over a scene like that.

Most of Elinor's muddy, wet hair was plastered across her neck or pasted to the shoulders of her ruined gown. One long, slimy hank hung over her right eye and directly across her mouth. She blew it away from her face in a sigh and saw her rescuer's lips twitch before he raised one hand to politely shield his expression.

Somehow, she didn't think he was about to sweep her off her feet into a life of romantic luxury.

"Thank you," she said stiffly, and stepped away from him. Her elbows, shoulder, and back felt like one big bruise; her dignity was far more battered. She turned painfully to pick up her valise, which had fallen to the ground a few feet away.

"I appreciate your help, sir, but I won't delay you any...*oh*," she breathed, staring at her own bare wrist. "Oh, *no*."

This time, her voice didn't squeak. It dropped a full octave.

Despair did that, it seemed. Elinor had finally noticed what she should have realised immediately: her reticule was missing.

It had been hanging around her wrist before the accident. Now, her wrist wasn't the only thing that was bare. So was the ground around her.

She lunged back towards the watery ditch and dropped to her knees in the dirt, heedless of any further damage to her gown.

"What is it?" said the man behind her. "What's amiss?" And then, as she leaned over to plunge her hand into the water, "Be careful! You'll fall back in."

Elinor ignored him. All of her attention was fixed on the muddy water below. She couldn't even see through the muck that filled it. She leaned further and further forward, swiping her hand desperately through it, until...

"*There*!" She finally felt it under her fingers: a plain cotton bag, squidged into a muddy ball.

"Wait!" Her rescuer grabbed her waist again just in time, as she began to slide back over the edge into the ditch. "For heaven's sake. Whatever it is you're hunting for, it can't be worth the risk."

"Oh, yes, it can!" Elinor straightened triumphantly,

holding the reticule high. "It's..." Her mouth dropped open. She finished, blank with shock: "It's empty."

The little reticule had come open in the ditch.

She stared at it. Her vision blurred.

Four shillings and sixpence, carefully saved over so many months...

Gone.

CHAPTER 3

Elinor had resolutely refrained from swooning, shrieking, or giving in to any other romantic self-indulgences across the last year of her life. But as she looked at the empty reticule in her hand now, she felt the insides of her head begin to spin in a decidedly ominous fashion.

"I say," said the man behind her. "Are you quite well? You weren't carrying too much of your money in that little bag, were you?"

"Everything I had." Elinor's lips felt numb. Little spots began to dance before her eyes.

"Hawkins!" Another man's voice called out from the open door of the carriage. "You won't believe this, but I've just found the most astonishing fallacy in De Groot's thesis. You'll laugh when you hear what he says about wingtips!"

She really must be losing consciousness, Elinor thought muzzily. She hadn't understood a word of what he'd said.

The man behind her sighed and stood up. "Look here, I think you'd better come with us."

"I beg your pardon!" Abruptly regaining her wits, Elinor scooted away from him and scrambled to her feet, while Sir Jessamyn chuckled ominously on the ground beside her. "I've thanked you for your help, sir, but—"

"Oh, yes, we have been terribly helpful, haven't we? Especially knocking you into the ditch in the first place, to lose you all your savings." He gave her a lopsided, self-mocking grin. "I can only imagine just how grateful you must be feeling right now."

"Regardless..." Elinor stiffened her shoulders and backed away. That grin was dangerous. It was exactly the sort of thing that persuaded defenceless young women to get into strange gentlemen's carriages, which marked the beginning of every warning story she had ever heard. "I don't require any more assistance, so—"

"Don't be absurd. You haven't any money, remember? Would you really rather sleep in a hedgerow tonight than allow my friend to give you supper and put you up at the local inn for a night as an apology?"

"Your friend?" Elinor frowned.

"It's his carriage, not mine. But he couldn't get out, because he was too busy. To tell you the truth..." Her rescuer ran one hand through his hair, rumpling it even more. "I don't honestly think he even noticed the collision. Wingtips, you see. It's a bit of an obsession."

"Wing tips?" Elinor echoed faintly. She didn't feel like swooning anymore—at least, she didn't think so—but his words still made no sense.

"You'll understand when you meet him," said her rescuer. "Come. I swear you'll be safe and unharmed by either of us. And you can hardly deny your dragon a meal, can you?"

"Oh, dear." Elinor looked down at Sir Jessamyn, who had curled into the tiniest possible ball behind her feet. "I suppose..." She swallowed.

Every ounce of propriety and common sense was telling her not to accept his offer. Unlike her sister Rose, Elinor had never believed that Fate would ever sweep in to rescue her. Anything that looked like a stroke of luck from the blue was far more likely to be an appallingly bad idea.

But her rescuer was right. She could not deny Sir Jessamyn food. So what choice did she have?

"Here, I'll carry your dragon for you," her rescuer said. "Pretty little fellow, isn't he? I've seen a few in London, but none quite so glittery as this one." He scooped up Sir Jessamyn easily and tickled him under his cobalt-blue chin. "I say, he's in a good mood, isn't he? He's actually laughing at me."

"What?" Elinor had been reaching for her valise, but now she straightened abruptly. "I think you'd better—oh, Sir *Jessamyn*!"

It was too late.

Her rescuer looked down at his slime-covered silver waistcoat for a long moment. Elinor tensed. “It wasn’t his fault!” she said. “You see, when he’s frightened—”

“Yes,” said her rescuer, gazing at his ruined waistcoat. “I can see, actually.” Then he looked up, met her eyes, and began to laugh as he adjusted the little dragon in his arms.

“Well,” he said. “Let’s hope that inn is close by, eh? Because—forgive me for saying this, but—you’re not the only one who could do with a bath.”

WITH SIR JESSAMYN safely back in her own keeping, Elinor opened the door of the carriage to find that the inside had been as elegantly designed as the exterior...or at least, the top half had been. She assumed that the same must have been true for the rest, too, but it was rather more difficult to tell. Both of the seats and the footwell in-between were completely filled with books and scattered sheets of paper. Even the fair-haired gentleman who sat inside the carriage, frowning down at a thin pamphlet with total absorption, was covered with massive flurries of books and papers from his knees up to his waist, as if the pages were slowly rising up to devour him.

She gaped at him from the doorway as even more pages fluttered past her ankles to fall onto the ground like leaves.

“Just tip some more into the footwell to make yourself a

space to sit," said the man behind her. "Trust me, it's the only way."

"Well...if you're quite certain it won't be a problem..." She edged inside, shuffling through calf-high piles of paper as carefully as she could. Holding Sir Jessamyn in one arm, she pushed aside just enough books to glimpse a dark green leather cushion underneath. While the other gentleman remained absorbed in his reading, she perched on the cleared edge of the seat, horribly aware of the mud that coated her gown and trying desperately not to touch anything.

It was a doomed attempt. There were more books in this carriage than she'd seen in all of Hathergill Hall.

Her rescuer pulled the carriage door closed behind him and swept a broad swathe of books off the seat across from her. It was only as he sat down that his friend finally seemed to notice his presence.

"Oh, are you here again, Hawkins? I have to tell you, De Groot—"

"Tell me later, old man." Mr. Hawkins rapped the roof of the carriage, and it rolled into motion. "We have company."

"We do?" The owner of the carriage peered up over his spectacles and blinked with visible surprise when his gaze passed over Elinor and Sir Jessamyn, seated directly across from him. "I say. What a perfectly marvellous specimen of *dracus domesticus*. Look at those ear ridges!" He leaned forward, dislodging a stack of paper from his lap and sending it cascading across Elinor's feet.

Sir Jessamyn's ears flattened against his head, but—much to Elinor's relief—he didn't chuckle, even when the man's silver-rimmed spectacles nearly brushed his head. Instead, he made a strange, clicking sound in the back of his throat, and his eyelids fluttered half-closed. He tilted his head back to expose his glittering, blue-and-green neck.

For heaven's sake, Elinor thought. Sir Jessamyn was preening. The little dragon looked positively coy.

"Beautiful," murmured his inspector, in a reverential tone. "Beautiful, beautiful. Just look at that arch! Now, if De Groot thinks he can explain *that* with medieval symbolism —!" He waved his pamphlet threateningly at his friend, with such vehemence that Sir Jessamyn scuttled back and pressed himself into Elinor's stomach.

Mr. Hawkins, on the other hand, wore a look of resignation. "I dare say," he said. "But the point remains." He coughed meaningfully. "Perhaps you may have noticed another occupant of your carriage, Aubrey? One without any ear ridges?"

"Eh?" Mr. Aubrey blinked at his friend. "Another occupant, you say?"

"Erm..." Mr. Hawkins tilted his head in Elinor's direction.

"Oh! Oh, I see. Yes. Quite. Miss—that is, Miss..." He frowned. "I beg your pardon, but I can't quite remember..."

"That," said Mr. Hawkins, "is because you haven't been introduced. Your horses knocked her over, not ten minutes ago, and sent her into the ditch. That is why she is in such disarray."

"I say!" Mr. Aubrey lowered his pamphlet, looking horrified. "I do beg your pardon, Miss...I'm afraid I don't recall your name. But we knew you already because...?"

"We didn't," said his friend patiently, "but now we do. She lost all of her money in the ditch when your horses knocked her over, so you're going to put her up at the local inn tonight and pay for her to eat a bang-up supper as apology."

"I am?" Mr. Aubrey's frown deepened into a scowl.

Heat crept through Elinor's cheeks. She pulled Sir Jessamyn closer to her chest. "If you would rather not, sir—"

"Oh, no," said Mr. Aubrey. "If we have inconvenienced you, we must make up for it, certainly. I was only trying to remember when we had decided all of this." He sighed. "I'm afraid the discussion has quite escaped my memory. How terribly embarrassing."

"No need to be embarrassed, my dear chap." Mr. Hawkins patted his shoulder. "This is the first you've heard of it. I was the one who made the decision."

"Aha!" The frown vanished; Mr. Aubrey beamed at Elinor, his angular face lighting up. "That's quite all right, then. It is a pleasure to meet you and your dragon, Miss—?"

"Tregarth," she said, and let out the breath that she'd been holding. "Elinor Tregarth. And this is Sir Jessamyn Carnavoran Artos."

"A pleasure." Mr. Aubrey's words were fervent as he tipped his head to one side, examining Sir Jessamyn again from a different angle. The spectacles slid slowly but inevitably along his perfectly straight nose as he inquired,

"How old *is* Sir Jessamyn, precisely? Have you noticed any peculiarities about him?"

"We still haven't finished our introductions." Mr. Hawkins sighed. "Miss Tregarth..." He sketched a half-bow from his seat, dislodging more books. "Benedict Hawkins, at your service. And this dragon-mad fellow is Cornelius Aubrey. One of Cambridge's finest, you understand, but without much experience in the non-scholarly world."

"I...see." Elinor looked at Mr. Aubrey, trying to gauge his age. Surely he couldn't be much more than one-and-twenty? "Are you a student at Cambridge, sir?"

"A student?" He lifted Sir Jessamyn's tail, peering closely at the scales underneath. "No, no. I study, only."

"Aubrey took a First at Cambridge at sixteen," Mr. Hawkins explained, "and never left. He's a genius, you see."

"Mm." Mr. Aubrey was tracing the under-scales with one long finger now, while Sir Jessamyn watched him nervously.

Yawning, Mr. Hawkins leaned back in his seat and crossed his trouser-clad legs. They brushed against Elinor's gown on the way, inciting quite a disconcerting sensation, but he shifted swiftly to grant her more space in the crowded footwell. "I do apologise, Miss Tregarth, for our tight quarters. Aubrey's on a visit now to one of his mad colleagues in Wales, you see, and was kind enough to give me a lift along the way."

"Wales!" Elinor's chest tightened with longing; for a moment, excitement pushed her to lean forward, drawing a breath. Her sister Rose was in Wales. Perhaps—?

But no. She could hardly beg a ride so far across the country with two strange gentlemen, no matter how kind and harmless they both seemed...and even if she did, Rose still wouldn't be allowed to take her in. There was no use in even asking the question.

Elinor sighed as she sat back and tried to remember her manners, despite the highly irregular situation. With her muddy hair drying stickily against her skin, it was uncomfortably challenging simply to keep herself from scratching her chest in public, much less to make any polite conversation. Worse yet, every time the carriage took a turn, her legs bumped unstoppably against those of either Mr. Hawkins or Mr. Aubrey. Thank goodness, Mr. Aubrey paid no attention to the contact, and Mr. Hawkins looked perfectly comfortable even with the noxious smell of his dragon-slimed waistcoat rising up to fill the carriage.

He really was unnervingly handsome. She'd never in her life sat in such close proximity to even one attractive gentleman, much less two in the same carriage—and as much as she reproved herself for her forwardness, she couldn't stop sliding discreet glances at Mr. Hawkins's broad shoulders, which were outlined far too well by his fashionable coat. His rumpled brown hair fell haphazardly across his brow, just begging for her to reach over and stroke it back into place...

No! She jerked her eyes away and kept her wayward hands firmly clasped around her dragon. Common sense was more than enough to inform her that the wealthy and too-appealing Mr. Hawkins was well beyond her reach.

Still, even after she forced herself to lower her gaze to the dragon in her lap, her whole body prickled with awareness at every carriage turn that brought the two of them together.

If she didn't distract herself soon, she might begin to drool, and that really would be unacceptable. So she forced herself to begin, with an air of polite interest, "How much further is your journey to—?"

"Here we are!" As the carriage pulled to a halt in front of the local inn, Mr. Hawkins straightened and jogged his friend's elbow. "Forget the dragon just for the moment, old man. There'll be plenty of time to inspect him over supper."

"I beg your pardon?" Elinor stared at him. "I thought you two were going to Wales and only leaving me here!"

"Oh, Aubrey is, but I'm not. I'll be staying in the area for quite some time," said Mr. Hawkins. "We're just sharing one last evening of leisure tonight before Aubrey goes on to Wales and I embark upon my great matrimonial adventure."

"Your great..." Elinor blinked. "Oh, you're betrothed?" *Wanton, Elinor!* How could she have allowed herself to ogle a betrothed man's shoulders? Her skin burned with the shame of it.

"Oh, no, I haven't even met the lady yet—and she's never heard of me." He opened the door and leaped to the ground, ignoring the folded carriage steps. "Come, let me assist you." He held out his arms. "It was enormously helpful to meet you today, actually. As a local yourself, you can advise me on my best matrimonial strategy over supper—you must have met the lady I'm meant to woo, if you've spent any time in this area."

"I must?" Elinor repeated. A hideous presentiment began to dawn inside her even as she leaned inevitably forward towards Benedict Hawkins's broad chest.

She had *known* this couldn't be as easy as it seemed, hadn't she? She had certainly known better than to ever step into a strange gentleman's carriage. And yet...

Mr. Hawkins closed his strong arms around her and swung her easily to the ground, sending a burst of entirely inappropriate heat throughout her mud-covered body. "Oh, you must at least have heard of her. Her father is a landowner of renown in this county, I've been told. And she is said to be unforgettable!"

He stepped back the moment that her feet touched the ground, lowering his arms with perfect courtesy to his sides and grinning his lopsided grin down at her. Even his noxiously slimed waistcoat couldn't make him look unappealing.

It was most unjust and disagreeable.

"Do tell me." Elinor swallowed. "What is her name?"

There *were* several young ladies in the neighborhood, after all. Only the cruellest, most unjust hand of Fate could possibly—

"Penelope Hathergill," said her rescuer. "*Have* you met? Is she as beautiful as they say?"

Elinor closed her eyes against his smile.

Fate was never on her side.

CHAPTER 4

There was only one stroke of luck for which Elinor could be thankful that evening as she stepped into the private room that had been reserved for their supper, carrying an alert and curious Sir Jessamyn on her shoulder.

She hadn't recognized any of the men in the crowded front room of The Lion's Head when she, Mr. Hawkins, and Mr. Aubrey had first arrived...which meant that the Singhs, who owned the bustling inn, had cheerfully accepted her identity as Mr. Hawkins's sister, rather than Sir John Hathergill's runaway niece.

Unfortunately, she still couldn't quite escape her relatives.

"So," Mr. Hawkins said, as he held out a chair for her at the weathered old wooden dining table, "you were remarkably cagey in our earlier conversation. Do I take it that you *are* acquainted with my future fiancée, Miss Tregarth?"

"Ah..." Elinor glanced around the room as she sat, hunting for inspiration.

Mr. Aubrey was immersed in a thick book, cheerfully oblivious to her entrance and their conversation; he had already scattered two sheets of scribbled-upon notepaper across his rice-covered supper plate and was rapidly jotting down notes on a third sheet now with a quill pen that spattered, spreading spots of black ink. A second book sat ready at his elbow, near the three thick candles that lit his studies.

A crystal goblet of wine on the oak sideboard behind him glinted darkly in the fading light from the narrow, grated windows, while two different curries—one chicken and one lentil—steamed pleasant clouds of spice into the air and large paintings of mountain scenes hung, shadowed, about the room.

As Elinor couldn't think of any way to step into any of those paintings to escape the topic at hand, she sighed and gave up, bending her head to start slicing the plain chicken breast that had been cooked for Sir Jessamyn. "'Future fiancée,' Mr. Hawkins? I'm not sure I've heard that term used before."

"Oh, she doesn't know it yet," he said cheerfully. "But she will soon."

"I suppose she'd have to," Elinor agreed, "if you are actually to be married." She fed Sir Jessamyn a bite of chicken, and he chirped happily, leaning over her shoulder towards the plate.

"Exactly." Mr. Hawkins poured three glasses of wine and set one of them firmly on top of his friend's second book. "Now for pity's sake, Aubrey, don't forget this is here and knock it over again, all right? It's actually a good brew this time—and you're paying a princely sum for it!"

"Mmm-hmm." Mr. Aubrey did not look up. "It's measurements that go wrong every time with these people! Why don't they ever take the time to *think*?" Still muttering to himself, he jotted a new round of angry notes.

Mr. Hawkins sighed and handed Elinor her glass. "You see, Miss Tregarth, you are the only one I can ask for assistance now. It's not that Aubrey isn't willing to help—he's already done a great deal by coming out of his way to drop me off here, as you see—but as far as I can tell, he's been dragon-obsessed ever since he was born. He has no helpful romantic experiences to share."

"Since he was born?" Elinor set down her glass, seizing upon the distraction. "But I thought—that is, *I* never even heard of real dragons until a few years ago. Until then, I thought they were a myth. Didn't everyone?"

She raised an apologetic hand to stroke Sir Jessamyn's warm, un-mythical back. He nudged her fingers aside, pointing his snout meaningfully down at the neglected chicken breast.

"Oh, I certainly did." Mr. Hawkins nodded as he sat down across from her. "But even before those Navy chaps down in

South America started writing back home about them, Aubrey already had it in his head that there was more to it than mere legends. He read through all the stories in his grandfather's library and started adding things up, apparently. And he's not the only one—by the time that first dragon landed back in England, there was a whole slew of obsessive scholars all ready to start arguing at the top of their lungs over its fine points, never mind the fact they'd never seen any before outside of fairy tale illustrations."

"*Fairy tales*, Hawkins?!" Mr. Aubrey looked up for the first time since Elinor had walked into the room. "Really, must you insult my hearing in that way? Haven't I explained to you often enough how insidious that outmoded and offensive terminology is, when discussing the matter of dragons?"

"Beg pardon, old chap." Mr. Hawkins scooped up a large portion of curry and dropped it onto his friend's rice-covered plate, shifting the sheets of notepaper out of the way just in time. "Here, take at least one bite before it goes cold." He handed Mr. Aubrey a spoon.

His friend took it, still glowering. "If people are going to spout any more gibberish about *fairy tales* in my presence..."

"I do beg your pardon, Mr. Aubrey," Elinor said, "but isn't that how most people first heard of dragons? I know my sisters and I—"

"Oh, well, in the *old* days." Aubrey waved a dismissive hand, nearly smacking his friend with his spoon in the process. Mr. Hawkins dodged with the apparent ease of long practice. "Now that we are living in supposedly more enlightened times, though, there ought to be a ban on spreading *that* particular disease."

"But—"

"Tell me, Miss Tregarth." Mr. Aubrey fixed his glare upon her. "Has Sir Jessamyn ever belched flame in your presence? Spoken a single word of English or displayed an eccentric fondness for riddles? Can he, in any sense of the word, be described as *magical*?" He pronounced the last word with unmistakable distaste.

"Ah..." Elinor turned to Sir Jessamyn. In his eagerness for more chicken, he was hanging halfway off her shoulder, his small, glittering face nearly touching the plate. She pushed him back into place, wincing as his long claws scrabbled against her skin through her cotton gown. "Really, Sir Jessamyn, have some manners!"

"Exactly!" Mr. Aubrey thumped the wooden table with his fist, sending even more ink spattering in all directions. "He is a beast, like any other. Perhaps, many centuries ago, larger specimens *may* have existed in Europe and even England itself. If so, they were no doubt hunted to extinction by louts afraid of their size and strength, who liked to exaggerate the creatures' danger and abilities as hunters always do. But there was certainly nothing magical about any of them, no matter what any *fairy tales* may say!"

He scooped up a heaping spoonful of curry and rice and shoved it into his mouth, glowering. "Fairy tales," he finished around a mouthful of lentils. "Ha!"

"Quite so," Mr. Hawkins said soothingly. "I'm sure Miss

Tregarth won't make that mistake again." He gave her an apologetic look. "Why don't you tell us how you came by your own dragon, Miss Tregarth?"

"Ah..." She took a bite of her own, filling her mouth to give herself a moment to think. Sir Jessamyn bumped his chin against her head, letting out a squawk of betrayal. "You can't have *all* of your supper before I even start mine," she told him as soon as she'd swallowed. "Don't be greedy."

Mr. Hawkins laughed. "You certainly seem comfortable with one another. Do you know, of all the ladies I've seen this season wearing dragons on their shoulders, you're the first I ever saw actually talking to one as if he understood you."

Elinor flushed. "Well, Sir Jessamyn is very intelligent." Mr. Hawkins glanced down at his waistcoat; her flush deepened. He'd changed clothing since the Incident, of course. His new waistcoat, a flowered yellow satin, was clean and dry. Still... "As soon as he's learned to control himself a bit better—"

"Oh, I don't disagree," said Mr. Hawkins. "Young puppies are much the same. He's fortunate in having a mistress who understands him. I've always thought it one of the oddest quirks of Society nowadays that a third of the creatures in every ballroom are treated as if they were inanimate." He lifted his glass of wine to her. "I didn't mean to insult you, Miss Tregarth, on my honour. I admire your integrity."

Integrity, Elinor reminded herself, hardly carried the same credit as beauty or wit. Still, she couldn't help the brief burst of warmth that flooded her. She lifted her own glass to hide her embarrassment. "I haven't had him long," she said. "I found him in an...untenable situation. We were both in rather awkward situations, actually. So we left. Together."

"Mm." Mr. Hawkins regarded her steadily. "It must have been an awkward situation indeed, to send you out onto the open road without a maid or any other chaperone, and with all of your money in one small reticule."

"Well..." She looked at Sir Jessamyn to avoid looking into the eyes of her cousin's future fiancé. Sir Jessamyn rubbed his scaly cheek against hers, chirping softly, and she fed him another sliver of chicken.

"I do understand awkward situations," said Mr. Hawkins gently. "I'm in the midst of one myself, at the moment."

Regaining control of her expression, Elinor looked back at him. "Is that why you've decided to court Penelope?"

"Exactly." He shrugged, half-smiling. "To be perfectly frank, Miss Tregarth, I'm in rather desperate need of Miss Penelope Hathergill—as are my three younger brothers, my five-year-old niece, and all of the tenant farmers on my father's estate. My *late* father's estate, that is. It's mine now, at least for the moment...but it won't be for long if my future fiancée doesn't take a liking to me. In truth, she is my final hope."

In other words, he was in desperate need of Penelope's famous dowry, not her love, in order to settle his father's debts. Elinor sighed. It was hardly a romantic realization to have about a man who looked like a hero...but she couldn't help understanding his perspective. After the last twelve months, she had come to understand a great many unromantic facts of life, like it or not.

"Have I shocked you?" Mr. Hawkins said. "I'm sorry for that. Perhaps I shouldn't have said anything."

Elinor shook her head. "No. My own parents..." She traced her spoon along her plate while Sir Jessamyn watched, his head snaking out on his long neck to mirror every move she made. "My younger sisters and I were surprised, on their passing, to discover that they had no savings left at all—not even the small dowries they'd always planned for us. It seems that my father had been persuaded to invest all of his capital in a South American investment scheme—"

"The great Brazilian bubble!" Mr. Hawkins let out a crack of laughter that contained no humour. "Our parents were birds of a feather, it seems. Or rather, considering the nature of the scheme, I should say they were dragons of a...hmm. Of a claw? Or perhaps an ear ridge?"

"*Your* father was drawn into the Brazilian scheme, too?" Elinor's head jerked up; she met his sympathetic gaze. "I could hardly believe it when I found out the truth. To think that anyone could ever imagine making such an unlikely fortune—"

"Dragons were considered to be mythical not five years ago," Mr. Hawkins said. "I suppose both of our fathers thought there might still be some magic left in them after all. Perhaps yours even imagined that it was his chance to give you all the larger dowries you deserved." His voice was gentle, but his eyes hardened as he slowly shook his head. "I'd give a great deal to find the blackguard who organized that scheme and then fled with the profits from so many innocents' livelihoods."

"Oh, so would I," Elinor said fervently. "When I think..." She bit her lip to hold back the torrent of passion that wanted to come pouring out.

"We are in a similar predicament." Mr. Hawkins sighed. "So tell me, Miss Tregarth. What is your scheme for salvation? I'd offer you a wealthy husband, but the only candidate I know of is Aubrey, here. He's far more interested in dragons than in wedlock, I'm afraid."

"Hmm," said Mr. Aubrey vaguely, without looking up. "It's the wingtips, you see. If you want to talk about domestication..."

Elinor met Mr. Hawkins's gaze. Her lips twitched. "Mr. Aubrey *is* very charming," she said sincerely, "but I don't believe I would make him happy."

The rules of propriety all confirmed that this was an unforgivably vulgar conversation. Indeed, Elinor ought to feel consumed by embarrassment at the very thought of discussing her potential mercenary marriage-hunt with an attractive single gentleman who was no member of her family.

Oddly, though, Elinor realized as she met Mr. Hawkins's warm and rueful gaze that she felt far more comfortable at this very moment than she had for over six months now... ever since she had said good-bye to her sisters.

Benedict Hawkins might *look* like a romantic hero, but in fact...

She smiled and lifted her wineglass to him. "I appreciate the thought regardless," she said.

In fact, he had all the makings of a friend.

* * *

...NONE OF WHICH, of course, made her feel any better as she lay in an unfamiliar bed that night, listening to the walls of the old inn creak and groan around her. Even the finest conversation couldn't make her forget her darker truths forever. A single evening of shared laughter and companionship could not change the future.

And the future for a girl without any prospects or protectors...for a girl without a single coin in her reticule but with a dragon who needed feeding...

Common sense might keep Elinor from weeping or swooning in the daytime, when there were urgent tasks to be done. Pride could always hold her chin high whenever witnesses were present. But in the middle of the night, Elinor found herself weeping with silent desperation into her pillow. Even Sir Jessamyn's increasingly anxious cheeping couldn't make her stop. When his pointed snout finally nosed past her hair into her bare cheek, all she could do was roll over and bury her face in the comfort of his warm scales.

"Oh, Sir Jessamyn," she whispered, "I'm so sorry. I wish I was wealthy enough to look after you properly. I wish I was wealthy and clever and powerful and..." An image of the fashionable Mrs. De Lacey, as she'd seen the lady sketched in so many newspapers across the years, popped into her head, and she choked on a sob. "Oh, I *wish*..."

Mrs. De Lacey wouldn't have to settle for mere friendship if she met an attractive, intelligent gentleman. How many famous and titled gentlemen had been numbered among her public admirers by now? Mrs. De Lacey certainly wouldn't have to walk away with quiet dignity into the jaws of poverty and terror while such a man was snapped up by *Penelope,* of all people! Mrs. De Lacey...

"Oh, *rubbish.*" Elinor pulled back from Sir Jessamyn and wiped her tears away with one hard swipe. Breathing hard, she forced down the final sob that wanted to escape her throat.

Who was she trying to fool? Even if she *had* been as wealthy as Mrs. De Lacey herself, Benedict Hawkins still wouldn't look twice at a crow like her when a true beauty like her cousin was available.

Penelope and her friends had been right all along. Elinor *was* dark and drab and insignificant. The only reason she hadn't realized her inadequacy before was because her sisters and their sweet, impractical parents had been far too unworldly to care for that sort of thing. She'd been so naïvely happy, safe and confident in the shelter of her family's love, that it had never even occurred to her to fear that other people would see her in a different light.

Now that she *was* left on her own in the outer world,

though, well outside the safe walls of their vicarage, no one would ever again look at Elinor and see anything of interest.

It was only too easy to see that unpalatable truth in the utter darkness of the room...and to whisper her secrets into the safety of Sir Jessamyn's warm scales, where no one else could ever hear them. "I just *wish* everyone could see me differently. If only I was as handsome and as stylish as Mrs. De Lacey..." Her words trailed off as Sir Jessamyn nudged her gently up to face him.

The little dragon leaned in close, until his snout pressed against her nose with surprising firmness. There was something odd about the intensity of his gaze in the darkness. She could feel it burning into her, even though she couldn't see his eyes.

Until...

"Sir Jessamyn?" Elinor whispered through her tears. "Are you...*glowing*?"

Sir Jessamyn opened his mouth wide. Shocking heat flared across her face. Light blinded her.

Elinor's final thought before she lost consciousness was: *I must tell Mr. Aubrey. Dragons* can *breathe flame after all!*

CHAPTER 5

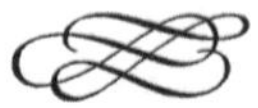

The first thing Elinor noticed the next morning when she woke was the warmth of bright sunshine against her eyelids—*too*-bright sunshine.

She never slept late! She certainly couldn't afford to sleep late today of all days, not if she wanted to leave the inn in time to avoid—

"I tell you, that girl is my niece, and I *will* see her account for her crime!" bellowed an all-too-familiar voice outside her door.

Too late! Elinor met Sir Jessamyn's golden gaze. He was sitting perched at the far end of the bed, shivering, with his long tail wrapped tightly around his body.

Elinor jumped out of bed, her pulse beating against her throat like a pair of wings fighting to get free. She ran to the window—

No. It was a three-storey drop onto the hard stone innyard. She would never survive that jump. Neither could Sir Jessamyn, with his poor, clipped wings.

"Sir John, really." That was Mr. Hawkins's voice, somehow managing to sound placating even when pitched at an unnaturally loud volume. "I'm sure there must have been some mistake. There's certainly no need to go charging into a lady's chamber before she's even dressed, is there? If you just wait downstairs and have a pint of ale to calm yourself before she wakes..."

He was trying to give her a warning—and an escape route.

Elinor bit her lip, torn between humiliation and gratitude. *If* it worked—if he could persuade Sir John out of the way—she could slip down the back stairs quickly with Sir Jessamyn. It would give her a slight head-start, anyway.

But to where? She hadn't the money for a trip to London or Bristol, to register with any employment agency. She hadn't even funds enough for a single meal.

She took a deep breath and looked back at Sir Jessamyn as the heavy weight of practicality sank through her. The little dragon was gazing up at her from the bed with trusting golden eyes. Something seemed oddly different about his face, but she hadn't time to worry about that, either.

Freedom had been such a beautiful dream. But it was long past time for Elinor to be sensible again, for both of their sakes.

"I can't let you starve," she whispered to Sir Jessamyn. "I *cannot*."

She squared her shoulders and reached for the valise that held all of her clothing. Before she could even pull out her only clean morning gown, though, she heard Sir John's voice rise with unmistakable finality.

"Damn it, man, my daughter will have her due!"

Sighing, Elinor snatched up her dressing gown, instead, from the spindly wooden chair beside the bed. She wrapped it tightly around herself as she hurried to the door, and turned the handle just as her uncle's fist sailed through the air to knock. Past him, Benedict Hawkins was reaching out to Sir John's bull-like shoulder, as if he were about to physically pull the older man away.

Both of them stopped and stared at her with as much horrified astonishment as if they'd seen a ghost. Her uncle's fist hung as if frozen in mid-air. Benedict Hawkins took a full step backwards, blinking.

Oh, for goodness' sake! Crow-like Elinor might be, but her appearance—even directly after a night of sleep, before she'd washed her face, dressed, or brushed her hair—couldn't be *that* frightening, could it? Or at the very least, they could pretend otherwise for courtesy's sake.

She lifted her chin, pride swelling to push aside her fear. "Well, Sir John?" she said coldly. If she was to be disgraced in front of Mr. Hawkins, at least she would bear it with dignity.

Her uncle shook his head. Then he shook it again, his big

jowls quivering. His meaty fist lowered; he gave it a horrified look.

"I beg your pardon," he said, to his fist. "I had no idea—that is, I thought—I was led to believe—" He whirled around to face Mr. Hawkins. "That fool of a maid *said* this was my niece's room, didn't she? You heard her as well as I did! I'll see her sacked for this. I'll—"

Elinor interrupted him for the first time ever. "Sir John? What is happening?"

He drew a deep breath that filled his broad chest, straining at the gold buttons on his striped waistcoat. "Mrs. De Lacey," he said heavily, and bowed. "I am so sorry to have disturbed you."

* * *

As Elinor's uncle bowed before her, she felt the world spin around her for the second time in two days.

I am dreaming, she thought. *I must still be asleep.*

She didn't *feel* asleep, though. She could smell the rich, well-spiced scent of cooking meat drifting up the staircase from the inn's kitchens, and she could hear men's voices far below. A clock was ticking nearby, her back still ached badly from her accident the day before, and she didn't think she could have dreamed the small brown mole in the middle of her uncle's pink bald spot. She had never even seen that before; he had never bowed to her.

And Benedict Hawkins was staring at her with gape-mouthed astonishment...until her gaze met his.

He closed his mouth with a snap. Then he visibly swallowed and straightened his shoulders. “Mrs. De Lacey, please forgive me for addressing you without any introduction, and in such awkward circumstances, too, but—”

“Mr. Hawkins?” She smiled weakly.

His eyebrows shot up. “You know who I am?”

“Ah…” She clutched the neck of her dressing gown.

He cleared his throat. “Forgive me, Mrs. De Lacey, but the young lady who was here last night—do you know if she’s safe and well? Or—”

“Of if she took my daughter’s stolen dragon with her!” Sir John straightened, glowering anew. “I’ll see her locked away for that treachery, family or no!”

Elinor stared at the two men. “Forgive me,” she said. “I was asleep until a moment ago, and I can’t—I don’t seem to understand—”

“Of course.” Mr. Hawkins winced. “We’ve woken you. Our apologies, truly.”

“Oh! Yes,” Sir John said, and bowed again. “*Deepest* apologies, Mrs. De Lacey. I can only hope it hasn’t given you too much of a distaste—gad, if I’ve offended you, my daughter will have my head! Now that you’ve finally condescended to visit us after all—that is, if I haven’t changed your mind—Good God, if I have…!”

He stopped, breathing hard, and snatched a handkerchief from the inner pocket of his bright red coat. He wiped it across his glistening forehead and then clutched it in his hand, crumpling it with the force of his grip. "*Please* do tell me you can forgive my rudeness, ma'am!"

Elinor swallowed hard and put one hand out to the corner of the doorway for balance.

"Perhaps you might do us the honor of meeting us downstairs when you're ready?" Mr. Hawkins suggested. "There is a private drawing room—"

"On the second storey," Elinor finished for him, sighing in relief.

His hazel eyes narrowed. "Yes. It is on the second storey."

"What a fortunate guess." Smiling weakly, Elinor shut the door on both of them. Then she slid directly to the floor and landed with a thump.

Sir Jessamyn was watching her from the bed. He cocked his head in curiosity as the men's footsteps thumped down the stairs beyond the door, their voices fading.

"They've gone mad," she told him blankly. "Completely mad. Both of them. They actually thought—well, I don't look *that* different in the mornings before I wash my face, do I?"

Sir Jessamyn chirped and craned his neck to look meaningfully at the door.

"I know." Elinor sighed. "You're hungry. I will find you breakfast. I'm sure that Sir John will agree to feed *you*, at least. But..." She frowned and stood up to cross to the bed. "Your face." She touched it with gentle fingers, stroking across his warm scales. "*That's* what's different! You never had any gold streaks around your mouth before."

Sir Jessamyn preened, half-closing his eyes, stretching his tail out luxuriantly along the bed, and clicking happily in the back of his throat as she inspected every detail. Round curlicues of gold swirled from the left edge of his mouth and along his chin, shining brightly against his glittering blue and green scales.

"Your new pattern is very beautiful," said Elinor. "But what on earth caused it?"

He opened his eyes and looked up at her...and Elinor suddenly remembered: that feeling of strange intensity burning through his gaze; Sir Jessamyn's scales glowing in the dark; flaming heat against her skin...

Her hand dropped away from his face as if she'd been scalded. "That was only a dream!"

Sir Jessamyn looked up at her steadily, his golden eyes glinting knowingly beside his startling new golden streak.

Elinor drew a deep breath. "I *must* get dressed. There's no more time for nonsense!"

She took the time to arrange every layer of her clothing with painstaking care, despite her uncontrollably trembling fingers. Finally, though, when she was fully dressed, she slowly turned towards the tiny, warped silver mirror that hung above her wash basin, a full five feet away and still angled safely away from her. She couldn't arrange her hair for the day without looking at that mirror, but she couldn't bring herself to move any closer to it, either.

It was utterly foolish to feel so nervous, she reminded

herself. Even if the two gentlemen outside her door had somehow become confused...

She reached back to un-do her plait. A long waterfall of hair fell loose over her left shoulder.

Her throat clenched.

Her hair was an entirely unremarkable shade of thick, straight brown. To be kind, her mother had always called its shade *chestnut*.

Luxuriantly curling waves of black hair tumbled over her shoulder now. Elinor reached up to stroke them, numb with disbelief.

She still *felt* her own hair, straight and thick, against her skin. But she *saw* her fingertip rise and fall over round curls that she couldn't feel. The contrast made her stomach swoop. A low whimper sounded from her throat, against her will.

Elinor stepped towards the mirror, feeling as if she were floating outside her own body.

The woman whose eyes she met there was at least fifteen years older than Elinor. She wasn't adorably beautiful like Penelope. Her nose was too strong for that and her chin too wide. No, *she* wasn't pretty or soft. No one would mistake her for a china doll.

But there was something about the striking curves and angles of her face and the confident glint in her dark blue eyes...something that Elinor recognized immediately, even though she'd never glimpsed it in her own expression.

It was the look of a woman who knew that she held

power...and no wonder. It was, after all, the face of the most powerful woman she'd ever heard of.

"Oh, my," Elinor said faintly. "Oh, my heavens."

She turned to stare at Sir Jessamyn. He chirruped proudly as he looked back at her. Gold glinted to the left of his mouth in the light that streamed from the square window.

"Oh, Sir Jessamyn," Elinor breathed. "What have you done?"

CHAPTER 6

Elinor walked into the second-floor drawing room ten minutes later with a rapidly fluttering pulse hidden behind her gown and Sir Jessamyn perched alertly on her shoulder. Both of their gazes went straight to the big, scarred wooden table in the center of the room...but for very different reasons.

Shining platters of traditional English breakfast foods covered the table, from toasted cheese to eggs to slices of cold chicken and assorted jellies. Sir Jessamyn wriggled so hard with delight that he nearly fell off Elinor's shoulder.

Elinor, however, barely noticed the mountain of food or even the teapot that steamed enticingly at the center of the table. She was too busy staring in horror at the empty chair beside Benedict Hawkins.

"Mr. Aubrey hasn't left already, has he?"

The other two men had already pushed their own chairs back from the table to rise and bow to her; Mr. Hawkins paused halfway from his seat, frowning. "You know Aubrey?"

"Who's Aubrey?" Sir John's voice was muffled by his own waistcoat as he bowed with a subservient flourish she'd never seen from him before.

Elinor swallowed hard as she searched for the right answers to give them both. Of course, there would be no reason for Mrs. De Lacey, of all people, to know of a young dragon scholar at Cambridge, no matter how brilliant. And as Sir Jessamyn seemed to have somehow turned her into an impossible vision of Mrs. De Lacey...

Panic fluttered against her chest. She fought the urge to turn and flee.

Sir Jessamyn craned his neck towards the table. His mouth hung open. His glittering golden eyes fixed on the chicken.

If she tried to leave now, he might well commit mutiny.

"Are you feeling quite well, Mrs. De Lacey?" Sir John started forward, holding out his arm. "Allow me to—"

"No!" She jerked away—then tried to mask her reaction by reaching up to adjust Sir Jessamyn on her shoulder. "Thank you for the offer, but...." She smiled weakly. "I don't require any assistance, Sir John."

The very last thing that she required, in fact, was for her uncle to touch her arm—which was far thinner than it currently appeared as the deliciously curved arm of Mrs. De Lacey—and feel the difference between illusion and reality.

Benedict Hawkins was watching her with a thoughtful frown. When she met his gaze, though, he only walked around the table to pull out a chair—the same one that she had sat in last night. "Mrs. De Lacey."

"Thank you, Mr. Hawkins." She sat, holding her chin high and making sure not to brush against him by so much as a hair.

She'd only dared this breakfast meeting in the first place for the sake of seeking Mr. Aubrey's advice...but now that she was here, it made sense to take advantage of the (terrifyingly impossible, *magical*) illusion and eat one final hearty meal. If she did somehow manage to escape afterwards, she would very likely go hungry for quite some time; and if, instead, Sir John realized who she was, he would certainly order her hauled off to prison on charges of dragon theft immediately afterwards.

Elinor didn't think she could face either prospect without a bracing cup of tea.

Both men were frowning now at Sir Jessamyn as he leaned precariously over her shoulder, gazing at her still-empty plate with glittering golden eyes. Elinor shook her head at the sight, relieved to finally be back within a realm she understood.

"Yes, I know. You haven't eaten for hours, and you're going to starve to death if you wait any longer. Just give me a moment, will you?" She reached for a pair of serving tongs.

Sir John reached them first. "Allow me, Mrs. De Lacey." He was still frowning at Sir Jessamyn, though, even as he piled heaps of meat and eggs onto her plate without waiting for her reaction. "Apologies for not arranging the proper service, ma'am, but I didn't want any of those witless inn maids overhearing our conversation. They will talk, y'know, no matter how well you pay 'em, and as you may have gathered, there's been a bit of an uproar within the family."

Elinor raised her eyebrows and set one hand on Sir Jessamyn's warm scales, as if to hold him in place. It was a good excuse to keep her hand well out of her uncle's reach. "Uproar, Sir John?"

He sighed heavily. "I wouldn't bother you with it if you weren't such an old friend of my wife, but..."

Benedict Hawkins interrupted. "May I ask how you long you've had your dragon, Mrs. De Lacey?"

"*My* dragon?" Elinor widened her eyes, feeling her breathing shorten. "Do you take a particular interest in dragons, Mr. Hawkins?"

"Not...generally," he said. "But that one looks remarkably similar to one I saw just last night. The resemblance is striking."

"Exactly what I've been thinking!" Sir John waved his arm so vigorously in agreement, he sent a pile of eggs flying from the serving tongs onto the bare wooden table.

Sir Jessamyn cheeped in protest at the lost food. His head snaked out to anxiously mirror the path of the waving serving tongs as Sir John continued, "That blue and green face, and those wings—"

"The golden markings on *my* dragon's face," Elinor said

sharply, "are said to be entirely unique. Surely *they* cannot be found on any other, less superior dragons you may have seen!"

Sir Jessamyn wriggled in protest as her fingers tightened around him. As Elinor dropped her hand, she found Benedict Hawkins watching her steadily.

"Yes," he said. "You're quite right. That is the one point of difference I can see." He paused, then added, "The *only* one."

"Hmm. The only difference, you say?" Sir John leaned closer to peer suspiciously at Sir Jessamyn.

With a squeak of dismay, the little dragon scuttled back, burying his bright face behind Elinor's hair. He had always been terribly nervous around Sir John, from the very first day he'd come home from the breeder.

Please don't chuckle, Sir Jessamyn, Elinor begged silently. *That would give everything away.*

Two dragons might look startlingly similar without proving anything conclusive...but for two such dragons to both share Sir Jessamyn's own nervous weakness? *No one* would ever believe that the great Mrs. De Lacey would choose to travel around the country with a dragon who couldn't contain himself in company.

She arched away as her uncle leaned closer, his breath far too hot. "Sir John, really—!"

"Beg pardon, ma'am." His sigh of frustration ruffled her hair, smelling of whiskey and the peppercorn seeds he liked to chew. Still, he sat back obediently. "Just trying to get a better look."

Sir Jessamyn vibrated nervously against Elinor's neck, and her spine stiffened in response. *I made a promise.* She might not have funds or a future, but she could at least keep anyone else from frightening him now.

Elinor glared at her uncle with every bit of outraged haughtiness she could imagine from the woman she'd read so much about. "Would you care to tell me *why* you have been gaping at my dragon in such a vulgar fashion, Sir John?"

Sir John scooted his chair back as hastily as if she'd slapped him in the face. "Well—that is—"

A strange exhilaration filled Elinor as she rose to her feet, tossing her napkin onto the table with dismissive flair. "Your local villagers may bow and scrape, but *I* do not personally find it amusing to have any gentleman breathe onto my neck without permission—*or* to ogle my dragon with such rudeness!"

She snatched up a thick slice of chicken to pass to Sir Jessamyn; his head snaked out to catch it with lightning speed before returning to the safety of the back of her head.

Sir John loosened his neckcloth, breathing hard, as he scrambled to his feet. "Mrs. De Lacey, I beg you—"

"I fear I have made an error in choosing to visit your family," Elinor said coldly. "Please inform your wife and daughter that I am once again...indisposed. You needn't pass on any apologies." She turned her back on him pointedly and started for the door, ignoring the choked protestations coming from behind her. "I shall start back for London directly."

And just in time, she finished silently.

If she was quick enough, she would be long gone before he discovered that the great Mrs. De Lacey had never officially arrived at the inn after all—and had certainly never stabled any carriage or horses there.

It would be a local mystery—fodder for gossip for weeks to come—but Elinor and Sir Jessamyn would be safe. By the time Sir Jessamyn's illusion faded, they would be well away. And then...

Well, she would think of something after that...she hoped.

Benedict Hawkins's voice stopped her only two feet from the door.

"Mrs. De Lacey, if you please—*do* you know what happened to the girl who was staying in your room last night?"

Ohhh... Even knowing that she shouldn't, Elinor stopped walking. She took a deep breath, her eyes still fixed on the brass door handle that led to safety. "Which girl?"

"There was a young lady," Benedict Hawkins said. "She began the night there, at least, and—"

"I arrived in the middle of the night." Elinor didn't turn around. She didn't dare. "The room was already empty."

"Were there any signs of distress? Anything left behind that might give a hint of where she's gone?"

Elinor couldn't help herself. She turned and met Benedict Hawkins's intent hazel eyes—which were, for once, completely free of laughter.

"I'm concerned about her safety," he said quietly. "She had no money and no one to help her. I don't see how she could survive on her own. I meant to give her what little I could before she left, but—"

"*On her own*?" Sir John's face reddened with remembered rage. "She had my daughter's dragon, sir! She *stole* my daughter's dragon, impudent as you please. She's no doubt sold it on already to the first blackguard she met. Wretched girl! After everything we did for her—"

Elinor forced her words out through gritted teeth. "Of whom can you possibly be speaking, Sir John?"

"My *niece*." He spat out the word. "Well, my wife's niece, anyway. Her fool of a sister married a man who couldn't handle his investments *or* his horses. He overturned himself and his wife in a carriage ride and left three daughters for someone else to look after. My wife insisted we ought to take one of them in to help our daughter Penelope, but—"

Benedict Hawkins choked. "Oh, good Lord. I beg your pardon, Sir John—and Mrs. De Lacey. I just—I'm afraid, I was so distracted, sir, that I hadn't quite put it all together until now. As we weren't properly introduced, I hadn't heard your surname, but—well, of course. Your daughter must be Miss Penelope Hathergill, then?"

Sir John blinked, interrupted in mid-flow. "Well...yes."

"So the girl who was here last night—Miss Elinor Tregarth—is her *cousin*?"

"Unfortunately." Sir John shrugged. "That minx couldn't care less for family loyalty, though. Yesterday afternoon she made a fool of herself with a hysterical fit in front of my daughter and my wife, and then she fled the house in disgrace with Penelope's dragon—who cost me a pretty penny, I can tell you. When I catch up with her, she'll learn her lesson!"

Elinor forced her breathing to remain steady as she watched Benedict Hawkins absorb the news. Different emotions chased themselves across his face...but he ended up shaking his head with a wry half-smile.

"She did say she knew Miss Hathergill," he murmured. "I suppose I understand, now, why she didn't share any further details."

It shouldn't matter what he thought of her. It *didn't*. After all, Elinor would never see him again after today. And yet...

"Perhaps there is more to the story than you've yet heard, Sir John," she said. "You weren't in the house yourself yesterday, were you?"

"No," he said, "but—I say, how did you come to know that?"

Elinor shrugged lightly with her less-burdened shoulder, while Sir Jessamyn quivered against her hair. "You would hardly have waited so long to chase her down if you had been at home when this supposedly occurred."

"True enough." He sighed. "It was the first thing I heard about when I arrived home, though. I can assure you of that. Before I even washed off my dust, I had the whole story from my daughter, so you may trust that I have *all* the facts in hand."

Elinor raised her eyebrows. "Is there no other side to the story but Penelope's?"

"How could there be?" Sir John snorted. "No, that wretch walked off with the dragon, all right, and she couldn't have had any intention but to sell it. There's no other reason for her to have stolen it—well, except to hurt my daughter, that is. Penelope says she was always perishingly jealous and showed it with all sorts of ill-tempered remarks. We're well rid of her from our household." Sir John took a long swig of his ale and squared his shoulders. "All the same, I'll have to spend the rest of the day chasing after her now to see justice done—she must be halfway to London by now, thinking to live high off the profits from her crime."

Elinor's fingers tightened around the skirts of her dress. "Perhaps you should simply let her go. She can't be worth such exertions on your part, surely."

"I'd rather not do much more traveling," he admitted. "But if you imagine my daughter will ever let her go..." He shuddered. "If you only knew how upset this has made Penelope..."

"You may not catch up with her at all," said Benedict Hawkins. "If she hasn't gone to London—"

"Where else *could* she go? There's nowhere else big enough for her to make that kind of sale and then vanish. She don't have any other family left but her sisters, and *they* can't take her in—but I suppose I'll have to see about them now, too. I'll write tonight to those poor fools who took the other girls in, to warn them of *their* danger." He shook his head dolefully. "They ought to know to expect Miss Elinor on their doorsteps—and more than that, as one sister's turned out to be a thief, it's only fair that I warn 'em not to trust either of the others."

Elinor's throat tightened. "Surely that can't be necessary."

"Ha! If you think Penelope will ever let me rest without seeing justice done—"

"*Perhaps* we can give Penelope something better to think about," Elinor said swiftly. "I hear she plans to début soon?"

His big shoulders slumped. "In just five days. But with that dragon gone and no time to order up a new one for her—"

"I think you had better forget the dragon entirely." Elinor listened to her own words with disbelief. How was her voice remaining so calm? But then, it wasn't *her* voice at all...and that would have to make all the difference from now on. "A dragon won't be necessary for Penelope, I assure you. She will have something far better on her side."

Her uncle frowned. "What could be more fashionable than a dragon at my daughter's début ball?"

Benedict Hawkins's frowning gaze rested on Elinor's face. Sir Jessamyn shivered against her shoulder, still hiding his own face from Sir John.

Elinor thought longingly of the door handle and of freedom, still close enough to touch. *Think of Rose*, she told herself. *Think of Harry*.

She lifted her chin. "Penelope will have *me*," she said coolly. "You're in luck, Sir John. On the condition that you abandon these tedious and petty schemes of revenge—which are far too vulgar for me to associate with in any fashion—I believe I *shall* condescend to visit your family after all. What could ever be better than that?"

CHAPTER 7

"You will?" Sir John surged towards her, his face breaking into a wide smile. "Oh, you won't regret it, ma'am, I promise you won't. You do us too much honor—indeed you do—but you shall enjoy every moment of your stay. Mrs. De Lacey—by Gad, ma'am, I could kiss your hand for what you've done for me today!"

Thus warned, Elinor swiftly clasped her hands behind her back. "Indeed," she said coolly, "we could hardly allow poor Penelope to suffer. But I expect you to escort me to Hathergill Hall yourself, Sir John, with no more nonsense about chasing errant nieces about the country or pursuing some sort of Gothic revenge upon their sisters."

"No, ma'am, of course not, if you don't like it. Certainly not." He pulled out his handkerchief and mopped his shining forehead. "Even Penelope couldn't...that is, you've done me an immense favor, Mrs. De Lacey, and I know it."

"Indeed," said Elinor, and tried in vain to determine whether hysterical laughter or a scream most wanted to escape in response to all of it.

"Ah..." Benedict Hawkins cleared his own throat.

With true relief, she turned to where he stood by the table. "You had something to say, Mr. Hawkins?"

He nodded, making a rueful face as he stepped forward. "Sir John, I *had* hoped to meet you in more fortuitous circumstances, but...I must tell you, I had indeed hoped to meet you today. It was the very purpose of my travel here."

"Oh, was it?" Still beaming with relief, Sir John waved an expansive invitation. "You said you'd heard of my daughter, young man, didn't you?"

"Why, yes, I have." Mr. Hawkins nodded. "Her praise has reached across the country—even as far as my own estate near Cambridge."

"Of course. Beautiful girl, Penelope," said Sir John. "An angel. That's what everybody calls her, you know!"

Elinor bit her lip and fixed her gaze purposefully on the wall beyond.

"I had heard something of the sort," Benedict agreed. "But in fact, it was you I've heard most about."

"Oh?" Sir John frowned. "I haven't heard your name before, Mr. Hawkins."

"No, but I know an old friend of yours." Benedict reached into the inside pocket of his jacket and withdrew a sealed letter. "Mr. Edmund Crawford was kind enough to write me a note of introduction. He hoped you might be willing to give me some advice on the running of estates and so forth, as I've so recently come into my own. I'll be staying here at this inn for the next week or two, and I'd be grateful if you could spare any time to take me in hand for his sake."

"Hrmm." Frowning, Sir John broke open the seal and began to read.

Elinor's uncle had never been a speedy reader. As the moments stretched on, Sir Jessamyn uncoiled himself enough to peer over her shoulder towards the table of food. He nudged her cheek with his snout, then looked pointedly back at the waiting table.

"Oh, very well," Elinor whispered. "Greedy monster." Still, she reached up to stroke his neck affectionately as she moved back to the table and resumed her seat...and she reached for the teapot, too.

With hysteria looming high on her emotional horizon, tea—even sadly cooled tea—had become a true medical necessity.

The two men took their own seats at the table a moment later, but she didn't raise her eyes to look at either of them. Instead, she focused on feeding Sir Jessamyn and taking restorative sips from her cup. Her own stomach was knotted far too tightly to consider any of the vast quantities of food on offer anymore.

Fortunately, that could never be a problem for Sir Jessamyn. From the voracious way he snapped up every bite, any new observer might well have imagined that he'd spent the last month subsisting on nothing but stale bread and water. Feeding him a steady stream of food—and stopping him from taking more at a time than was good for him—was the perfect excuse for Elinor not to meet the gazes of either gentleman at the table.

She badly needed that time to think, because the words she had spoken on desperate impulse were resonating throughout her body now...and flooding her with a cascade of increasingly horrifying realizations.

She had no carriage or horses. She had no maid. She had no piles of expensive luggage, nor clothing that was fit for anything but the poor relation she was.

What was I thinking? Illusion or no, she could never fool everyone at Hathergill Hall—not for five full days, the length of time that she would have to wait for Penelope's début to take place. Perhaps Rose could have managed it in these circumstances; *she* had the confidence and strength of will to carry off any daring masquerade. Harry was quieter but so clever that she could have planned all sorts of persuasive details.

Elinor, though? As everyone knew, she was plain and sensible; the polar opposite of the dashing Mrs. De Lacey and her set. *A crow, trying to pass herself off as a peacock?* It was laughable.

"Ha!" said Sir John.

Elinor gave an involuntary start. Sir Jessamyn missed his next bite, and cold scrambled eggs fell across her bare hands.

Fortunately, Sir John wasn't looking at her. "I haven't seen old Crawford for years," he told Mr. Hawkins, leaning back in his seat. "Not since our university days. Dab hand at billiards, that man—or at any rate, he was thirty years ago."

"He still is," said Mr. Hawkins. "He played against my late father several times."

"Yes, he says so in the letter. Says your father was a fine fellow, too."

"He was." This time, Mr. Hawkins's voice was low. "Without him, I wouldn't be here."

Still wiping the greasy remnants of eggs off her fingers, Elinor slid him a glance and found his handsome face looking startlingly grim...or, perhaps, haunted.

With a visceral twist of pain, she suddenly remembered the night after her parents' death, when she'd made her own discovery of the disaster left behind them in the wake of that terrible, fraudulent investment scheme, the one that—according to her father's earnest correspondence—"could not fail."

She would never stop loving her kind and hopeful father. She simply couldn't do it. A childhood of love and warmth and safety would never be canceled out by a single mistake and a too-trusting nature.

But there had been times, as she and her sisters had sat in the empty vicarage, their bellies growling with audible hunger as they'd waited to hear which unknown relatives would agree to take them in and separate the three of them forever...

Oh, yes. Elinor took a slow, deep breath as she admitted the bitter truth to herself.

She was still absolutely furious at her father for what he had done to all of them.

It would have helped to share that tangled feeling with Mr. Hawkins now; or at least, to give him any sign of the empathy she felt. But Mrs. De Lacey, of course, could know nothing of his father's losses. Mr. Hawkins had worked too hard to keep those secret…and if he was to save his younger brothers, his niece, and all those dependent workers on his estate, it was vital that Sir John, of all people, not be allowed to ever guess that he was penniless.

So there really was only one thing that she could do.

Elinor looked up, met her uncle's gaze, and steeled herself to be Mrs. De Lacey once more.

"Mr. Hawkins is a fine young man, too," she said brightly, "and his estate is meant to be delightful. He'll be quite a catch for some lucky young lady!" She paused, then widened her eyes as if struck by sudden inspiration. "Why, perhaps you ought to invite him to Penelope's début! The timing is so fortuitous, after all. Aren't you and Lady Hathergill putting together a houseparty for the event?"

"Well…" Sir John frowned, glancing down again at the letter in his hands. "We've invited a few people to come down this week to make up numbers at the dance, but…"

"Perfect," Elinor said, and smiled with the serene confidence of a woman who never worried about other people's opinions. It felt astonishingly liberating. "How fortunate that the two of you should meet in this way."

"I...don't know," Sir John said. "I can't think what Penel—that is, what my wife would say. It's not a full houseparty, you see, just a few—"

"I'm quite certain your wife would be delighted to have such an eligible young man in attendance for Penelope's début," Elinor said. "After all, you are inviting other gentlemen to stay at the house, aren't you?"

Sir John frowned harder. "Only a few friends from town. I thought we needed more numbers in attendance at the dance, so..."

"Well, then," said Elinor briskly. "Lady Hathergill will be delighted to have such a handsome young guest for Penelope to dance with at her début. *And* so will Penelope, I expect."

Mr. Hawkins cleared his throat. A faint flush tinged his cheekbones. "Mrs. De Lacey—Sir John—you are too kind, both of you, but I wouldn't wish to cause any inconvenience. As I said, I was planning to make my stay at this inn, rather than imposing on Sir John's hospitality in such a way."

If Elinor *had* been herself, she would have let the matter drop already, her cheeks burning with embarrassment. But Mrs. De Lacey, she was certain, would never give up so easily—and more importantly, she knew which other guests had been invited. She'd written out most of their invitation cards herself. Benedict Hawkins would need every advantage he could get if he was to compete with those gentlemen of fortune and debt-free estates.

"Nonsense," she said. "How could it be an imposition? Sir John, do you really mean to say that the hospitality of Hathergill Hall is too limited—too *provincial*—to host a young man of good estate, recommended to you by an old friend?"

"Er..." said Sir John. "No, but...well, no. Of course not." He squared his bull-like shoulders. "Of course we'd be delighted to have you stay, Hawkins. Couldn't possibly let you languish in an inn, could we? Not when old Crawford himself recommended you."

"Well..." Benedict Hawkins hesitated. For a moment, Elinor thought she saw a flash of actual reluctance cross his face.

For heaven's sake. He wasn't going to turn the offer down, was he? She found herself leaning forward, as if she could mentally urge him on.

If he wanted to marry Penelope, he couldn't possibly refuse! If he still wanted to marry Penelope...

"You are too kind, Sir John," said Benedict Hawkins, and smiled. "I accept."

Elinor subsided back into her chair. Her pulse was beating faster than it should have been. Disappointment, illogical and fierce, clutched her throat.

Of course he still wanted to marry Penelope. Why wouldn't he?

And now she was going to help him do it.

Sir Jessamyn burped loudly, in perfect satisfaction, straight into her face.

* * *

IT WASN'T until the end of breakfast that the awkward questions arose.

"Shall I order your carriage, Mrs. De Lacey?" Sir John said. "I can't leave my own horse here, but if I ride alongside—"

"My carriage?" Elinor gave a light laugh. She'd had the whole of breakfast to prepare, but she still felt her chest tighten as she widened her eyes in a semblance of surprise. "Why would I still have my carriage?"

Both of the men at the table looked at her as if she had suddenly started speaking Spanish.

"I've sent my carriage back to London," Elinor said, and let the concluding phrase "*of course*" linger unspoken in her tone. "I knew I shouldn't need it here, and I expected that you would be relieved not to stable my horses during my stay."

Both men were still staring at her wordlessly.

She tried to give a trilling little laugh, like Penelope's. It came out more like a squawk, half-strangled by nerves. Sir Jessamyn's head swung around, and he angled his head to stare at her inquisitively.

"I beg your pardon," said Mr. Hawkins, "but do you mean to say you arrived in the middle of the night and didn't even keep your carriage with you until the morning?"

She shrugged, taking care not to dislodge Sir Jessamyn. "It was only unfortunate that my luggage—including all of my clothing and my travel purse, too—was still in the carriage when it drove away."

Sir John's mouth dropped open, revealing a wad of half-chewed eggs still on his tongue.

Benedict said, his voice sounding weak, "And...your maid? She didn't realize either?"

This time, Elinor's shrug was so jerky that Sir Jessamyn let out a chirp of dismay and had to dig his claws in to retain his perch. She had a dire suspicion that her smile had become manic. "Oh, I sent her home, too. Useless girl! I thought I'd just let one of the maids at Hathergill Hall take care of me."

"Good *God*," said Sir John.

Elinor's shoulder burned where Sir Jessamyn's claws dug into it. Panic rang clanging alarm bells in the back of her head.

She asked, "Are you saying that you don't have enough maids to assist me after all, Sir John? Because I can, of course, still return to London. I'll simply send my coachman a message and—"

"No!" he said hastily. "No, no. Never fear. I'll start after your carriage immediately. I should catch up with it by—"

"No need." Elinor smiled. "There was a case of clothing in my room when I arrived. Left there by your niece, I presume." She touched one finger to the gown she was wearing, in demonstration. "Luckily, her clothing fits me well enough. I find it rather amusing to wear such different attire for a week. It is rather a novelty, don't you think?"

Both men's gazes dropped to the drab material of her gown, which was every bit as ugly as it had been inexpensive. Elinor would have winced in humiliation if she had been herself. Instead, she beamed at them with all of her might.

Fashionable and wealthy women were allowed to be eccentric and authoritative, where lesser women had to be sensible and submissive. Mrs. De Lacey was the most fashionable and wealthy woman of them all. Therefore, if they really believed she was Mrs. De Lacey...

"Well," said Sir John, "we had better find you another carriage."

But for the first time, she saw a hint of suspicion in his eyes.

CHAPTER 8

"My friend Aubrey has a carriage he might lend us for an hour," said Benedict. "You did ask about him earlier, didn't you, Mrs. De Lacey?"

"Oh, he's still here?" Elinor could have wept with relief. "That would be ideal! Do you think he could escort me himself?"

"Aubrey?" Sir John turned his frown to Benedict. "Who *is* this fellow you keep nattering about?"

"A scholar at Cambridge," said Elinor. "A specialist in dragons. In fact, I've been hoping very much to consult with him about my pet." She tilted her head to rest against Sir Jessamyn's warm face as he contentedly chewed his latest chicken slice. For once, she was the one vibrating, not him, as excitement shivered through her fingertips. If Mr. Aubrey *was* still here—if she could tell him everything—then—

"A *scholar*, eh?" Sir John snorted with disgust. "Never seen the point of those bookish fellows, myself. Not what a real man chooses to do with his time." He shrugged and turned back to his ale.

Irritation passed over Mr. Hawkins's face before he masked it. "He's also the grandson of Sir Toby Grayling."

Ale spattered across the table as Sir John jerked to attention. "Grayling the *banker,* you mean? The one who got himself knighted for paying off all the Prince Regent's debts five years ago, after Prinny built that monstrosity of a new palace?"

Mr. Hawkins nodded. "My friend is Sir Toby's only heir."

"Good Gad! Good..." Sir John's jaw worked in silent agitation. "His *only* heir, you say? Well, he'll just have to come and stay with us, too, then, of course!" He drew himself up. "We could hardly be so rude as to not invite *him*, when we're asking you to stay. Wouldn't want to offend any friend of yours, would we?"

Mr. Hawkins's eyes widened. "I feel I must warn you, Sir John, that he isn't the most sociable of fellows. He—"

"Balderdash!" Sir John's voice hardened. "If *you* are to come to Hathergill Hall, he must as well. I won't hear another word spoken against it! Do you understand me, sir?"

Mr. Hawkins paled. "Ah..."

Elinor's conscience twinged. If she truly meant to aid Benedict in his pursuit of Penelope, she ought to intercede with Sir John, shouldn't she? It couldn't do Benedict's courtship any good to be compared to a man who—judging by Sir John's reaction—possessed a truly mouth-watering inheritance.

But...

No, Elinor thought firmly, and for once, she turned a deaf ear to her conscience.

Mr. Aubrey was hardly likely to take any notice of Penelope—not unless she developed ear ridges and scales, anyway. And Elinor could hardly turn down such a heaven-sent opportunity.

"What a delightful idea," she said. "I shall look forward to meeting him as soon as possible!"

Mr. Hawkins looked from her to Sir John, sighed, and shrugged. "Then I'll see what I can do."

FORTY MINUTES LATER, Elinor was sitting once more in Mr. Aubrey's paper-flooded carriage, while Benedict Hawkins sat on the opposite bench beside his friend, who'd hunched tightly over the book in his lap. With bright sunshine pouring through the expensive glass windows and Sir Jessamyn curled up on her own lap, it should have felt just like the ride she'd taken the day before, with all of its ease and subversive, tingling pleasure.

It didn't.

This time, they rode in near-silence, broken only by Mr. Aubrey's occasional, low-voiced mutters of disgust with the book he was reading. Outside, the sun was shining every bit as brightly as it had before, but the temperature in the carriage felt as if it had dropped several degrees. Yesterday, Mr. Hawkins's stretched-out legs had come perilously close to brushing against Elinor's at every turn of the road. Today, he held himself carefully rigid in his seat, several polite—and chilly—inches away, and with no flow of easy conversation to lighten the mood. Instead, he frowned out of the window, his face set in weary lines.

Even after just one day of acquaintance, Elinor knew that grim silence was unlike him.

Was he regretting yesterday's generosity now that he'd heard Sir John's side of the story? Perhaps he, too, was remembering yesterday's journey...but wishing that he could turn time back and leave her in the ditch where he had found her. It was what Sir John would have advised him to do, certainly.

It didn't matter, Elinor told herself. It couldn't matter, if she was to maintain her charade. And for all her undeniable temptation to break that grim silence now by revealing the truth—to tell him her side of the story and hope that he believed it...she *was* still Elinor Tregarth beneath her magical façade. She hadn't entirely lost sight of common sense even in this desperate escapade.

Benedict Hawkins's only chance of saving his family and estate lay in persuading Penelope Hathergill to marry him. Therefore, he could never be allowed to know the truth—not when he'd win Penelope's favour in an instant by turning over Elinor to justice.

Elinor sighed and gave Sir Jessamyn a gentle pat for comfort.

That sigh finally caught Mr. Hawkins's attention. He turned away from the window, his face easing into a not-quite-natural smile. "I beg your pardon, Mrs. De Lacey. I've been terribly rude with my wool-gathering."

"You appeared to have grave matters on your mind."

He opened his mouth as if to speak, then shook his head. "Nothing of importance. Only..." He compressed his lips. Then he sat forward with a sudden burst of intensity, looking into her eyes. "Mrs. De Lacey—"

"In the name of God!" Mr. Aubrey burst out. He snatched off his spectacles and glared around the carriage wildly. "When will they learn to catalogue properly? *When*?!"

Sir Jessamyn reared away from that accusing glare, letting out a startled clicking sound of alarm. Elinor let out a half-breath of shaken laughter.

Sighing, Mr. Hawkins shook his head and sat back in his seat. "I'm sure you're right, old fellow, but perhaps—"

Mr. Aubrey's wild gaze landed on Elinor. "*You'll* understand me! Miss Tregarth, as the owner of a dragon yourself, you must surely—"

"I beg your pardon!" Elinor's breath stuck in her throat as she met his burning gaze. "What did you just call me?" she whispered.

He knew. How could he know?

"*Not* Miss Tregarth, Aubrey." Benedict sighed and shot

her an apologetic glance. "That was yesterday, remember? This is a different lady."

"A different lady?" Mr. Aubrey replaced his spectacles and leaned across the seat to frown at Sir Jessamyn. "But surely—"

"Mrs. De Lacey, remember? She's been wanting to consult with you about her dragon."

"But this is Miss Tregarth's dragon, clearly." Mr. Aubrey lifted one finger to Sir Jessamyn, who nosed forward cautiously in response, face lowered in nervous submission. "If you look at the very particular shape of those ear ridges..."

Elinor sat frozen in her seat as Mr. Hawkins's eyebrows drew together. "But the markings on its face—"

"Markings?" Mr. Aubrey frowned, and gently tilted Sir Jessamyn's chin. "What mark—? Oh. Ah, yes. Hmm. I hadn't noticed these before." He inspected the golden swirls on the left side of Sir Jessamyn's face with interest. "Remarkable. I've never seen anything quite like them."

"Never?" Elinor's query came out as a croak.

He shook his head, tracing the swirls with one careful finger, while Sir Jessamyn leaned into his hand, eyes drifting half-shut with pleasure. "Never. I've seen pictures, of course —Kelsham has an illustration in his latest treatise of a few mature dragons in South America with such markings, but I've never seen one myself...not on a living specimen, at least. There was one stuffed specimen brought over by a Navy surgeon that displayed something similar, but it was so degraded by the quantity of seawater that had overwhelmed it during one of their pointless battles—"

"During their heroic sea-battles against the French, you mean," Mr. Hawkins prompted patiently, "during the long wars against Bonaparte."

"As you say, as you say." Mr. Aubrey shrugged impatiently. "It was a desperate waste of a good specimen, though! They couldn't manage to bring back a single live dragon until they finally gave up on all that cannon-shooting."

"When Bonaparte was bravely defeated by our armies, you mean," said Mr. Hawkins, with more resignation than hope.

Elinor moistened her lips. "But you must have seen a number of adult dragons yourself in the past few years, Mr. Aubrey, since they were first imported to England."

"Oh, yes. Ladies' *pets*." Mr. Aubrey's voice held the same note of disdain with which Sir John had uttered the earlier word "scholars."

"Ahem." Mr. Hawkins looked pointedly from his friend to Elinor and back again. When Aubrey didn't react, he said, "Mrs. De Lacey herself—"

"Oh, I know, all the ladies who follow fashion must have them, and *we're* all meant to be grateful just because they pay to bring dragons here for study. But, Hawkins, even you can hardly claim that the true pinnacle of dragonhood comes from riding about on a lady's shoulder at a ball. Of course they're hardly *magical*, as some fools in history thought, haha..."

"Ha," Elinor repeated faintly. "Ha?"

"...But when you think of the size they must once have been, before the larger ones were hunted to extinction—when you think of the mark that they made upon history and legend...well!" He sat back in his seat and shrugged. "One can hardly look at such a degradation with any pleasure."

Sir Jessamyn let out a cheep of protest as Aubrey's petting hand retreated. The scholar nodded to him courteously in response. "Not that I blame the dragons, of course."

"Of course." Mr. Hawkins rolled his eyes.

"But Mr. Aubrey," Elinor persisted, "those facial markings—"

"And I still fail to understand what could possibly be essential about my presence at Hathergill Hall!" Aubrey scowled at Mr. Hawkins. "My colleague is *expecting* me in Wales, you know. He *claims* he's made some very interesting discoveries related to the work of a local dragon breeder. It's all nonsense, of course—his theories are impossible—but who is to convince him of his foolishness if not for me?"

"And you will," said Mr. Hawkins. "Only wait a single week, for my sake, please."

"A week!" Aubrey sighed dolefully. "And what exactly am I to do during this week? Sir John may have a vast quantity of dragon scholarship in his library, as you say, if he is a great reader..."

Elinor let out a strangled cough.

Mr. Hawkins winced. "I only said that he *might*, not that

he definitely would. But the point is, old chap, Sir John wouldn't hear of refusal. If you don't come, I can't either, and..." He slid a wary glance at Elinor. "...Well, you know why this visit matters to me."

Mr. Aubrey banished discretion with an impatient wave of his hand. "Yes, yes, pretty girl, large dowry, salvation, I remember." Beside him, Mr. Hawkins closed his eyes with a look of pain, but Aubrey took no notice as he lifted a sheaf of papers and shook them in the air. "Of course I want the best in the world for you, man, but what of my own work? How am I supposed to accomplish *that* at Hathergill Hall?"

"Surely a scholar can work anywhere," Elinor said, taking pity on both of them. "Isn't most of the work you do that of the mind, sir?"

"Well..." He shrugged irritably. "I suppose so. But those dragons in Wales—"

"I have several questions about my own dragon, actually." This time, Elinor was the one who aimed a wary glance across the carriage. "He's been displaying some...ah, some decided *peculiarities* related to those facial markings, and—"

"Indeed?" Aubrey's face brightened. "What sort of peculiarities have you noted? In detail, if you please."

"Indeed," said Mr. Hawkins. "Do tell us, Mrs. De Lacey. Please."

She smiled weakly. "You could hardly be interested, sir. Perhaps later, when Mr. Aubrey has a moment for a private consultation—"

"Oh, nonsense." For the first time since they'd met,

Aubrey set down his papers and firmly pushed aside the book he had been reading. He even gave Elinor a sickly-looking smile—his best attempt at ingratiation, she supposed—as he added, "Hawkins is far less ignorant about dragons than most laymen, I assure you."

"It's true." Mr. Hawkins gave Elinor a rueful smile. "Trust me, after so many years of friendship, it's impossible to avoid *some* knowledge of the species."

"He won't cause us any trouble with stupid questions," Aubrey said briskly. "I have him well-trained. So, Mrs. De Lacey! Exactly which peculiarities have you observed? And exactly when did they begin?"

"Ah..." Elinor looked from one expectant face to the other. "I really think it would be better if—"

A rap at the glass window cut off her words—and made her realize for the first time that the carriage had rolled to a stop.

These windows might not open, but Sir John's bellow, trained on hundreds of hunting fields, was more than capable of reaching through a mere layer of clear glass.

"Mrs. De Lacey!" He waved expansively. "My humble home! At your service!"

Hathergill Hall spread before them: expansive, grey, and only too nauseatingly familiar. Elinor's stomach plunged at the sight.

It hadn't even been twenty-four hours since she had escaped.

Was it her imagination, or had a curtain just fluttered at

the front of the house? Penelope always did like to know which visitors were arriving.

Elinor took a deep breath as her heart began to race frantically behind her chest. She had always pitied the red foxes who were mercilessly run to their deaths by her uncle and his friends. But she had never felt so much empathy for their situation...and she was about to walk voluntarily into her own hunters' home.

Her fingers twisted painfully together in her lap as her breath shortened.

Rose, she reminded herself. *Harry.*

And then: *Mrs. De Lacey.*

Her spine stiffened. Her chin lifted.

No one called Mrs. De Lacey helpless prey. *No one!*

"Excellent." Elinor's smile felt as jagged as an icicle waiting to fall and shatter to the ground. "I can hardly wait to get started."

CHAPTER 9

Elinor might have imagined that first curtain-flutter from Hathergill Hall, but she couldn't have missed the second one as Sir John flung the carriage door wide. She didn't miss the flash of golden curls behind curtain, either...and it made her stomach clench with visceral dread.

She'd stepped out of another carriage in this spot six months earlier, still weary with grief and desperately missing her sisters but also brimming with a naïve, foolish hope. She had been so determined to make herself a new home. She'd imagined that she might be welcomed—even liked—by her extended family once they came to know her.

You're not the despised poor relation anymore, she reminded herself. *As Mrs. DeLacey, you're the one Penelope ought to fear.*

It was more than difficult to believe—but at least she didn't have to suffer long in anticipation. The front door of

Hathergill Hall was already opening as Elinor started down the carriage steps, steadfastly refusing Sir John's offers of assistance. Penelope, still tying her china-blue bonnet ribbons under her chin, started out of the house—then jumped back, one hand flying to her mouth in theatrical astonishment.

"Oh my goodness! Papa, I had no idea you were already back. And with visitors!"

"I am indeed." Sir John puffed himself up with delight. "Caught you on your way out for a morning constitutional, have we, pet?"

She smiled enchantingly, peeping out from under the broad brim of her bonnet like a naughty angel. "The weather is *so* lovely, I simply couldn't help myself. You know how I dote upon nature!"

...And yet Penelope, Elinor noted, wasn't wearing a walking dress or even outdoor shoes. If so much as a speck of dirt smudged those pink silk slippers—newly ordered from London—she was certain to throw a royal fit.

Had anyone else noticed?

Apparently not. Sir John was beaming down at his daughter on the drive, Aubrey was muttering to himself in the carriage as he selected the three or four bucket-loads of papers that absolutely *had* to be carried in his own hands to the house, and Mr. Hawkins...

...Benedict Hawkins was standing at the top of the carriage steps, gazing wide-eyed at Penelope, as if caught in a trance.

Elinor bit down hard on the inside of her cheek as she turned away. *Stupid, stupid, stupid.* How could she be disappointed? Gentlemen always looked at Penelope that way, even when she wasn't smiling in the sunshine, golden hair glinting beneath her bonnet. As Elinor looked from Mr. Hawkins to Penelope, all the smothering despair and suffocation of the past six months sank once more across her shoulders with a crushing weight.

Had she actually forgotten, even for an instant, the kind of contrast that she and her cousin always formed? Of course he'd believe anything that Penelope said about her from now on.

She took a step backward without even realizing it. As Sir Jessamyn scrabbled to hide his face behind her head, her own chin sank down. Her eyes lowered, too, forming the image of invisibility and perfect submission that she'd learned to perfect during the last several months. No one ever wanted to look at her or be reminded of her existence... and when she was with Penelope, she was never allowed to forget that.

This time, though, Sir John gestured her forward, clearing his throat portentously. "Now, then, Penelope! Can you guess who I've brought you?"

The words brought Elinor to her senses with a snap. Sir Jessamyn was shivering against her neck. She swung her chin up and her shoulders back, desperately sweeping up the cloak of Mrs. De Lacey-ness around her.

Mrs. De Lacey wouldn't be intimidated by Penelope. Mrs.

De Lacey knew *herself* to be the most interesting woman in any room.

Elinor raised her eyebrows into an arch of haughty expectation and willed Sir Jessamyn not to lose control all over her. *Not this time!*

Penelope had looked straight past her when they'd first arrived, of course, because Penelope was never interested in other ladies, especially older ladies, when there were gentlemen about. Now, though, at her father's words, she turned with a pretty, expectant smile. It lasted only a moment.

Then her eyes widened. "Papa! It isn't—you can't mean to say—"

"My dear." Sir John positively glowed with pleasure. "I found her at The Lion's Head, already on her way to meet you. Mrs. De Lacey, may I present my daughter Penelope?"

"Delightful." Elinor forced herself to meet Penelope's gaze, and offered her hand as courtesy demanded. She dropped it, though, at the very first brush of fingertips, and turned immediately back to Sir John, taking care to keep Sir Jessamyn's face safely pointed away from her cousin. He was trembling with long, silent shivers, but as long as he couldn't see her, he seemed able to bear it. "And your wife?" Elinor said expectantly to her uncle.

"Ah...well, *she's* inside somewhere, I suppose, but..." His gaze darted back and forth between her and Penelope, whose lips had begun to push into a pout. "Penelope, Mrs. De Lacey has generously agreed to help with your début."

"Oh!" Penelope's incipient pout vanished, transformed into a beaming smile. "Then I am *so* pleased you could come after all, Mrs. De Lacey! It will be a marvelous ball, you know. The very best people will be coming from miles around. I *knew* you couldn't bear to miss it, even with a sore throat. No matter what Elinor—well. *I* knew that you must choose me in the end!"

"Indeed," Elinor murmured. "My throat is...much improved."

"We must write to the newspapers immediately, Papa! When everyone reads that Mrs. De Lacey will be in attendance at my début ball—"

"I beg your pardon," Elinor said, "but we won't tell the newspapers beforehand, if you please!"

"What?" Penelope and Sir John both spoke at once.

"*Not* tell the newspapers?" Sir John demanded

"But—but—!"Colour mounted on Penelope's cheeks.

"Not until after I've left Hathergill Hall," Elinor said firmly. "I am having a quiet rural retreat. I don't wish it to be disturbed."

"A quiet rural retreat?" Penelope breathed. "*Quiet? Rural*? But *my début*—"

"We'll write immediately after your début, pet, once Mrs. De Lacey is gone," said Sir John. "I'm sure she won't mind that."

"If you must." Elinor tried not to imagine what the real Mrs. De Lacey's reaction when she saw that notice.

Elinor would be long gone by then, and this illusion would be safely past, too. *Surely*.

She slid a nervous glance at Sir Jessamyn. He had finally stopped shivering, but he was hunched with unusual stiffness on her shoulder, head lowered, peering carefully away from Penelope through slitted golden eyes.

With a pang of empathy, Elinor recognized the pose. He was trying to be invisible...just as she had when they'd first arrived. It appeared that they had both learned that lesson in their time here before.

How dared Penelope make him feel so small and helpless? For the first time since she'd arrived, Elinor didn't have to pretend the assertiveness that held her chin upright and her eyes raised in absolute equality with everyone around her.

No one had the right to make Sir Jessamyn feel that way. Elinor was *damned* if she would ever let it happen again!

"I believe there are more introductions to be made, Sir John." She waved a careless hand at the men behind her without turning to look back. If Benedict Hawkins wanted to keep on gaping at Penelope, let him. "In the meantime, though, my dragon will require more food soon, and I should like to retire to my chamber to rest from my journey."

"Of course, of course. The maids—"

"—Will show me to my room, I am sure." Elinor swept past him, ignoring the gathering storm on Penelope's pinkening face.

"But my début—! You can't leave before we even begin to—"

"I'm sure it can all be arranged this afternoon." Elinor kept a steadying hand on Sir Jessamyn's back as they brushed past her cousin, and she felt the long shiver that rippled through his body. But there was no tell-tale chuckle as he tucked himself even tighter around her neck. *Brave dragon*, she thought, with fierce pride.

Out loud, though, all she said was, "Goodbye, Penelope."

IT WAS the first time she had ever gone against her cousin's wishes without a punishment. Perhaps it should have felt like victory. But as Elinor followed a hastily-summoned maid up the main staircase of Hathergill Hall, exhaustion wrapped around her like a fog. All of the piled-up drama and panic of the last twenty-four hours felt so heavy, she nearly staggered under its weight. If she could only make it to her bedroom and be safe...

"Ma'am?" The maid's voice pierced her fog. Elinor snapped back into awareness to find the girl staring at her in open puzzlement. "I'm afraid we haven't quite reached your room yet."

"I beg your pardon?" Elinor frowned—then felt a lurch of horror as she looked down at her own hand. Her fingers rested on an all-too-familiar door handle. Without even thinking, she'd already begun to swing open the door...

...Into the bedroom that she'd slept in for the past six months.

She snatched back her fingers as if she'd been burned. "Ah. I see. That is..." She drew a deep breath, searching for inspiration.

Had she ever really looked at this particular maid before? She knew Carter, Lady Hathergill's abigail, only because Carter also arranged Penelope's hair. The housemaid who stood before her now, though—was her name Sally? Or was Elinor only imagining having heard the housekeeper address her that way?

At home, before her parents' death, Elinor had known not only the names of their two maids, but all the familiar details of their families and lives. Saying goodbye to them had been one of the many painful wrenches of the past year. But Elinor's home, comfortable though it had been, had been no Hathergill Hall. Matters were run very differently here.

Sally was only one of the many maidservants in Hathergill Hall who lit the fires and cleaned the rooms, neat in their uniforms and utterly impenetrable in their silence—at least in front of the Hathergills and their guests. Elinor had never paid close attention to her, any more than—she'd imagined—Sally or any of the other servants had ever paid close attention to Elinor, a poor relation whose opinion and influence could not matter.

Now, though, she looked into Sally's startled grey eyes and remembered with a jolt that these servants might be too well-trained to draw the attention of any members of the family...but that didn't stop them from observing everything around them with keen intelligence.

It wasn't only her own family that Elinor had to fool this week with her disguise.

Forcing a laugh, she stepped back. "No, I can see that this wouldn't be my room. It's rather small and dark, isn't it?"

Then she remembered who she was talking to, and winced. The maids in this great house slept two to a room in the dark upper attics, without any windows to brighten their cramped quarters.

"Yes, ma'am." Sally lowered her eyes submissively. "If you'll follow me..."

Elinor followed, silently cursing herself at every step.

When she'd first arrived at Hathergill Hall, she'd been surprised and chilled by the anonymity of the servants, as well as by Penelope's treatment of them. But perhaps she had absorbed more than she'd known—or hoped—from her cousin's attitudes.

The room Sally led her to instead was large and airy, with long windows overlooking the gardens and wallpaper striped a bright yellow and white. It was exactly what Mrs. De Lacey would consider her due, but it took Elinor a long, frozen moment at the door before she could bring herself to step inside as if it truly belonged to her.

Foolish, she told herself as she sank onto the canopied bed at last. *Dangerously foolish.*

"May I bring you anything else, ma'am?" Sally asked.

"No," Elinor said, and then added, because she couldn't help herself, "thank you."

She saw the flash of surprise on the girl's face even as Sally dipped her head in a curtsey. The door closed quietly behind her, and Elinor closed her eyes with a groan. "Argh!"

Sir Jessamyn nosed her cheek with an inquiring cheep. She sighed and reached out to stroke his face. "Oh, don't worry. I'm fine. I'm a fool, that's all."

The cuddling helped, though. After a few minutes, she managed to open her eyes again, and Sir Jessamyn seemed to take it as a sign. He uncoiled himself and hopped down onto the bed. As he paced around the flowered bedcover, searching for the best patch of sunlight in which to bask, Elinor opened her eyes, rubbed her forehead and forced herself back to work.

All she wanted was write to her sisters now, to unleash the unhappiness and fear that she felt. But any letter that she wrote would be passed through the butler at Hathergill Hall, and Mrs. De Lacey couldn't possibly write to Elinor's sisters, not without arousing the suspicion of the household. Mrs. De Lacey would only send letters to her fashionable friends, her London correspondents, or...

"Oh!" Elinor straightened with a jerk that made Sir Jessamyn raise his head, golden eyes glittering with lazy curiosity.

"That's it!" she said. "Oh, Sir Jessamyn. I couldn't afford to travel to London to search for employment. But I don't need to anymore! Sir John orders all of the newspapers from

London and Bristol. I'll search the advertisements and apply for a post from here!"

She stood up, filled with new resolution. "All I have to do is ask for the morning papers to be delivered to me every day once Sir John is finished with them. Who knows? By the end of the week, I may have found us a new home. If they're reasonable people, they might even pay for our transportation."

Sir Jessamyn lowered his head back to the cotton bedcover, clearly unexcited about going anywhere. His jewel-coloured body sprawled in a long line of contentment, bathing in the sunlight from the windows as Elinor started for the bell-pull that hung by the door.

"Where do you think you should like to live?" she asked him. "Clifton is said to be a lovely town. Or perhaps Taunton or—oh!"

A soft knock had sounded on the door. Elinor blinked, her hand still halfway to the bell-pull. Had Sally somehow known that she was wanted without being asked? No, that was absurd. Why would a maid bother to knock? It had to be one of the family members—probably Lady Hathergill, roused to unusual exertions by news of her famous guest.

"Come in," Elinor called.

She smoothed down her gown and lifted her chin, ready for her final reintroduction. Lady Hathergill, at least, had never said anything openly cruel in all of Elinor's time here. So she mustered quite a creditable smile as she turned towards the opening door. "How nice—" she began.

Then her mouth dropped open as she saw who stood just outside her bedroom.

"Mrs. De Lacey," said Benedict Hawkins in a low, urgent whisper, "I beg your pardon for such a shocking intrusion upon your privacy, but I really must speak with you in private."

CHAPTER 10

"Mr. Hawkins!" Elinor took a step back in surprise before she recollected herself. "What on earth are you doing here?"

"I know it's shockingly improper." Taking a careful step back from the doorway of her bedroom, he glanced around the deserted hallway with a wince. "I'm afraid I couldn't help myself, though. You see, I tried to ask you an important question in the carriage, but Aubrey interrupted us, and I lost my nerve. Now I don't know how else to ask in private. Mrs. De Lacey..."

"Yes?" Elinor felt her pulse beating swiftly against her throat. He couldn't know the truth, she told herself. It was too impossible, too unlikely. But the way he was looking at her... it was as if he could read the secrets hiding behind her disguise.

He stepped closer to the doorway, his green gaze intent. "Mrs. De Lacey, I must ask you, in the strictest confidence: what truly happened to the young lady who left the inn last night? Elinor Tregarth?"

"What?" She let out her held breath in a whoosh of surprise and relief as she stepped forward to meet him, lowering her voice to a discreet whisper. "I beg your pardon? Mr. Hawkins, surely you heard me tell Sir John—"

"Yes," he said. "I heard what you told him. But, ma'am..." He smiled ruefully as he looked her up and down, from the top of her head to the bottom of her cheap, unfashionable brown gown. "I understand that eccentricity can be fashionable, and I was impressed by how well you told your story... and yet, I'm afraid it didn't quite convince me. Not when there was a much simpler explanation for your situation that made so much more sense."

"Oh?" She braced one hand against the doorframe and raised her eyebrows. "I can hardly wait to hear it. Do tell me what wild story you've concocted."

"Well..." Linking hands behind his back, he took a breath. "*If* Sir John is to be believed about his niece's character, then there's one rather obvious explanation. Miss Tregarth could have stolen your carriage, with all your clothing inside, and taken off into the night like the criminal her uncle calls her."

"Fascinating." Elinor fought to keep her voice level and her eyes on his. "Is that what *you* think happened, then? You apparently met Miss Tregarth, Mr. Hawkins. Did she strike you as a wicked criminal and a fugitive from justice?"

"Did she—?" Letting out a stifled half-laugh, he turned away from her, his gaze fixed on the empty passageway and his expression frustratingly impossible to read.

"It doesn't matter how she struck me," he said at last. "There's a rather more compelling fact in play. Why would you let a fugitive escape so easily? Why would you allow yourself to be robbed without a single word of complaint?"

"Perhaps I take all of my possessions lightly." Elinor could hear a roaring at the back of her head; she had to force herself to relax her fingers around the wooden frame of the door. "Perhaps I have so many carriages and clothes to spare that I don't mind losing a few here and there."

"Or..." He turned back to face her. "Perhaps you're the one who suggested it in the first place."

"Suggested that I be robbed?" Elinor let out a laugh that creaked with strain. She shifted a few inches backwards, her arm falling to her side. "Mr. Hawkins, as entertaining as it may be to listen to these flights of fancy—"

"No, listen," he said. "You can trust me!" He stepped forward, eating up the distance between them, and Elinor couldn't bring herself to move away. "I met Elinor Tregarth. I understand. She needed help. Good God, she deserved far more help than *I* could give her—I only realised how much today, when I met her uncle and understood how much trouble she was in. If you did choose to help her—to give her your case of clothing and order your coachman to drive her to any safe harbour you knew—I will be infinitely grateful, ma'am. But..." He swallowed visibly. "Please, you must tell me, so that I can stop torturing myself about what's become of her!"

Elinor blinked, twice. "You've been worrying about her?"

"Of course I have!" He spun away, grasping the doorframe with one big hand as if it were an anchor. "She hasn't any money at all—not at *all*, did you realize? Our carriage knocked her into a ditch. She lost everything from her reticule—and I'd wager there wasn't much in there to start with! She had no means of supporting herself in the world, no relatives to offer her any protection, not even a maid to stand with her against the dangers of the road—and if you think of all the rogues only waiting to prey upon helpless young women like her…!"

Elinor shook her head. "I don't understand. You heard Sir John—"

"I heard exactly what he said," Benedict Hawkins snarled. "And after talking to both Elinor Tregarth and her uncle, I know exactly which one to believe." Turning back to her, he fixed her with a grim look. "Forgive me for speaking disrespectfully of any acquaintance of yours, Mrs. DeLacey, but can you honestly tell me that *you* would trust Sir John's word over that of any young lady?"

Elinor thought of one in particular. "It would depend upon the lady, I suppose."

He dismissed that with a quick gesture. "Elinor Tregarth is painfully honest."

"Ah." Elinor swallowed uncomfortably and shifted another inch backwards.

"She has far more integrity than is good for her. Otherwise she would never have found herself in such a situation in the first place! If she stole that dragon, she had a reason for it." He took a deep breath and straightened his shoulders. "Mrs. De Lacey, please. I must know. Did you spirit her away in your carriage last night or did you not?"

Elinor opened her mouth. No words came out.

Elinor Tregarth is painfully honest.

She felt Sir Jessamyn watching them from the bed, his golden gaze intent.

If Mr. Hawkins truly meant everything that he had said... if he would actually believe her, or even take her side...

Wait.

"Tell me, Mr. Hawkins." She brushed down her gown. It gave her an excuse to look away from his too-compelling eyes. "You're very agitated for Miss Tregarth's safety, but you don't seem to have considered the other side to this story."

"What other side? She's alone, friendless—"

"Her cousin," Elinor said sharply. "Miss Hathergill. What was it Mr. Aubrey said of her? 'Pretty girl, large dowry, salvation'?"

Mr. Hawkins winced. "Ah. Yes. I was...rather hoping you hadn't caught that."

"Were you indeed?" She raised her eyebrows. It was as haughty a 'Mrs. De Lacey' look as she could imagine, but at that moment, it came entirely naturally. "Are you telling me that he was incorrect?"

"No," he said. "Aubrey wasn't incorrect."

"I see." Elinor met his gaze full-on. "Then you are hoping to persuade Miss Hathergill to marry you?"

He stood as rigid as a soldier at attention. "Yes. I am. I must."

"And Miss Hathergill is the one whose dragon Miss Tregarth stole. The one who sent her father out to hunt Miss Tregarth down."

Benedict frowned. "Sir John did seem to be implying as much, but that hardly seems likely, does it? I'm sure he was only using her as an excuse."

Disappointment tasted bitter in Elinor's mouth. "Indeed," she said. "We can always hope as much. But now perhaps you'd like to leave the way you came? You'll have to forgive me, Mr. Hawkins, but I don't believe I owe any account of Miss Tregarth's whereabouts to Penelope Hathergill's future fiancé."

The angry, hurting words were out of her mouth before she could even think them through...and Benedict Hawkins went still at the sound of them.

"'Future fiancé'?" he repeated.

Oh, Lord. Elinor's chest tightened. "Well?" She swallowed before her voice could crack. "Isn't that what you are? Or, at least, hope to be?"

He was staring at her, his hazel eyes wide. "It's an ear-catching phrase. Not one used every day."

She managed a brittle smile, without meeting his eyes. "Are you accusing *me* of being ordinary?"

"No-o," he murmured. "Not that. But..." His voice dropped away.

The silence between them hummed with tension. Elinor could feel his frowning gaze resting on her face. She barely breathed, all of her focus on staying perfectly still, not making a single move that might reveal the truth.

Be Mrs. De Lacey, she told herself. *You are Mrs. De Lacey. You are—*

And then suddenly it was perfectly simple. Would the real Mrs. De Lacey ever allow herself to be trapped by a stranger's questions in her own bedroom—for the second time in a day, at that?

Elinor waved her arm in a truly magnificent gesture of dismissal. "This *has* been an entertaining interlude," she said, "but really, Mr. Hawkins, I think you may have gone a little deaf. Did you not hear me say that it was time for you to leave?"

"I did." The tension in the air released with his sigh. "Again, I must ask you for your forgiveness." He began to turn but then paused, his frown deepening. "I won't pursue you any further for answers, Mrs. De Lacey. But from what little you've told me...you'll have to expect me to draw my own conclusions."

"You may think whatever you choose," Elinor snapped, "so long as you do it in your room rather than mine—and *don't* allow anyone to see you leaving! I'd prefer not to have any scandalous rumours spread about me on this visit."

"I understand. And I thank you." He stepped forward, the tips of his toes just passing the barrier into her room. As his rueful smile caught her gaze, he reached out—and before she even realized what he was doing, he had taken her hand and raised it to his lips.

"Aah!" She jumped backward, yanking herself free...too late.

He had kissed her *actual hand*.

Her knuckles tingled where his dry, warm lips had brushed against them. Her fingers tingled with reaction, too—her true fingers, which were *at least* half an inch smaller and stubbier than the long and elegant fingers of Sir Jessamyn's illusions. He had just felt them in his grasp...

And now he was staring at her as if he had seen a ghost.

Panic rang clanging bells of warning in her ears. "You may go now!"

"I..." Blinking hard, he shook his head and then took a step forward. "But you—"

"*Now*, Mr. Hawkins!" Elinor scrambled backwards.

He turned and left the room without a word.

ELINOR SANK down onto the bed, gasping for breath. Faintly, she heard Sir Jessamyn cheep with concern behind her. She couldn't bring herself to turn around, not even for him.

Benedict Hawkins had kissed her hand—but that wasn't the important part, no matter how much her mind wanted to linger on every irrelevant sensation. *Think, Elinor!* He had felt the truth behind the illusion. And then...

"No," she said. "No, no, no!" She lunged up from the bed. "He does not know me. He does *not*."

Too many prickling emotions were swamping her at once. She paced through the room, struggling to shake them off. *Be sensible*, she told herself. *Don't let emotions carry you away! You're not a romantic heroine, remember?*

Perhaps Mr. Hawkins *had* felt the wrongness and dissonance between the illusion he'd seen and the truth he had touched for that one, fleeting moment. But it would be madness for him to leap to the impossible, true conclusion based on that moment of startlement. If Elinor carried off her next meeting with him with panache, he would be forced to set it down to a trick of his own mind.

She was safe. *Of course.* She was safe from Benedict Hawkins in every way.

And now she was lying to herself, too.

Elinor tipped her head against the glass of the window, letting out her breath in a sigh. Outside, the gardens of Hathergill Hall spread out in neatly ordered rows, every flower marching in perfect order. Each one could be confident of its place in the world...just like everyone in Hathergill Hall except for her.

Elinor Tregarth is painfully honest.

She wanted to shut her eyes against the truth, but she couldn't.

Her knuckles still tingled where Benedict had kissed them. She remembered every word he had said about her. She already knew—no matter how hard she tried not to—that she would hear them again before falling asleep that night, and for many nights to come.

She wondered if she would ever manage to forget them...

But no matter how much common sense railed against it, she couldn't bring herself to forget the impractical, impossible truth now that she had finally admitted it to herself.

Elinor had fallen head over heels in love with Benedict Hawkins, her cousin's future husband.

CHAPTER 11

It took longer than she would have liked, but by the time Lady Hathergill's abigail, Carter, finally arrived to prepare her for luncheon, Elinor had regained self-control...and formed a plan, too.

"It was kind of my cousin to send you," she told Carter. "However, as you can see, I've managed to dress myself already, and I don't need you to arrange my hair."

As an upper servant—and one who worked regularly with Penelope, at that—Carter was, of course, far too well-trained to disagree with her employers. Her horror was clear to read on her face, though, as she looked at the plain, tight, high knot that Elinor had scraped her hair into—the only style Elinor had ever successfully managed on her own, and the one that had been deemed most appropriate for a despised poor relation during the last six months.

Carter was not merely a ladies' maid; she was a true artist, an acknowledged genius with hair. "Yes, ma'am," she murmured, dipping a polite curtsey...but she sounded as if she were gagging on the words.

Elinor felt a sudden stab of uncertainty. Benedict's earlier words rang in her ears: *"Eccentricity can be fashionable, and yet..."*

Rapidly, she revised her plans. "Actually, what I should really like would be for you to show me how to arrange it better!" She smiled brightly. "I've never done without an abigail before, but I'm determined to prove that I can manage. I think it would be *most* amusing to learn how to dress my own hair. Don't you?"

Carter blinked twice in a row. Her face twitched. "Yes...ma'am."

Carter really *was* highly professional, Elinor reflected. Thus far, the woman somehow hadn't uttered the words: *You inane fool*...even though they must have been positively choking her.

"It's for a wager," Elinor added. "My friend, Lady"—she paused, searching for a name from the gossip columns—"Lady Featherstone said that I could never manage it. So I *must* prove her wrong. You see?"

"Yes, ma'am. I do see." Carter's shoulders relaxed, and Elinor let out a silent sigh of relief.

Everyone knew that wealthy and idle people made nonsensical wagers all the time. There was a thin line between eccentricity and implausibility...but this time, Elinor had landed on the right side.

She seated herself at the elegant dressing table, watching Carter's face in the mirror. "Please," she said firmly, "do not touch my hair *at all*—even the slightest brush of your fingertips would count as cheating, by the terms of our wager. If you could simply explain what I should do with it?"

She walked into the front parlour half an hour later, carrying Sir Jessamyn proudly on her shoulder. Her dark grey gown was as cheap and unimpressive as ever, but her hair was arranged high on her head in a reasonably elegant updo that even sent dark ringlets down to frame her face.

"At least you needn't take the time to curl *those*," Carter had said with approval, as she'd directed Elinor in the arrangement. "Your hair has all the curl it needs already, doesn't it, ma'am?"

Elinor could only smile and nod...even as she felt the straight brown hair against her fingers, hanging behind the illusion of thick black curls. The difference between what she'd seen in the mirror and the physical substance she'd touched with her fingers had made the entire procedure twice as difficult as it should have been. It wouldn't have been easy even without the illusion...but she knew how astonishingly, miraculously lucky she was that it had worked at all under these circumstances. Apparently, Sir Jessamyn's illusion was clinging tightly to the truth and following her own physical features and actions as closely as possible.

Elinor was grateful, too, that she'd taken the time to do that painstaking work under Carter's patient direction. Every member of the Hathergill household was gathered now along the two long couches and the cluster of straight-backed chairs, along with Benedict Hawkins, Mr. Aubrey, and—the muscles in Elinor's back tightened as she recognized them—two young ladies whom she knew only too well: Penelope's closest friends and admirers, Lucinda Grace and Millie Staverton.

Lucinda's and Millie's avid gazes went straight to the gray gown that Elinor wore. "Isn't that—?" Lucinda's whisper pierced the room.

Millie's eyes opened wide with delighted horror. "Why, Penelope was right. She really *is* wearing—"

"Mrs. De Lacey!" Sir John surged to his feet, followed by Mr. Hawkins.

Mr. Aubrey was the only gentleman in the room to remain seated. Elinor took no offense at his lack of attention; he was, of course, reading a book, and judging by his expression of furious disgust, this author was clearly as hopelessly deluded as every other dragon scholar...apart from himself. She doubted that he could be roused from such satisfying outrage without the use of physical force, but she did wonder just how much time and effort Penelope, Millie and Lucinda had wasted in the attempt.

That thought made her lips quirk and her spine relax enough to allow her to move somewhat gracefully forward and take her own seat—*not* in the spot that Sir John had indicated, on the couch between him and Penelope, but beside his wife, on the couch opposite. Of all of the people in this room, she most trusted her aunt not to make any sudden movements.

Sir Jessamyn had also tensed when they'd first walked into the room and he had seen Penelope, but now he climbed down Elinor's arm and onto her lap, where he curled up in a warm, glittering pile of blue and green scales and buried his face beneath his tail.

"My dear friend." Lady Hathergill roused herself to give Elinor a sweet, vague smile from the other side of the couch. "How glad I am to see you again after so long. I do hope the trip from London was not too difficult for you?"

"Mama!" Penelope let out a sharp titter. "How can you even ask such a thing? Only look at her. Do you imagine Mrs. De Lacey would *ever* wear one of my cousin Elinor's dreary gowns if her trip had not been *difficult*?"

Lucinda and Millie giggled in perfectly enthralled unison...and Elinor's chest tightened by instinct. She knew that sound.

For the past six months, whenever Penelope had been most dangerously bored, one of her favourite solutions had been to summon Elinor to do her assigned sewing—assorted plain mending for the household—in the sitting room on command. Then Penelope would enjoy making all of her keenest witticisms, while Lucinda and Millie giggled in delighted appreciation and whispered their own addendums into Penelope's ears.

Elinor, of course, could never respond with anything but courtesy...and even when she *was* there in the room to hear them, Lady Hathergill had only ever closed her eyes and drifted safely away into her own world, far from the unpleasantness that surrounded her. So Elinor had taught herself to endure those moments by wearing an expression of solid stone, keeping her back stiff and her face firmly lowered over her work.

Mrs. De Lacey, though, didn't have to endure any of it—so Elinor was finally free to fight back.

"Don't you care for your cousin's gowns, then?" She cocked her head in inquiry, her voice like honey. "I am all astonishment, Penelope. I had heard *so* much about your generosity to your poor cousin. You *were* the one who chose all of her clothes from the moment she arrived, were you not?"

"Well..." A pretty flush rose in Penelope's cheeks. "I *did* allow her to use my own dressmaker, because I felt so sorry for her, but—"

"*And* you chose the patterns and quality of cloth that would be available to her, did you not?" Elinor smiled sweetly. "That is what I was told. So—as you were so motivated by generosity, and *of course* only desired to help her—this gown must be what *you* consider most attractive, must it not?"

Penelope stared at her, open-mouthed and silent. In the corner of her vision, Elinor saw Mr. Hawkins's brows lower into a frown as he watched. Millie let out an uncertain giggle —but it cut off as Lucinda glared her into silence.

Sir John smiled fondly at his daughter. "You *were* only too generous to your cousin, weren't you, pet? Aye, there's the danger of innocence, Mrs. De Lacey. You never know when your own acts of kindness can betray you."

"*Yes!*" Penelope's chest rose and fell; tears sparkled in her blue eyes as she seized control of the new conversational direction. "My cousin stole *everything* from me," she whispered. "When I think of how I trusted her and was so cruelly betrayed..."

This time, it was Elinor's turn to be struck dumb. Millie and Lucinda, however, were more than ready to leap into the breach.

"She really *was* terrible, Mrs. De Lacey," said Millie. "If you had only seen the way she used to sit there scowling at everything and everyone—"

"She looked exactly like a crow crouched in the corner of the room," Lucinda said. "Penelope *tried* to make her choose gowns in brighter colours, but she actually refused. Refused! Can you believe that anyone would choose that shade of grey?"

Mourning, Elinor thought distantly. *I was mourning. For my parents.* But Mrs. De Lacey couldn't know that. No, wait. Could she?

Her head was beginning to cloud with rage, making it difficult to think through what she could or couldn't say. Sir

Jessamyn had lifted his own head from his tail and was humming worriedly in the back of his long throat as he looked up at her. She stroked his neck gently, fighting for control.

Millie scooted her chair closer, brown eyes sparkling with excitement. "Do you know, Penelope said she *never* saw her cousin laugh. Not even once! She—how did you say it, Penelope? Oh yes—*she* said Elinor could never have been introduced to a sense of humour. It wouldn't even know what to do with a stormcloud like her. Ha!" She beamed. "*That*'s what Penelope said. She's *so* clever, you know! Everyone thinks so."

"What a pity that Penelope's cousin was so unappreciative of her wit." Elinor knew she had to take better control of her tone, but it was becoming more and more difficult, especially as she caught Mr. Hawkins shifting uncomfortably in his chair.

"The weather today..." he began.

"Oh, she was poor company in *every* weather," said Penelope. "No matter how I tried to like her..."

Elinor was trying with all of her might to focus on the warmth of Sir Jessamyn's scales under her hand and the support of his glittering, golden gaze focused so very intently on her face. "Perhaps she didn't hear anything that amused her."

"Oh, no, that couldn't have been it!" Lucinda sniffed. "She was just grim. Grim, grim, grim! And *so* very plain, you would never have even guessed that she was Penelope's cousin from looking at her. Oh, and..."

Elinor couldn't bear to see Mr. Hawkins. So she turned to look at her aunt, whose eyes were carefully averted from the scene while her expression—as always—looked gently pained.

She had sent gifts, from time to time, to Elinor and her sisters, when they were younger. Her letter of invitation had been signed with affection. And she looked, even now, so much like Elinor's mother that it made her heart twist. "*Is* all of this true?" Elinor asked her.

"Well, of course it's true!" Penelope snapped. "Haven't you been listening? When you think of everything we did for her—!"

Elinor still couldn't catch Lady Hathergill's eyes, but she watched the grooves in her aunt's cheeks deepen. "What would *you* say, though?" she asked tightly. "You *are* Elinor's aunt. You must have some opinion."

"Oh..." Wincing, Lady Hathergill slid a glance at her daughter. "You mustn't ask me," she said. "I'm sure that Penelope...well..."

"She was *terrible*," said Penelope firmly. "Awful! Ungrateful and sneaking and untrustworthy and—"

Lady Hathergill's eyes fell shut. Elinor knew the finality of that action. But it had never before burned quite so badly as it did now, listening to Penelope and her friends while Benedict Hawkins sat nearby, a silent, watchful audience.

She couldn't let it go to make peace. Not anymore.

"She is *your niece*," Elinor said. "Your younger sister's

daughter! You promised her a safe home. *Would* you describe her to me in the way Penelope has?"

Sir Jessamyn rose to lay his head against her chest. Lady Hathergill grimaced helplessly but kept her eyes firmly closed.

"There's no use asking Mama about it," said Penelope. "*I* am the one who knew my cousin best. And really—"

"No," Elinor gritted through her teeth. "I wish to know. *What does your mother really think?*"

Millie's high-pitched scream of terror broke the tension in the room....just as flaring warmth erupted directly against Elinor's chest.

"Good God!" Mr. Hawkins leaped to his feet. "Mrs. De Lacey, are you badly injured?"

Millie was still screaming. She pointed at Sir Jessamyn as she scooted her chair away in frantic, farcical hops. "He breathed—he breathed—*I saw flame*!"

"I say." Mr. Aubrey finally looked up from his book, blinking. "Are you speaking of a dragon, by any chance? Dragons do *not* breathe fire, I can assure you. That is a historical misapprehension which—"

"*That*," said Benedict Hawkins grimly, "is one point of scholarship upon which we will have to disagree—because I just saw, with my own eyes, Mrs. De Lacey's dragon breathe fire." He started forward. "I don't know how you escaped serious injury, ma'am, but you had better set that creature aside and—"

"No!" Elinor tightened her arms around Sir Jessamyn protectively. "He would never hurt me."

Mr. Aubrey and Benedict began to argue in increasingly heated voices, but for once, she didn't pay either of them any attention. All of her focus was on the dragon in her lap.

Sir Jessamyn nestled comfortably against her stomach. His eyelids drifted downwards as he curled himself into a perfect ball.

As she watched, a second set of golden markings crept slowly but inexorably down his long, blue and green throat, beginning just beneath his chin and looping in bold, sweeping curves towards his chest. Elinor's skin prickled at the sight.

Sir Jessamyn, what have you done now?

The sound beside her was so unfamiliar, it took her a long moment to even realize what it was. It was the sound of Lady Hathergill pointedly clearing her throat and then—as everyone turned to stare—straightening in her seat to sit perfectly upright, with her eyes wide open.

Lady Hathergill shook her head sadly as she looked about the room. "I do wish you would finally learn some manners, Penelope, but I am afraid that it is probably too late for you. I admit I am partly to blame—I allowed your father to overrule me at every turn, which did you no favours. I was never brave like my own sister, though; that was why I quarreled with my dearest friend, all those years ago, when she tried so hard to rouse me into courage. I did hope, though, that you *would* learn better one day—or, at least, that you would learn to be a bit more convincing whenever you pretended to be kind."

Penelope's gasp hit ear-piercing levels of horror and outrage...but Sir Jessamyn closed his eyes and went to sleep on Elinor's lap with evident satisfaction.

CHAPTER 12

Elinor had already had the most unlikely day of her entire life, but as she sat now on the long, forest-green couch and listened to the words streaming out of her aunt's mouth, she felt physically dizzy with disbelief.

"...And I never cared much for your last governess, either. I suppose the reason you never chased her off, though, unlike all of the others—"

"Mary!" Sir John had been sitting in pole-axed silence since she'd first begun to talk. Now he finally broke in, staring at his wife as if she'd developed a second head. "What the devil has come over you?"

"*Over* me?" She frowned at him in obvious confusion. "Why, whatever can you mean? I am just the same as ever, Sir John. I have never thought any differently."

"But—"

"I must say, though, I do feel better than I have in years," she said. "I believe this new tea that Mrs. Braithewaite ordered must have beneficial properties!" She looked over his head and smiled at the maid who stood, open-mouthed and staring, in the doorway. "I see that luncheon is ready. We had better go in now, my dear. Food will settle your nerves—and, we may hope, Penelope's temper, as well."

Lady Hathergill swept out of the room with a confident stride and one hand on her befuddled husband's arm, leaving the rest of the household to gather themselves up somehow behind them. Millie and Lucinda traded nervous glances as they flocked to Penelope's chair.

"I'm sure she didn't truly mean—"

"Oh, Penelope, are you—?"

"She—she—!" Penelope's cheeks flushed deep pink. Her eyes sparkled with outrage. She looked, Elinor had to confess, magnificent. "My mother has gone mad!"

"Ah." Benedict cleared his throat. "Miss Hathergill, if I may?" He bowed and held out his arm to escort her into the next room.

"Oh! Mr. Hawkins..." Penelope bit her lip and lowered her eyelashes. Tears hung, diamond-like, from her lashes. "How can I even bear to meet your eyes, sir, after what you've witnessed?"

"Please don't trouble yourself, Miss Hathergill." Benedict smiled at her with what Elinor recognized, with a pang, as real sympathy. "Every family quarrels from time to time. If you had seen some of the scenes between me and my brothers when we were younger—or heard my grandfather when his gout was paining him..."

"You are *so* kind," Penelope breathed. Looking up at him meltingly, she set one hand on his arm. "I do wish I could accept your escort, Mr. Hawkins. But I believe, in terms of precedence, that Mr. Aubrey—"

"Mr. Aubrey," said Elinor, "must escort *me*, in terms of precedence. How right you are, Penelope, to remember such niceties." She gave her cousin a thin smile, not missing the quickly-hidden flash of resentment that she received in return.

Penelope, it was clear, knew already who Mr. Aubrey's grandfather was, and exactly what sort of fortune he stood to inherit—so there was no time to lose. Elinor gently nudged Sir Jessamyn awake. Grumbling, he allowed her to pour his limp body onto her shoulders. Once there, he nestled his head into the left side of her neck and curled his tail around her right shoulders, so exhausted by his efforts that he barely even twitched as they passed Penelope.

"Shall we, Mr. Aubrey?"

"Eh?" He blinked up at her from his book, frowning. "You aren't here about that *flaming* nonsense, are you? I told Hawkins very clearly—"

"It is time for luncheon, Mr. Aubrey," said Elinor. "You may explain all the details to me while we eat."

"Oh. Well. I suppose, if you're hungry..." He picked up his book again. Then, at a pointed cough from his friend, he sighed. "Am I meant to be coming with you?"

Millie's startled giggle competed with Lucinda's gasp of horror. Elinor rolled her eyes inwardly. "If you would?"

"Oh, very well. Ridiculous habit, though. I had plenty to eat at breakfast." He stood up and held out his left arm with a long-suffering air, still clutching his book tightly in his right hand. "In the wild, you know, dragons forage whenever they're hungry. There's no such thing as set mealtimes, to them."

"Indeed." Elinor set her hand just above his arm, keeping a careful half-inch of distance between them. Mr. Aubrey was the last person in Hathergill Hall who would ever pay any attention to what she looked like...but there was no point in courting danger. When she did ask him for his advice later on, she would do it in privacy, well away from Penelope and her friends.

Penelope flashed Elinor a quick, triumphant smirk as her own escort helped her to her feet with pleasing attentiveness. "Oh, Mr. Hawkins, you are *too good*!"

It was for the best, Elinor told herself, as she walked beside Mr. Aubrey out of the room. It was what Benedict and his family needed. It was what she wanted for him.

She slid a glance over her shoulder. Penelope was smiling waveringly up at Benedict as she brushed away the last of her tears...and Benedict smiled back down at her while Lucinda and Millie both watched with wide, delighted gazes.

"I'm actually afraid to go in there," Penelope murmured. "Isn't that absurd? But the thought of hearing even more cruel things said about me—and in front of *you*,

Mr. Hawkins—! Who could ever possibly bear such a thing?"

Elinor yanked her gaze firmly forward and quickened her steps as much as she could without leaving Mr. Aubrey behind. Still, she couldn't help overhearing.

"Please don't worry, Miss Hathergill," Benedict said. "I'll be sitting beside you, and I promise I've no liking for hurtful gossip of any kind."

"Oh," she sighed, "you are *so* kind! And you make me feel so safe. Will you promise to talk to me for the entire meal?"

Elinor tasted something bitter in her mouth.

"Do you know what, Mr. Aubrey?" she said briskly. "I think you may be right about luncheon, after all. Set mealtimes *are* a ridiculous habit, aren't they? Let us go and talk about dragons instead." She aimed a bright smile at her cousin. "*Do* pass on our excuses to your mother, won't you, Penelope?"

Before anyone could respond, she freed her hand from the crook of Mr. Aubrey's arm and set off at a quick stride, placing one hand on Sir Jessamyn's back to ensure his safety on her shoulders while he slept. Multiple voices rose in shock behind them, but she didn't let them slow her down.

Mrs. De Lacey was allowed to be rude...and even if she wasn't, Elinor found that, for once in her life, she didn't truly care what anyone else thought about her. All that she wanted —no, *needed*—was to escape...and luckily, she knew just where to go.

No one was quick enough to stop her as she led Mr.

Aubrey swiftly through the house to a never-used back parlour, still decorated in the style of the last century. Stalking through it, she pushed open the plain and unimpressive door at its opposite end, hurried through a crowded foyer that was stacked with odds and ends from the past two decades, and finally stepped outside with pure relief.

Fresh air and sunshine poured like a blessing across her skin as she walked into the hidden garden that sat between the main house and the stable block, with high hedges planted carefully on all sides to protect it from general view.

Unlike most of the gardens outside Hathergill Hall, this one was surprisingly small and unassuming. It grew vegetables for the kitchen rather than flowers, and only one—rather uncomfortable—rustic wooden seat was set nearby, under the shade of an oak tree. As far as Elinor knew, no one in the family had ever spent any time there.

That was why it had become her refuge in the last six months.

The green, vibrant scents of the growing plants mingled with the richer and more intense smells of the stables nearby. A breeze rustled through the thick hedges and the branches of the oak tree, and Sir Jessamyn sleepily lifted his head in response, stretching out his neck as far as he could and opening his mouth wide to taste the air current.

Sunlight sparkled off Mr. Aubrey's spectacles as he looked around the garden in bemusement. "Is this really where luncheon is being served?"

Elinor laughed for the first time that day. "No," she said.

"Forgive me, Mr. Aubrey, for abducting you. We've abandoned the official luncheon, actually. If you find that you are hungry after all—"

"Oh, no," he said. "No, this will do quite well. I enjoy reading outside, you know. So much less interference, except when the wind blows my papers away."

"I can imagine," Elinor said. And she could. But the idea of Mr. Aubrey chasing his papers around the garden, while it brought a smile to her mouth, was far more endearing than laughable. She liked Mr. Aubrey. She thought that Benedict Hawkins had good taste in friends.

It was a pity that...*no*. She cut off that train of thought with a snap.

Penelope might have spent the last six months being vile to Elinor, but that was no reason for Elinor to keep on returning the favor. Poisonous thoughts had been her only viable recourse as a poor relation, but over time, they had become a too-addictive habit that needed to be sharply cut off before she turned hopelessly bitter.

Releasing her held breath in a sigh, she walked across the garden to the big oak and set one hand against its wide, rough trunk. Its warmth sank into her skin like a blessing as she let her frustrations sink away. "I will leave you to read here undisturbed, Mr. Aubrey. I had hoped to ask your advice first, though."

"About your dragon?" Mr. Aubrey perked up, his gaze sharpening as he turned to Sir Jessamyn. "You did mention in the carriage that he's been exhibiting peculiarities. What are they, exactly? We can dismiss all that nonsense that Hawkins was gabbling about *fire-breathing*, of course."

"Well..." Elinor moistened her lips. In the warmth of the open air, with the familiar hum of insects buzzing industriously around the garden, it did seem impossible that anyone could ever take her story seriously. But she looked at the hand that she'd set upon the tree trunk—its fingers long and its palm wide—and she summoned her courage. "Do you remember how you called me 'Miss Tregarth' in the carriage?"

"Eh?" He frowned. "Ah, yes. I was confused, you see. The lady who rode with us yesterday—"

"Was me," Elinor said. "I *am* Elinor Tregarth."

"I beg your pardon?" He blinked. "I could have sworn that Hawkins said—"

"*He* thinks I'm Mrs. De Lacey. Everyone does. I look just like her now, you see."

Aubrey shook his head impatiently. "This is all very confusing. Mrs. De Lacey—Miss Tregarth—or whatever you choose to call yourself today—I *still* don't see what this could have to do with dragons."

"It has everything to do with them!" Elinor met his gaze with all the earnestness she could summon. "Mr. Aubrey, I know this may sound entirely fantastical, but Sir Jessamyn, my dragon, is the one who did it! He breathed fire on me last night after supper, and when I woke up this morning, my entire appearance had changed."

Mr. Aubrey's eyes widened behind his spectacles. "What did you say?"

"I was weeping before bed," Elinor said quietly. "I was... unhappy about various things. So I said..." She tried to remember, even as Sir Jessamyn stood up on her shoulders, shook himself off, and wandered down along her outstretched arm to examine the tree she was touching. "I wished I was as handsome and stylish as Mrs. De Lacey, I think? At any rate, he looked me in the eyes and breathed flame upon my face, and when I woke up..." She shrugged helplessly. "I looked like Mrs. De Lacey in every way."

"He breathed flame on your face and transformed you," Mr. Aubrey repeated flatly.

His voice sounded decidedly odd, but Elinor pounced on the words with relief.

"Exactly! And then this morning he did it again. When I said I wished to know what my aunt—Lady Hathergill, that is—what she was thinking, he breathed flame upon me, and then she suddenly started talking!"

"Your aunt began to talk," he repeated, even more flatly than before.

"*Yes*! You can't know how unlikely that was, as you've only just met her, but you may take my word for it that it was unprecedented. And the things she said—!"

"Let me see if I understand you correctly," Mr. Aubrey said, interrupting her. "You are telling me that your dragon can perform...magic?"

"Yes!" Elinor could have wept with relief. "You *do* understand. Thank goodness. But I don't know what to do about it! I have to break the illusion somehow. I can't look like Mrs. De Lacey forever! But if anyone at Hathergill Hall discovers who I really am..."

"He breathed flame and did magic," Mr. Aubrey said, and this time, his voice was nearly unrecognizable.

"Yes?" She looked at him with growing concern. "Is there something amiss? Mr. Aubrey—good heavens, Mr. Aubrey, are you quite well?"

"Am I quite well?" Mr. Aubrey repeated. "*Am I well*?" His voice rose to a roar. "Good God, madam! Have I not suffered enough?"

She blinked at him, taking a step backwards, while Sir Jessamyn hurried back along her arm to take shelter upon her shoulders. "I don't understand."

"I am meant to be in *Wales*!" he shouted. "I am meant to be pursuing desperately needed research, but no, my friend needed me, so here I am. I am *here*, of all the godforsaken places in England! I ask you, madam, have you even *seen* this house's library? Can you *possibly* imagine any way for me to work in such a place?"

"Ah..." She winced. "I do understand the inconvenience, but—"

"But can I leave?" Aubrey demanded. "No! I cannot even depart now as I ought, because I promised Hawkins. I gave him my word that I would stay, no matter how many young ladies giggle at me or how much horrifying talk of *hunting*, of all abominations, may take place. And now—now, when I am already dealing with deprivation and ignorance at every turn!—now, of all times, you've decided to *play a practical joke on me*?"

"No!" Elinor gasped. "Mr. Aubrey, please—"

"Oh, you may find me very amusing," Aubrey said bitterly. "Society ladies generally do, I believe. But madam, I am no joke. I am a scholar. And now, if you will do the honor of excusing me..." He swept her a breathtakingly beautiful bow. "I have *real* work to do."

He stalked back towards the house, gait stiff with outrage.

"Wait!" Elinor picked up her skirts and ran after him. "Mr. Aubrey, wait. I can prove it! The markings on my dragon's face—they've changed again since this morning. And..." In desperation, she grasped his closest sleeve and pulled the cloth towards her, dragging his arm with it. "Here! Feel my face—you can *feel* it's different, underneath, from the illusion you see. Just—"

The door swung open a moment before she could force Aubrey's hand to touch her cheek. She gasped in surprise. Her hand fell off Aubrey's sleeve.

Benedict Hawkins stood in the open doorway, staring at them. "I beg your pardon." His gaze went from Elinor to Aubrey, still standing close together. He looked at Aubrey's furious face, and then at Aubrey's arm as it dropped to his side. When Mr. Hawkins looked up once more at Elinor, his expression was chilly and his tone coldly polite. "Have I interrupted something?"

"I—Mr. Hawkins..." Elinor swallowed hard, searching for

an explanation. “I was only—that is, I was asking Mr. Aubrey…”

“You haven’t interrupted anything,” said Mr. Aubrey. “Trust me, Hawkins. There is nothing this lady has to say that could *ever* interest me.”

CHAPTER 13

Mr. Aubrey stalked into the house and slammed the door behind him...leaving Elinor and Mr. Hawkins in the garden, staring at each other.

Heat flooded Elinor's cheeks. She took a deep breath. *Be Mrs. De Lacey*. She tried for a careless, unaffected laugh. "Well! That was rather..."

"I think I had better warn you, Mrs. De Lacey." Mr. Hawkins's voice was clipped and colder than she had ever heard it. "My friend may seem distracted from everyday life, but he is no fool."

"I—what?" Elinor frowned. "Mr. Hawkins, I don't know what you imagine—"

"Other ladies have tried to trap him into marriage before," Mr. Hawkins said, "but he has escaped every single time, even from the most determined. I would advise you not to waste your effort on the attempt."

Elinor gaped at him. "You think I—*what*? You cannot be serious!"

Mr. Hawkins's expression did not warm. "He may be the heir to one of England's greatest fortunes, but he is not available as an additional source of income, nor as an accessory for your entertainment. It would make him utterly miserable to be taken away from his university studies...and no matter how much wealth his wife might gain, I can promise that she, too, would be miserable after using my friend in such a way. He is one of the best men I know, not a pawn to be manipulated for anyone else's comfort."

"The way you plan to use Miss Hathergill, you mean?" Elinor glared back at him.

A flush crept up from Benedict Hawkins's jawline. "I have great respect for Miss Hathergill."

"Oh, really? Is that 'respect' what brought you here in the first place?"

"That is an entirely different situation." He crossed his arms. "If Miss Hathergill agrees to marry me, I will do my utmost to make her happy for the rest of both of our lives. My friend Aubrey would *never* be happy to be ripped away from Cambridge and forced to attend Society balls as the puppet of a fashionable wife."

He swept her with a scathingly dismissive look. "You may be accustomed to everyone in London falling down before your reputation, Mrs. De Lacey, but Aubrey cares nothing for fashion or popularity, and your status means nothing to him. Don't waste your time, or his, by pursuing him any further."

"You really think I was trying to entrap him." Elinor shook her head wonderingly. "So much for what you said about me earlier!"

"I said..." Benedict's face tightened. "I thought I saw something different in you. Better. Clearly, I was mistaken."

"Clearly." Tears burned behind Elinor's eyes, but she was far too angry to allow them to escape. "I was wrong about you, too, Mr. Hawkins. I think you and Penelope are perfectly suited to one another, after all!"

She stalked towards the door, head held high and vision blurred. Sir Jessamyn let out a cheep of protest as they neared the house, but she ignored it. He nudged his face against her cheek, trying to push her back towards the tree and the rest of the outdoors.

"Later, Sir Jessamyn," she whispered under her breath. "Later."

Later, when they were alone, she would sit outside with him in the fresh air and enjoy the beautiful day...*without* any other company. First, though, she had to sweep past Mr. Hawkins in a way that made her disdain *perfectly* unmistakable, for the sake of her remaining pride.

"What did you just say?" Mr. Hawkins's voice sounded strained as she approached, but then, her heartbeat was thumping so loudly in her ears, it muffled every other sound.

Still, Elinor tilted her chin another half-inch higher, the better to look down her nose at him despite their difference in height. "*I* was talking to my dragon," she said. "You and I have nothing left to say to each other, Mr. Hawkins."

She swept straight past him, ignoring the unfairly appealing warmth that rose from his body and the soft, swishing sound that her long skirts made as they brushed against his boots. She pulled the door open.

He pushed it closed with one hand.

She gaped up at him. "What on earth do you think you're doing?"

"*You* just called your dragon Sir Jessamyn."

They stood only half a foot apart. His strong arm, holding the door shut, nearly brushed against her shoulder. His broad chest rose and fell with his quick breaths.

Elinor's own chest felt so tight that she could barely breathe. "You must have misheard me."

"I don't believe I did." He leaned closer, his hazel gaze fiercely intent. "You called him Sir Jessamyn. That was the name of Elinor Tregarth's dragon."

She felt herself leaning forward, tugged by invisible threads like magnets drawing her into his warmth. They stood so close now that she could feel his warm breath against her face. Her voice came out as thin as gossamer. "What exactly are you suggesting?"

"Did you paint those markings on his face to confuse people? If you have Elinor Tregarth's dragon—"

"*Yes*?" She only shaped the word with her lips. She couldn't summon enough air to speak out loud.

"She would never have given her dragon to a stranger for

any reason." Mr. Hawkins's voice hardened; his face drew into a scowl. "What have you done to her, Mrs. De Lacey?"

"Oh, for heaven's sake!" Elinor jerked backwards. Air flooded back into her chest in a rush that left her reeling. "How absurd can you possibly be?"

"*Nothing* would have induced Elinor Tregarth to betray her dragon's trust." Benedict Hawkins stood as stiff as a soldier, glaring down at her. "He was no mere toy or ornament to her. She truly *loved* him, unlike any other Society lady I've met. There is no payment so high that she would have sold him to you!"

"Then it is a good thing I never asked her to," Elinor snapped. "This is *my* dragon, no matter what his name might be, and those markings on his face are not painted, they are real. You may feel them for yourself if you require any proof."

He frowned down at Sir Jessamyn, who reared his own head back on his long neck to return the inspection with open curiosity. "Why does he have more markings now than he did this morning?"

Elinor ground her teeth. "You will have to think up an answer for yourself. I have nothing more to say to you, Mr. Hawkins—and as you have already insulted me in every possible manner, *you* can have nothing more to say to me, either." She narrowed her eyes. "Now, will you let me pass through that door unimpeded, or must I walk all the way around the house to find another way inside?"

Slowly, Mr. Hawkins stepped away from her. He swept a graceful bow.

Elinor stalked past him without a word.

Voices rose in the distance, but she headed directly for the grand staircase, bypassing the closed dining room door. She felt Mr. Hawkins's presence behind her like an itch, but she refused to give him the satisfaction of looking around or even speeding her steps at any turn.

At the first-floor landing, he finally turned in a different direction. That sudden coolness at her back was a blessed relief. Still, she kept her pace steady, even after she knew he couldn't see her anymore. She walked with dignity down the long corridor to her room, opened her door, stepped inside...

...And stopped short as she saw the maid who sat at her dressing table, holding open the packet of Elinor's private letters from her sisters.

Sally looked up without any sign of embarrassment.

"Miss Elinor," she said wonderingly. She shook her head. "How in the world have you managed it?"

THERE WAS a long moment of silence before Elinor heard her own voice, as if from very far away, ask: "Whatever do you mean?"

"It can't be a mask." Sally was peering at Elinor's face with open curiosity, now, in the reverse of her earlier submissive posture. "It's too good to be a mask, no matter what that Carter says."

Elinor closed the door carefully behind her. "Carter thinks I'm wearing a mask?"

"Oh, her." Sally shrugged dismissively. "It was the only reason *she* could think of why you wouldn't let her touch your hair. But where you'd find a mask that good, *she* couldn't say, nor where you'd find a wig so fine in only half a day's journey from the Hall. That was why she gave up in the end and said you must be Mrs. De Lacey after all, only touched in the head by too much sun."

"But you don't believe that." Elinor met Sally's gaze as the maid stood up, still holding Elinor's letters in her right hand.

Sally smiled ruefully. "You and your family might not know us in service, Miss Elinor, but trust me—we *all* know you. Even if you hadn't tried to walk right back into your old room as if you'd never been away, I haven't ever seen any fine lady but you say please and thank you the way you do. Mostly, though..." She raised the packet of letters high in the air and waved it teasingly. "*Everyone* knows you'd cut off your own hand before you left any of these behind, no matter how fast you were running."

Elinor knew every swirl of ink from Rose and Harry on those pages, every story they'd related, every word of love. She'd read them a thousand times across the last six months, whenever she was safely alone in her room.

But servants went into every room in Hathergill Hall, as a matter of course...and there was no way to ever be completely private.

"I see." Elinor drew a long breath. Sir Jessamyn was a

warm presence on her shoulder, watching Sally with his head alertly cocked. She wished—as absurd as it would have sounded even to her a mere day earlier—that she could ask him for advice. She had no idea what to do next.

All she knew was that she couldn't run again...because Sally had been correct. Elinor would never leave those letters behind.

"I haven't any money," Elinor said flatly, standing still. "I cannot pay for your silence."

Sally's eyes widened. They were a lighter brown than her hair, which was pulled back into a knot so tight, Elinor could barely see any of it beneath her cap; but after a moment of petrified surprise, laughter shook her whole body so hard that several strands of thick, dark hair fell loose from underneath her cap to dance around her shoulders.

"You think—you actually think I—!" Sally sank back down onto the chair and hung onto the back of it as she shook her head, still laughing.

Elinor crossed the room and sank down onto the bed. Sir Jessamyn crawled down her arm and sat down next to her on the bedcover, his neck stretched high and his warm body pressed tightly against her side. Together, they waited for Sally to stop laughing.

When she finally did, Elinor spoke before the maid could say a word. "Forgive me," she said. "I've insulted you."

"You have." Sally shook her head, but she was still grinning. "Were you really afraid I'd try picking your pockets, Miss Elinor? I'm no fool. If I was going to blackmail anyone for money, I can promise it would be someone who had at least a penny or two to her name. Just a *bit* of a waste otherwise, don't you think?"

"A great waste," Elinor said, and felt the last remnants of tension inside her relax into a sigh. "How *do* you explain the way I look, anyway? It isn't a mask, nor a wig, I assure you."

"Well, you have a dragon now, don't you?" Sally shrugged. "Jem the footman saw yours breathe fire in the sitting room not even an hour ago, so who knows what else it can do? Everyone knows they've got some magic in 'em."

This time Elinor was the one who laughed, although it sounded broken to her own ears. "Everyone except the dragon scholars," she said. "Mr. Aubrey didn't believe me when I tried to tell him."

"Scholars!" Sally's tone was scornful. "What do they know outside their books? And why would all the old fairy stories talk so much about dragon magic if they didn't have any?"

"Well..." Elinor bit her lip. She wasn't thinking about scholars, though. Not anymore.

She was remembering the scene with Benedict Hawkins in the garden, and how angry his accusations had made her—how offended she'd been that he would even consider them as possibilities. He'd had far more evidence for his horrible assumptions about her than she had had about Sally, when she had accused the maid of attempting blackmail. Perhaps...

Then she finally caught the meaning of Sally's earlier words.

"Wait," she said. "You're not blackmailing me *for money*?"

"Well, of course not," Sally said easily. "You're as poor as a church mouse, aren't you?"

Elinor looked into the maid's amused, intelligent brown eyes, and felt something clench inside her. "So...what are you blackmailing me for, then?" she asked.

Sally smiled. It was an open, friendly smile—the smile of someone Elinor would have quite liked to be friends with, under any other circumstances. Just at the moment, though, it filled her with dread.

"Don't you worry, Miss Elinor," Sally said. "What I need should be no trouble to you...or no trouble for *Mrs. De Lacey*, anyway." She patted the packet of Elinor's sisters' letters as she tucked them neatly into the pocket of her apron. "And just so long as you help me with what I need, there'll be no reason for me to tell Sir John what I know. So you can just think of me as a partner from now on, can't you?"

Elinor's eyes locked on the letters in Sally's pocket. All she had to do was lunge forward to try to wrestle them away...

...But she couldn't escape Hathergill Hall again. Not with Rose and Harry depending on her to keep her promise to Sir John and remain here all week. And if Sir John was given enough reason to start asking hard questions...

Elinor drew in a deep, shivering breath that rattled every bone in her body. With a worried look up at her, Sir

Jessamyn leaned even more tightly into her side—but for once, his warm support couldn't make any difference. Not with her sisters' letters so close...and so completely out of reach.

"Very well." Elinor's shoulders sagged. "Tell me what you want me to do."

CHAPTER 14

An hour later, when a different housemaid brought Elinor the message that Miss Penelope was waiting for her in the gold drawing room, it was all that Elinor could do not to hide her head under the covers.

Penelope wanted the famous Mrs. De Lacey to make her country début a success. Benedict Hawkins wanted to protect his friend from Mrs. De Lacey's nonexistent marital traps. And Sally had laid down her own ultimatum: 'Mrs. De Lacey' had to expose Penelope's friend Lucinda Grace as a thief.

"A thief?" Elinor had gaped at Sally when she'd heard her pronouncement. "Lucinda? Truly?"

"Oh, she's kept it very quiet," Sally said. "But believe you me, all the servants know it. You can't protect any little trinkets that catch *her* eye whenever she comes into a room.

Usually, the gentry just think they've gone missing, so no one's harmed. But then she took it too far." Sally's brown eyes narrowed. "Her family had that big supper party last month —do you remember? The one Miss Penelope threw a fit about, because her dressmaker couldn't get a new gown ready in time?"

Elinor grimaced. "I remember. She didn't end up going after all." It was impossible to forget, because Penelope—furiously betrayed by the injustice of life and recalcitrant dressmakers—had made the next few days an abject misery for the rest of the household.

"Of course she didn't. Couldn't show off in front of her friends if she didn't wear a fancy new gown for it, could she?" Sally rolled her eyes. "*Other* people did, though. And the Graces hushed it all up afterwards, but the truth is, by the end of that evening, Mrs. Knighton was shrieking her lungs out about theft, because her new fan had gone missing."

Elinor winced, imagining the scene. Mrs. Knighton might be the wife of the local vicar, but Elinor doubted that she had ever listened to a word of her husband's sermons about charity. "How on earth did they keep that quiet? If Lucinda was caught—"

"Oh, *Lucinda* wasn't caught. Not her." Sally crossed her arms. Her round face had looked friendly before, but now it was set in dangerous lines. "No, Lucinda's no fool, not like that Millie Staverton who only follows her and Penelope around like a puppy-dog. Our Lucinda thought on her feet."

Elinor's heart sank. "What did she do?"

"Well. Everyone knows who to blame whenever things go missing, don't they?" Sally gave a derisive snort as she leaned back in her seat, resting against the dressing table. "No one ever trusts a servant when a fine lady's weeping. And when Lucinda disappeared for ten minutes, then claimed she'd seen one of the maids take it—said she'd suspected the girl of such things even before...well, then our innocent young miss led them all up to the servants' quarters, where they found that fan *and* several other pieces that had gone missing in recent times, all tucked up right underneath Daisy's covers."

Elinor sighed. It was only too easy to imagine. "What happened to her?"

"Well, she lost her position, didn't she? She would've been hauled up in front of Sir John as the magistrate, too, only the Graces wanted it kept quiet. So she was sent off without any pay or any references and warned not to show her face again in the neighborhood." Sally's face tightened, but not quickly enough; Elinor had already spotted the pain mixed in with her fury. "Now she's been sent away and can't get another position anywhere, and no one even cares if she ends up starving on the streets, all for the sake of Miss Lucinda's reputation."

"Someone cares," Elinor said, watching her. "Is she a friend of yours?"

"Oh...you might as well know that she's my sister," Sally muttered. "I was the one who found her that position—and I talked her into taking it, too, so we'd be close. But *that* didn't work out so well, did it?" She gave a jerky shrug and seemed to fold more tightly into herself. "So, she needs a new position." She looked pointedly at Elinor. "That's where you come in."

Reluctantly, Elinor shook her head. "It's not that I don't sympathize," she said, "but you know my situation. I can't afford to hire her myself. Even if I wrote her a reference, her new employers would only have to ask the real Mrs. De Lacey to discover that it was forged. And—"

"Don't be daft!" Sally said. "I know all of that. I could write her a reference myself, if all I wanted was a worthless piece of paper that would only get her into even *more* trouble! But *you* can see her name cleared after all if you show Lucinda Grace as the lying thief she is."

"Me?" Elinor stared at her. "What if she doesn't steal anything in front of me? I can't accuse her without proof."

"So you'll just have to make certain she does steal something. *You're* clever; we all know that. So I know you can find a way...if you care enough to try." Meaningfully, Sally tapped the pocket of her apron, where she'd stashed the packet of letters from Elinor's sisters.

Elinor dragged her gaze away from the apron, forcing herself to think. "Even if I do expose her, that doesn't mean your sister will be re-hired. The Graces will hush up any scandal, and the Hathergills will help them, for the sake of Penelope's friendship. For Lucinda's family to publicly admit that she'd lied about their maid...I can't imagine any way they would agree to it."

"Well, I don't care what you can imagine," Sally snapped, "*or* how you do it. All *I* care about is fixing what she did to my baby sister, no matter what it takes!" She stood up, her colour high, and shoved her loose strands of hair back into place underneath her cap, shaking out her shoulders and jerking her chin high. "So, you *will* expose Lucinda within the week, Miss Elinor, or I'll make sure *everyone* knows who you really are. Then you'll be the one facing magistrate's charges...*and* you'll lose these letters for good. Do you understand me?"

All too well. But in the hour that had passed since that conversation with Sally, Elinor still hadn't managed to come up with a sensible solution to the problem.

There was only one consolation she could find, as she walked down the staircase to the gold drawing room. If they really were to hash out all the interminable details of Penelope's début, then it would be only reasonable to order plenty of tea and cakes as accompaniment. Sir Jessamyn wasn't the only one who was starving, after they had both missed luncheon. If Elinor was really lucky, her mind might start to work better once she'd eaten.

Unfortunately, when she stepped into the drawing room, the sight before her turned her stomach.

"Oh, I shouldn't even be speaking to you!" Penelope waved her embroidery frame threateningly at Benedict Hawkins as she shifted away from him on the couch—but Elinor knew her cousin, and she was not fooled.

Penelope would never be caught dead near household mending, but she embroidered beautifully, and she brought out her embroidery frame whenever she wished to look particularly feminine, accomplished and industrious. She had begun this particular piece long before Elinor had first arrived at Hathergill Hall, and she was still nowhere near finishing it...but visitors always oohed and aahed over it, and even Elinor had to admit that it was truly beautiful—a cluster of bright flowers and vibrant green leaves that spilled across the fabric in a design of Penelope's own invention.

As Penelope batted Mr. Hawkins's arm with it, pretending —adorably—to scowl, sunlight poured through the windows onto them both and surrounded them in a golden glow. Neither of them had noticed Elinor's arrival yet. Lucinda and Millie, on the opposite couch, were far too busy ogling the spectacle before them, and whispering excitedly to each other, to take note of anything else short of an explosion.

"*You* promised to sit beside me all through luncheon to protect me, and what did you do but disappear? So for all your fine words now—"

"I beg your pardon with all my heart," said Mr. Hawkins. "If my friend hadn't needed me so urgently..."

Elinor froze. He wouldn't have passed on his suspicions to Penelope, would he?

A chill passed through her as cold reason splashed icily across her foolish hopes. *Of course he would.* Mr. Hawkins wished to marry Penelope, didn't he? Once they were wed, he would share every secret with her, as a matter of course. How could Elinor expect him, in the meantime, to respect the privacy of a woman he despised?

"Oh, *well.* I do understand that scholars can be distracted by their work, I suppose." Penelope gave a martyred sigh. "But surely you could have asked one of the footmen to bring him his luncheon, rather than doing it yourself?"

"I wish I could have," said Mr. Hawkins, "but I knew he would be hungry after missing breakfast, and I couldn't let him go without another meal. He might have sent the footman away without eating, you see, if he was absorbed in his books."

Elinor let out her held breath. Offensive and absurd as Mr. Hawkins's accusations had been, at least he hadn't shared them with anyone else at Hathergill Hall.

Not yet.

And the real Mrs. De Lacey would never hover nervously in a doorway, only waiting to be noticed.

She gathered herself up and swept into the room. "Penelope." She nodded graciously to her cousin and let her gaze skim carelessly across Mr. Hawkins's suddenly-blank face. "Mr. Hawkins. Miss Grace, Miss Staverton."

"Mrs. De Lacey. You've come down at last." Penelope began to pout, then stopped herself. "We have *so* much to discuss."

"Of course." Elinor sat down on one of the spindly, elegant chairs near the couch, keeping her gaze purposefully averted from Mr. Hawkins. On her shoulder, Sir Jessamyn tucked himself as low as possible, his scaly belly pressing hard into Elinor's shoulder and his golden gaze locked nervously on Penelope's face. His earlier exhaustion might have swamped his fear, but now it was apparently back in full force.

Elinor rubbed his long neck comfortingly and brushed his scaly cheek with hers. "Perhaps we can order refreshments before we begin?"

"Oh, no, I'm not hungry." Penelope dropped her embroidery onto a side table and leaned forward. "Now the *first* thing to discuss—"

"I should like some tea first," said Elinor firmly, "and I'm quite certain your mother won't mind if we order cakes—and a bit of meat for my dragon. He hasn't had his own luncheon yet."

"You needn't fret about *that*." Penelope snorted contemptuously. "Dragons always act as if they're hungry. Hadn't you noticed? I had one—he was quite like yours, actually—who pretended he was starving all the time, even if he'd eaten barely half an hour earlier. They are *such* greedy creatures! They'll take the greatest advantage of you if you allow it, so you mustn't pamper yours, you know."

Elinor gritted her teeth. On her shoulder, Sir Jessamyn had begun to shiver with real panic. She laid her palm soothingly across his back. "What a thoughtful piece of advice," she said. "I do thank you for your consideration, but—"

"They are pathetic, honestly." Penelope leaned closer, her blue eyes fixed scornfully on Sir Jessamyn. "Only look at yours! He's acting as nervous as anything, only because—"

Sir Jessamyn made a soft noise in the back of his throat. It sounded disturbingly like the beginning of a chuckle.

Elinor abandoned courtesy as a lost cause and lunged for Penelope's metaphorical underbelly. "Where is your mother, Penelope? I'd expected her to be here for our discussion. I'm sure she must have opinions of her own to share."

"Ha!" Penelope jerked back, letting out a huff of irritation. "My mother's *opinions*—!"

"Lady Hathergill wasn't feeling well," Millie supplied hastily.

"Not well at *all*." From the venomous tone of Penelope's voice, she would have liked to make her mother feel a great deal worse. "And if she thinks anybody is going to pay *any* attention to what she says from now on…!"

Lucinda cleared her throat, cutting off her friend. "Lady Hathergill decided to take a rest."

"What a pity." Elinor turned to Lucinda. "Would you mind ringing the bell for us, Miss Grace?"

"Of course not, Mrs. De Lacey." Lucinda rose with all the grace of her name and hurried to the golden bell-pull in the corner, while Penelope vibrated with irritation on the couch.

Elinor ignored her cousin. She barely even noticed that Mr. Hawkins's brows had drawn into a frown. Elinor was busy watching Lucinda, with Sally's words ringing in her memory.

She had spent the last six months trying her best to ignore Penelope's friends and close her ears to the words they said—or whispered—about her. Now, though, for the first time, she took a long look at Lucinda Grace.

Objectively speaking, Lucinda was pretty, although not as

pretty as Penelope, of course—no friend of Penelope's ever would be. But she had a clear complexion, a neat figure, and shining dark hair, well arranged. Her gown was fashionable, by country standards, and like both of the other girls' gowns, it was made of thin sprig muslin and cut high at the waist, with short, puffed sleeves that showed off her bare arms. Elinor couldn't see a single safe spot in which stolen objects could be hidden.

Elinor's gaze returned to the couch where Lucinda had sat next to Millie. *There*! Lucinda's reticule was a large, squashy, red and purple beaded bundle, which she had sewn herself. Elinor remembered that sewing party only too well, as she'd been forced to complete Penelope's own reticule after Penelope had lost interest in it.

If Lucinda had pocketed anything today, the only place it could be hidden was inside that reticule.

Elinor drew a deep breath. A strong infusion of tea and confidence had suddenly become more essential than ever...because it was time to find out exactly how daring 'Mrs. De Lacey' could be.

CHAPTER 15

Lucinda's unopened reticule tugged at Elinor from the corner of her vision, but the arrival of food was enough to brighten Sir Jessamyn's mood immediately. He raised himself from his wary crouch on Elinor's shoulder to stretch his neck hopefully towards the tea tray, and when Elinor took the plate of meat onto her lap, he only let her feed him politely for a moment before scampering down her arm to take over the job himself.

Penelope's nostrils flared with disgust as she watched him tear into his meal. "I cannot believe you allow him to eat in front of you."

Elinor, accustomed to her cousin's views, only rolled her eyes inwardly and prepared to change the subject.

Before she could say a word, though, Benedict Hawkins

asked, "How did you feed your own dragon, Miss Hathergill?"

"Well, I didn't feed him myself, obviously!" She shuddered. "The servants took care of that. Or Elin—well, anyway, I would never dream of letting him eat while he sat on my lap, of all places. That would be like—well, like letting a dog roam around your very own sitting room!"

"Ah..." He blinked. "You don't like dogs either?"

"Penelope has always been afraid of dogs." Millie beamed with self-importance as she passed on the news. "Ever since we were little, we always had to put our dogs away when she—"

"I am not afraid of dogs!" Penelope glared at her friend, even as Lucinda nudged Millie reprovingly. "I don't *like* them, that's all. Horrid, slavering creatures. My father would never allow any in our house!"

"Oh." Benedict visibly adjusted to the news. "Perhaps, if you met the right sort of dog—my niece's pug, for instance, who—"

"I would *never* allow a dog to run free in my own house," said Penelope. "Honestly, they all do very well outside in kennels, and I *do* think they prefer it, really. If their owners weren't so fussy and unreasonable, they'd all be kept outside, where they belong! It is better to treat animals as animals, don't you think?"

Mr. Hawkins hesitated. Hurt crept into Penelope's expression. "Oh, I suppose you're about to say something horrid to me, like everyone else does. My cousin—that is, *some* people have been completely unreasonable and cruel to me in the past, but I'd thought that you were kinder than that. Especially when I've just suffered such a terrible loss…" Tears clogged her voice. She turned her face away. "She stole him away from me, you know."

"Your...dragon." Reluctance was etched across Benedict's face. "Your father did say that your cousin had taken him, but—"

"She stole him," Penelope said, "out of my very arms! When I had chosen him myself, and named him and loved him, and he was my father's most expensive gift to me, *ever…!*"

Sir Jessamyn swallowed the last of the meat on the plate and let out a belch of satisfaction. Penelope's nose crinkled in distaste. She scooted another inch away from him.

Lucinda seized the opportunity to lean forward and catch Benedict's eye. "It really was quite shocking," she said. "If you had known Miss Tregarth and seen what a perfect pretense of self-righteousness she wore—if you'd heard all of her fine words about his treatment, as if *she* were a veritable saint herself!—well, you would be shocked at the hypocrisy of her theft."

If anyone should know about hypocrisy, it would be Lucinda...but suddenly, Elinor was rather looking forward to exposing her thefts after all.

"She probably needed the money," Millie pronounced with satisfaction. "*My* parents say she had absolutely nothing to live on. She must have taken him to sell him. He's probably living in a traveling circus right now, being used for unholy rituals."

Elinor blinked. Her gaze met Benedict's. For a moment, despite everything, she felt their mutual connection return in full force as both of them reacted to Millie's words.

His lips twitched; she cleared her throat. "Exactly what sort of unholy rituals do you imagine they would want him for in a public circus, Miss Staverton?"

"Well!" Millie's eyes sparkled with delight at the invitation to unburden herself. "My father's undergardener says that *he* heard from his cousin's friend—"

"Only a week before my début!" Penelope wailed. Tears flooded her cheeks; she snatched a handkerchief from her reticule and buried her face in it, muffling her next words. "She wanted to ruin me, that's all. She did it to hurt me and punish me for being kind to her when no one else ever was, and I will *never* forgive her for it."

"Luckily," said Elinor briskly, "you are not going to be ruined after all. In fact, I think you will do very well without a dragon."

"But every young lady in high society—"

"Precisely." Elinor set down her tea cup with a clatter. "Do you wish to be one of a thousand young ladies, Penelope, all doing exactly the same thing?"

"Well..."

Elinor sighed. "Would you attend a ball wearing the same gown as every other débutante?"

"Of course not!" Penelope lowered her handkerchief.

"Then why should you want to imitate all the rest? You will set your own fashion by daring to do without a dragon!"

"Lucinda and I don't have dragons," Millie said helpfully. "We don't mind, do we, Lucinda?"

Elinor winced. Penelope's face, which had looked so hopeful for a moment, was beginning once again to crumple.

Lucinda and Millie, of course, could not afford to have dragons any more than they could afford to have expensive London seasons afterwards. Penelope had flaunted her own dragon in front of her friends as the greatest symbol of her triumph.

If Elinor didn't act fast, she would lose all the ground that she had gained...and some other poor dragon would be in for a miserable servitude. Elinor leaned forward, her eyes intent and her voice infused with certainty.

"You," Elinor said to her cousin, "will *choose* not to have a dragon, unlike all those dreary, unoriginal young misses you meet in London. You will carry something else instead, something that will make you stand out from the crowd."

"I will?" Penelope said, with tearful hope.

"She will?" Lucinda frowned.

"But *what* will she carry?" Millie asked.

Benedict raised his eyebrows and waited.

Elinor searched her brain for inspiration...and came up empty-handed.

"You will carry..."

Even Sir Jessamyn was looking up at her expectantly now.

Elinor searched the room around her for anything suitable. *Nothing, nothing, nothing.* She swallowed hard. "You will carry..."

A raucous cry split the moment in two. Elinor jumped; so did everyone else, even Sir Jessamyn.

"Oh, those peacocks." Penelope rolled her eyes, laughing as she re-settled herself on the couch. "They are beautiful, but so noisy! Now, what were you saying, Mrs. De Lacey?"

"That's it," Elinor said. *All or nothing.* She fixed a smile of pure, blazing Mrs. De Lacey confidence on her face. "You will carry...a feather!"

"I beg your pardon?" Penelope blinked rapidly.

Lucinda and Millie stared. Benedict's eyes narrowed.

Elinor seized the moment, before anyone could spoil it. "You will carry a single feather from one of your father's peacocks—and you will wear it attached to your shoulder, exactly where everyone would expect a dragon to sit!"

"But..." Penelope's brow furrowed. "I don't quite see—"

"It will make a daring statement." Elinor summoned the power of every description she had ever read about the latest London fashions to infuse her voice with certainty. "It will say: *I know what you expect from me...but I shall not bow down to fashion!* It will be amusing, it will be powerful, and it will mark you out as a force to be reckoned with."

"Well..." Penelope's frown became more thoughtful.

Millie leaned over to whisper excitedly in Lucinda's ear.

Could they actually be persuaded? Elinor held herself as

still as she could, not even daring to breathe in case it broke the spell.

Benedict Hawkins shook his head…but a smile was tugging at his lips. "Do you know, Mrs. De Lacey, I believe you may be right."

Elinor let out the breath she had been holding. "Of course I am. When have I ever been wrong about fashion?"

As she saw the look of excitement grow on her cousin's face, though, a wave of unexpected guilt attacked her. Even after everything Penelope had ever said or done, it still felt cruel to do this…but truly, Elinor asked herself, was a shoulder-feather any more ridiculous than the real Mrs. De Lacey's many more famous sartorial inventions?

"Do you really think people will be impressed?" Penelope said. Her eyelashes fluttered appealingly, but her blue eyes were full of intense calculation.

Elinor thrust aside her guilty conscience and nodded firmly. "Trust me," she said. "With me standing by your side at your début, you will set the fashionable world alight."

And it *had* to be better than letting Penelope buy another dragon.

At the moment, though, Elinor had an even more pressing concern. "Now," she said. "Shall we think about exactly where to fix it? Perhaps…" She turned, letting her gaze sweep the room…until it landed on Lucinda's plump, beaded reticule, tucked into Lucinda's side on the couch nearby.

"Miss Grace." Elinor smiled sweetly. "You must have

something in your reticule that can aid us. A pin, perhaps, that we could fit to Penelope's gown to mark the spot for her feather?"

"Um..." Lucinda frowned, but picked up her reticule obediently.

"It has to be just the right feather," Penelope said. "If it's too small, no one will notice."

"Of course," Elinor said absently. She wasn't looking at her cousin anymore, though. She was watching Lucinda untie the ribbons that held her reticule closed. "You certainly mustn't carry the wrong sort of feather..."

Drat. Lucinda had opened her reticule...but only by half an inch. She peered inside, then reached inside to rifle among its contents. The angle of her hand kept the inside of the reticule fully hidden from view.

Surely she was being too careful. If she hadn't anything to hide...

"Why don't I look for you?" Elinor said, and held out her hand. "I know exactly what I'm looking for, after all."

Millie gave a squeak of surprise. Even Penelope broke off her chain of thought to stare.

Lucinda's hand froze in place as she met Elinor's gaze. For the first time since Elinor had met her six months ago, she saw a flash of cold, wary intelligence in the other girl's eyes.

Then Lucinda's face eased into a smile. "You needn't worry, Mrs. De Lacey," she said. "I've already found a pin for Penelope. You see?"

She drew out a shining hairpin, with a rounded end.

"Oh, good." Penelope reached across to take it from her. "Shall we put it here, do you think, Mrs. De Lacey?" She pointed to a spot on her shoulder. "And if the feather is just the right length..."

Penelope's words faded into the background of Elinor's hearing. Lucinda's head bent over her reticule as she tied the ribbons closed. As she finished, she looked up, met Elinor's gaze, smiled sweetly...and lifted the reticule across her lap to deposit it on her other side, safely out of Elinor's sight.

Elinor smiled back at her...and thought of Lucinda smiling just as sweetly when she'd led all of her parents' horrified guests to that poor maid's quarters, full of her own stolen goods.

Sir Jessamyn let out a cheep of protest. With a start, Elinor realized that her fingers had been digging hard into his sides.

She let go, with a quick murmur of apology. When she looked up again, she forced herself to look at Penelope...but she could feel Lucinda watching her.

She would have to tread very carefully from now on. Lucinda was already suspicious, but if Elinor let the matter go for the rest of the afternoon's visit, her suspicions might be allayed.

On the other hand, who knew when Lucinda would come to Hathergill Hall again? It might not be for days, and Elinor had less than a week.

"You can find a way...if you care enough to try," Sally had said.

Elinor thought about the letters in Sally's pocket and swallowed over a suddenly-dry throat.

She cared. And when she imagined how she'd feel if Lucinda had done it to one of *her* sisters...

"My goodness," she said, "Penelope certainly was right about dragon appetites. I believe my dragon is still hungry, despite all that meat he ate."

Sir Jessamyn looked up at her with surprise, but Elinor had no fear that he would betray her. If there was one thing that could be relied upon with the little dragon, it was a never-failing appetite when food was available.

"Miss Grace..." She smiled ruefully. "I do hate to burden you again, but would you mind ringing the bell one more time?"

Lucinda began to rise from the couch—then hesitated. She glanced briefly at the reticule, reached out as if to pick it up...

"I'll do it this time, Lucinda." Millie bounced up off the chair. "I wouldn't mind eating a few more cakes, too. Penelope?"

"Oh..." Penelope waved impatiently. She was leaning towards Benedict, in the middle of a question about her pin. "I'm sure that will be fine."

"Thank you," Lucinda said, and sank back down onto the couch.

"How kind of you, Miss Staverton." Elinor forced a smile.

Lucinda sat between her and the reticule. The table stood

in the middle of their cluster of couches and chairs, still holding the half-full tea urn and the empty cake plates.

If only Harry was here! Elinor's youngest sister always had a creative solution to hand. If Harry was the one who had to do this...

Penelope leaned even closer to Benedict, pointing to the pin as she moved it about her shoulder. "Here, do you think, Mr. Hawkins? Or here?"

His cheeks flushed, but he kept his eyes manfully raised from her only-partially-hidden bosom. "I'm sure it would be charming anywhere, Miss Hathergill."

"Oh, but..." Penelope pouted. "Don't you have an opinion? Where do you think it would be most attractive on me?"

Enough. Elinor hated gambling, but she couldn't stand to wait any longer—and if she could put right even one injustice in this house, perhaps she could bear all the rest so much more easily.

She stood up, setting Sir Jessamyn down on the couch in Millie's place. "I'll just pour my own tea, shall I, and—oh!" She gasped dramatically as the teapot twisted in her hands. "Oh, Miss Grace! I am so sorry! Your lovely gown!"

Lucinda leapt to her feet, slapping at the skirts of her gown. The tea might be no longer hot, but it spilled just as quickly when it was cold.

"Oh, and your poor reticule, too—here, while you deal with your gown, let me...."

With a lunge, Elinor had hold of the sopping wet reticule. She untied the laces—

"Let's get this aired out, shall we?"

—up-ended it over the couch before Lucinda could react...

...And a cluster of completely unremarkable objects fell out.

Five hairpins, two hatpins, several assorted coins, a rock and a letter... Elinor stared at the pile and tasted despair.

"How kind of you, Mrs. De Lacey." Lucinda held out her hand for the empty reticule. "I can take care of the rest by myself now."

Elinor met Lucinda's eyes and read the message in them.

"Yes," she said, letting the reticule go. "I do believe you can."

Lucinda knew exactly what she was after...and Elinor had lost her wager.

CHAPTER 16

Elinor had no time to contemplate her failure. Running feet sounded in the corridor outside—servants hurrying to answer an unexpected summons. A moment later, Elinor heard the unmistakable sound of Hathergill Hall's front doors opening and closing again.

Loud, jovial voices emanated from the front hall.

"We're hideously early—"

"Never mind, never mind!" That was Sir John's booming voice. "Delighted to see you, young man. Come in. And Miss Armitage, charming, charming...do you need to retire to your rooms, or d'you want to come straight in for tea?"

A woman's rich, melodic voice said something Elinor couldn't quite catch, even though everyone in the sitting room had gone still and silent to listen.

Sir John's laughter was easy to hear. "A lady after my own heart!"

Oh, dear, Elinor thought.

"Come in, come in!" Sir John's voice came closer. "I believe my daughter is just in here..."

Penelope jumped a full foot away from Benedict on the couch and set the hatpin down on the table. Millie hurried back to the couch, her face alight with excitement. With a cool nod to Elinor, Lucinda sat back down, swishing her skirts into place and covering as much of their tea-stain as possible with her large, wet reticule. Elinor sank down onto her own seat, gathering Sir Jessamyn back onto her lap. She couldn't help glancing at Mr. Hawkins, whose face was set in rueful lines.

The first of Sir John's invited guests had arrived...and the first of Benedict's serious rivals for Penelope's attention.

The door opened, and noise and colour billowed into the room. Sir John and the gentleman beside him were both laughing over something that had just been said by the lady who stood between them, wearing a bright crimson traveling gown that perfectly matched the crimson and silver scales of the dragon on her shoulder. As they stepped into the room, Sir John cut off his own laughter and cleared his throat importantly.

"My dear," he said to Penelope, "we have the unexpected pleasure of welcoming two of our guests already! Mr. Armitage, Miss Armitage, may I present my daughter Penelope, her friends Miss Staverton and Miss Grace, and our guest Mr. Hawkins? And..."

He puffed himself up, eyes gleaming with self-importance as he turned to Elinor. "Mrs. De Lacey," he said, "may I present our guests to you? Mr. Armitage of Stanton Court, and his charming sister, Miss Armitage."

"Delighted," Elinor said politely, and inclined her head in a nod, while Sir Jessamyn, stiffening, watched the new dragon warily from her lap.

Miss Armitage's dragon, as far as Elinor could tell, hadn't even noticed Sir Jessamyn's existence. He—or she—was sitting perfectly still on Miss Armitage's shoulder, with golden eyes focused on Miss Armitage's face and every line of his body positively shouting of attentiveness and obedience.

Clearly, Miss Armitage must be either a perfect goddess of dragon-training or an absolute ogre.

All that Elinor knew of either of the Armitages was what she had read in the past year's society columns, in combination with what her uncle had told Penelope and Lady Hathergill three weeks ago over dinner. Put together, though, it was more than enough to give Benedict cause for concern. Mr. Armitage was an acquaintance Sir John had made at an important London dinner party, and he was known to be a young man of undisputed wealth, although he and his sister had only recently come to the attention of larger society.

He had recently purchased a very fine estate, and over the past several months, he had received regular mention in the society columns as *"that well-favoured young man Mr. A—who is so highly regarded nowadays."* Even if Mr. Armitage had been the ugliest man in existence, Penelope would have found everything else about him attractive—and Mr. Armitage, Elinor had to admit, was anything but ugly.

Shining blonde hair, arranged in perfect waves around his head, made him the ideal counterpart to Penelope's golden beauty. His broad shoulders showed to advantage in his perfectly-cut black coat as he bowed…and his warm brown eyes widened with surprise as he saw Elinor's face.

"Mrs. De Lacey! Good heavens, I had no idea you would be here."

"Ah…" Elinor blinked, rapidly reassessing the situation. *Drat.* Of course, if he was well-known in Society, he would know Mrs. De Lacey, wouldn't he? She'd been so busy worrying about fooling her own family, she had completely forgotten that she would have to fool their fashionable guests as well. She moistened her lips, trying to think quickly. "I hadn't planned to come originally, but—"

"It must have been a very sudden decision indeed. When I mentioned this house party to you at the Rothershams' rout—that was only four nights ago, was it not?—I could have sworn—"

"Well," Elinor said weakly, "you made it sound so charming. How could I possibly resist?"

He raised his eyebrows skeptically, but, to Elinor's relief, did not pursue the matter. Instead, he turned to the woman beside him…and all of Elinor's relief melted away as she heard his next words: "Of course you know my sister already, Mrs. De Lacey."

"Of course," Elinor repeated, and cursed inwardly. How well did Mrs. De Lacey know his sister? Were they on first-name terms? Would she be expected to know their family history?

"Oh, Gavin, I'd be astonished if she remembers me." Miss Armitage's deep curtsey was a model of grace, leaving the dragon on her shoulder perfectly composed and not even forced to shift by half an inch. "We've only met once, and at *such* a crush, I wouldn't blame you if you don't recognize me, Mrs. De Lacey."

"But of course I do." This time, Elinor's smile was perfectly genuine. She could have kissed Miss Armitage in gratitude for saving her. With automatic courtesy, she began to hold out her hand—then caught herself and snatched it back as she remembered the illusion.

Miss Armitage's dark brows rose in surprise, but she lowered her own hand in response. She was quite dissimilar to her brother in appearance but every bit as attractive, with hair so dark that it was nearly black, deep blue eyes, and a curvaceous figure. She couldn't have been more than Elinor's own age—perhaps four years her brother's junior—but she turned to Penelope with all the ease and confidence of an established matron.

"Miss Hathergill, we do so regret descending upon you like this, a full two days early. I'm afraid your mother may never forgive us! But I'm afraid we were let down by our friends in Bath, who'd offered to host us along the way. Their child had caught scarlet fever, and as we could hardly intrude upon their house at such a time—"

"Oh, no!" Penelope said. "Only imagine if you caught it?"

"Quite," said Miss Armitage, sitting down beside Lucinda. "Only imagine! And so I'm afraid we have landed much too early on your doorstep. I do feel terribly guilty about the inconvenience we are causing you."

She smoothed down her skirts with perfect equanimity, and the dragon on her shoulder assumed a posture of perfect alertness, like an educational statue of Obedience. It was, Elinor thought, almost unnerving. She gave Sir Jessamyn an extra scratch behind his head, just in case he needed any reassurance.

"Nonsense!" said Sir John. "We're delighted to have you, aren't we, Penelope?"

"Oh, yes," Penelope said. She gazed meltingly at Mr. Armitage from under her long eyelashes. "We were just about to order more tea—would you care for some?"

"I should like it beyond anything," said Mr. Armitage, and dropped himself neatly into the foot-wide gap on the couch between Penelope and Mr. Hawkins, forcing Benedict to move aside. "Oh, those roads! Outside London, no one even seems to know how to build them anymore. At my own estate—sorry, old man, you don't mind me sitting here, do you?"

"Of course not." Benedict gave him an easy smile. "You're

clearly exhausted from travel. It takes many gentlemen that way."

"Ah..." Mr. Armitage's teeth flashed perfectly white in his smile. "I don't think we've met, but I do know your name. Hawkins, wasn't it? You aren't the Hawkins of Kennington Park, by any chance?"

Benedict's smile remained, but Elinor saw the sudden tension around his eyes. "I am. Have you visited my part of the country?"

"Oh, not for some time," said Mr. Armitage. "But I met your father once or twice. A good fellow, wasn't he?"

"That's what my old friend Edmund Crawford says," agreed Sir John. "He asked—"

"There was something I heard about him just last year, though." Mr. Armitage's brow creased in a thoughtful frown. "What was it? Oh, yes. The rumours *I* heard said that before his passing, he'd been drawn into a rather regrettable—"

"How was your journey, Miss Armitage?" Elinor asked hastily.

"Oh, well, if I can forget all the many miles of my brother's complaints about the road..." Miss Armitage rolled her eyes but aimed a fond smile at her sibling. "He is on fire to make improvements to his own estate, you see, and the first thing he wants to put money into is the road that leads to it from London."

"Well, we can't have people claiming it's too difficult to get there for a weekend, can we?" Mr. Armitage turned to appeal to Penelope. "What do you say, Miss Hathergill—isn't the best use of a good country house to hold the most popular house parties imaginable?"

Penelope's face glowed with delight. "Oh, I should so love to attend a house party! I have never been to one, you know. But then..." She aimed a reproachful look at her father. "I have never been to London, either, if you can believe it."

"One more month, kitten," said Sir John. "Then you'll be able to enjoy your Season."

"But we've had the good fortune of meeting you early!" Mr. Armitage gave her a smile that could only be described, Elinor thought, as intimate. Even from four feet away, it gave her a reluctant tingle of appreciation, especially as his voice deepened. "You wouldn't deny us that opportunity, would you, Miss Hathergill?"

Penelope's eyelashes fluttered; her face flushed lightly pink. "Oh, well, if you put it that way..."

"Do you two live in London for most of the year, then?" Millie asked breathlessly. "It must be such a wonderful place! The balls and the theater and the—"

"—And the routs, and the Venetian breakfasts, and the opera, and the masquerades..." Mr. Armitage laughed. "Oh, yes, London is beyond anything. Don't you agree, Hawkins?" He tossed a careless glance at Benedict over his shoulder. "But come to think of it...I've never seen you there. Are you one of those fellows who prefers the tedium of the countryside?"

Benedict's laugh sounded forced. "I wouldn't put it quite that way."

"Oh, no," Miss Armitage agreed, with a warm smile. "The countryside can be delightful. On a beautiful day, with the lilacs flowering and the sun shining above—"

"On the one day of the year it isn't raining, you mean." Her brother rolled his eyes. "Give me a ballroom crowded with five hundred people and a thousand candles, with all the ladies' diamonds glittering like stars. Wouldn't you agree with me, Miss Hathergill?"

"Ohh..." Penelope's face softened into a look of true yearning. "It sounds utterly perfect."

"It is," he said, and looked at her with an intensity impossible to mistake. "I cannot wait until you experience it yourself."

Millie's long, wistful sigh filled the room.

Miss Armitage smiled indulgently and turned to ask Sir John a series of polite questions about the history of Hathergill Hall.

Gazing into Mr. Armitage's eyes, Penelope fluttered with delight.

Lucinda's eyes narrowed with ill-concealed envy.

Sir John beamed proudly at his daughter and her newest suitor.

Elinor couldn't stop herself from giving Benedict Hawkins a sympathetic look, despite everything that had passed between them that day.

He wouldn't have an easy time of his pursuit, after all.

CHAPTER 17

The party broke up an hour later. The newcomers were escorted to their rooms to rest from their journey, Penelope retreated to her bedroom to begin her preparations for the evening, and Millie and Lucinda left for their own homes with open reluctance.

Elinor rose to leave, too, but Benedict held out a hand to stop her.

"If you wouldn't mind, Mrs. De Lacey..." He aimed a frowning glance at the door, which had been left half-open to preserve the proprieties. "We still have some time before we need to prepare for supper. Would you care to take a turn around the garden with me first?"

Elinor hesitated. The correct answer, of course, was *no*. On the other hand...

No, she told herself again, more firmly. She was not going to make a fool of herself over Benedict Hawkins, no matter how much she might be tempted. It would be ridiculous enough in her own guise—plain, uninteresting and impoverished—but it would be even worse now, when she was disguised as a woman more than ten years older than him…a woman he'd already accused of being unethical and mercenary.

She raised her eyebrows and forced her voice to sound as cold as he deserved. "I seem to recall a rather unpleasant encounter in a garden earlier, Mr. Hawkins. Perhaps we'd better not repeat it."

He grimaced, but humour danced in his eyes. "Believe me, Mrs. De Lacey, I haven't forgotten that incident either. But if you wouldn't mind, I'd prefer to make my apologies outside, where no one else can hear me."

Elinor had to fight to repress the smile that wanted to escape, as something tight inside her chest relaxed for the first time since their argument. "What a cowardly admission to make."

"Utterly cowardly," he agreed as he rose. He offered her his arm, and one corner of his mouth turned up in a half-smile. "What do you say? May I grovel in private, after all?"

She clasped her hands firmly in front of her and walked before him to the door. "Luckily for you, my dragon enjoys the fresh air."

"Excellent," Benedict said. "I knew there was a good reason that they'd become so popular."

Sir Jessamyn lifted his head with eager attention, golden gaze flicking back and forth expectantly.

And really, Elinor told herself a few minutes later, it hadn't only been an excuse. As they stepped out of the house, Sir Jessamyn tipped his head back in pure bliss. His thin, forked tongue darted out to taste the air; he gave a shiver of delight.

Benedict laughed appreciatively and reached over to stroke Sir Jessamyn's back, which glowed and glittered with colour in the open sunlight. "I see what you mean. He is much happier now, isn't he?"

"Well, dragons weren't meant to live in drawing rooms," said Elinor. "Or in houses at all, for that matter."

"You should hear Aubrey on the topic." Benedict's smile slipped as their gazes met, and their earlier conversation echoed silently between them. "Mrs. De Lacey, I must—"

"Wait." They were still standing directly in front of the house, overlooked by the windows to Penelope's bedroom. Elinor turned away from Benedict and set out across the carefully-manicured lawn. "There's a little wilderness on the east side of the house," she said. "We can talk there."

He followed her in silence, until they'd walked through the gap in the low stone wall that enclosed the Hathergill's "wilderness." It was, Elinor had always thought, the most orderly wilderness she'd ever seen, but still, there were enough rocks and bushes and long-branched trees to make it feel nearly natural. Better yet, it was completely private.

She reached out to touch the tallest rock—really an ornamental boulder, set beside a long stone bench—and Sir Jessamyn ran down her arm to bask on top of it. When she looked up, she found Benedict studying her with disconcerting intensity.

"You knew exactly where to come," he said.

"I asked a housemaid for advice, earlier," said Elinor. "Maids know everything."

Unfortunately, she added silently.

She had failed in her first attempt to earn Sally's silence and her own letters—and after that first failure, the second attempt would be infinitely more difficult.

Benedict opened his mouth as if to speak—then shook his head and turned away. He was facing the drooping willow that spread its branches across the small pond nearby, and he might have been appreciating its beauty, but Elinor saw the stiffness in his shoulders and was not fooled.

"I owe you an apology, Mrs. De Lacey."

Elinor drew a deep breath and sat down on the bench. "Yes," she said, "you do. How did you realize?"

He let out a half-laugh. "Well, I certainly knew I was being offensive at the time, but it wasn't until I spoke to Aubrey that I knew I'd also been mistaken."

Elinor's fingers curled around the cool stone of the bench. "You spoke to Mr. Aubrey?"

"I knew what I believed I'd seen, but you were so outraged...I thought I had better make quite certain of my facts." He still hadn't turned to face her.

Elinor swallowed. "And what did Mr. Aubrey tell you?"

"Very little." He shook his head, reaching out to run one finger along the line of a willow branch. "He kept muttering about fairy tales and practical jokes. I take it he didn't care for what you asked him about your dragon?"

"No," Elinor said, "he didn't. But..." Her fingers were beginning to ache; she forced herself to ease her grip on the bench. "He wasn't any more specific than that?"

"Unfortunately, no." Amusement crept into Benedict's voice. "When I made the mistake of trying to press him, he launched into a fiery lecture on how fairy tales have been the ruin of dragon scholarship. He thinks they should be banned, and all existing collections burned, by order of the King. I wasn't sure whether first to enlighten him on the Prince Regent's part in our government or try to argue over the literary merits of fiction...so I took the coward's way out and left him to his studies."

"Very wise of you." Elinor's voice sounded thin and airy.

He still didn't know the truth, after all. She was relieved that Mr. Aubrey had kept her secret. She *was*.

But she also, irrationally, felt bereft.

Absurd, she told herself, and stiffened her spine. "And? What about your accusation that I stole my dragon?"

"That..." Benedict finally turned to face her, but he still didn't meet her eyes. "That was an unjust conclusion to leap to, I'm afraid. There was no reason, if you'd helped Elinor Tregarth in other ways, that you should have turned against her in that despicable fashion. By far the most sensible conclusion, I finally realized, is that you are looking after her dragon for her until she finds a more stable situation."

"*If* I have her dragon at all," Elinor pointed out. "The golden streaks aren't painted on his face."

"I know. But I'm afraid..." He took a deep breath. "I've been rather shaken ever since this morning's conversation, in your room. You see—and I realize you may well think me mad for saying this, but I have to tell someone, and Aubrey was in no mood to listen..."

"Yes?"

He looked straight into her eyes, his face grimly set, as if braced for a blow. "For a moment, just at the end of our conversation...just for a single moment...I could have sworn that your appearance changed."

"I beg your pardon?" Elinor stared at him. She could feel her heartbeat fluttering in her throat.

"For just a moment, after I touched your hand, I could have sworn that when I looked at you, I saw..." He broke off, wincing, and began to turn away. "Never mind."

"No." Elinor leaned forward, the flats of her hands pressed against the bench. "*Tell me*. Who did you see?"

"Elinor Tregarth," Benedict said, and smiled, wryly, as her expression changed. "You see? I knew you'd think me mad."

For a moment, Elinor couldn't speak. Too many contradictory emotions and thoughts were rushing through her.

Benedict spoke again, before she could gather her thoughts. "Don't worry," he said. "I know it was only a trick of my eyesight—I haven't completely lost my wits yet. But, you see, you remind me of her in so many ways."

"I do?" Elinor blinked. Ever since this morning, she'd been acting the part of Mrs. De Lacey with all of her might. "But she's—I mean, everyone says that Elinor Tregarth was—"

Benedict waved a dismissive hand. "Obviously, she intimidated her cousin and her friends. When a lady has that much poise and confidence—not to mention intelligence—she's bound to intimidate some people."

"Poise and confidence?" Elinor repeated blankly.

Now her head was really whirling. Had he completely forgotten the way they'd met?

His face eased into a grin. "Do you know how we first became acquainted? Aubrey's carriage knocked her off the road, into a ditch. When I helped her out, she was half-covered in mud, her hair had come undone, and God only knows what muck she'd had to swallow in that filthy water... but she looked me straight in the eye and held herself like a queen. Thanked me for helping her and prepared to set off on her way without asking for an ounce of help." He shook his head admiringly. "Now, *there's* poise."

"I...suppose so." Elinor remembered that moment, how

she'd felt the mud caked on her face and hair and *known*, with agonizing certainty, how ridiculous she must appear.

But he'd actually thought this of her, instead?

She couldn't even take it in.

"She must have told you something about me before she left," Benedict said. "Otherwise you couldn't have recognized me this morning and introduced me to Sir John."

"Well..." Elinor hesitated, but couldn't think of any other explanation. "She did mention you, yes."

Benedict's face brightened. He took a quick step forward. "What did she say?" At the sight of her rising eyebrows, he added, "I mean...you certainly couldn't have heard of me from anyone else but her—my estate was never *that* magnificent, even before my father's mistake. But you've been acting the part of a friend to me ever since this morning—asking Sir John to invite me to the house, encouraging my cause with Miss Hathergill..."

"Yes." Elinor sighed. "I have."

"So I can't help being curious." He smiled, but Elinor could have sworn she saw a flicker of anxiety cross his face. "What did Miss Tregarth say about me, exactly?"

"Really, Mr. Hawkins, you could hardly ask me to betray a confidence," Elinor said tartly. She frowned at him, trying to interpret the odd anxiety she'd glimpsed on his face.

What on earth could he be angling for? Honestly, what *would* she have told an older woman, newly met, except...

Oh, no. She cringed.

What if he had noticed her attraction to him yesterday?

She'd tried so hard to hide it during their carriage ride and at the dinner table. She had thought—she had *hoped*—that she had kept it safely secret. It would be too pathetic otherwise! If he had noticed her reactions, after all...if he had been worried that he had hurt or disappointed her, or...

Good God! She couldn't bear the thought of it.

Elinor made her voice as brisk as possible. "Miss Tregarth was grateful for your and Mr. Aubrey's kindness, of course. She mentioned both of you as benefactors to her."

"Both of us," Benedict repeated flatly. "Oh."

"And she *certainly* recommended you both to my generosity," Elinor finished sweepingly. "So I was only too glad to offer you a bit of help with your courtship this morning. And of course, after Miss Tregarth's description of Mr. Aubrey, I knew that he was the man to go to with my questions about my dragon."

"Yes," Benedict said. "Yes, I can see that. So...she didn't say anything about me in particular, then?"

He *had* noticed. He must have. Elinor felt humiliation seize every inch of her spine. She swallowed hard and kept her face a blank.

"Should she have?"

"No," Benedict said quietly. "No, of course not. Why should she? We had only just met that day."

"Quite." Elinor could have choked on the embarrassment that filled her. She searched desperately for a different topic as escape. "But speaking of people who have heard of you...I thought you'd kept your financial issues secret. Hadn't you? I only knew because Mr. Aubrey spoke of them in the carriage this morning, but—"

"But Gavin Armitage seems to know all of the details." Benedict's voice hardened. "I could have sworn no one outside the family ever knew that Father had been caught in that confounded fraud of an investment scheme. How the secret slipped out—and to *him*, of all people—"

"He only spoke of it as a rumour," Elinor said. "He cannot know it as a certainty."

"But if he passes that rumour on to Sir John..."

"We'll have to see that he doesn't." Elinor stood up and straightened her skirts with two vigorous shakes. "I'll speak to his sister and make certain she knows that I think the rumour false. He won't want to make a fool of himself by libeling you, after that. Then all you'll have to do is persuade Penelope of your cause."

"Yes," said Benedict. "Of course. I must."

Elinor gave him a quick, bright smile. "Of course," she said. "Miss Tregarth told me all about it. You have a five-year-old niece to look after, don't you? And—"

"Three younger brothers," Benedict said. "Yes. Colin and Randall and Julian. Julian is only eight. Did she mention that? Not to mention all the workers on the estate. They came to me in a group last month, when they realized how matters stood. I promised them—all of them—that I would make things right again."

"And so you shall. I am sure of it." Elinor nodded firmly

and scooped Sir Jessamyn off his boulder. "Now if you will excuse us..." She set off before he could answer.

"Mrs. De Lacey?" Benedict's voice reached her just before she could reach the door in the wall.

Reluctantly, she turned back. "Yes?"

"When you spoke to Miss Tregarth..." He paused. When he continued, his voice sounded strained. "When she spoke of my plans to marry her cousin," he said, "what exactly did she say?"

Oh, God. He really did suspect her feelings.

"She was delighted," Elinor said, and lifted her chin. "Why wouldn't she be?"

She turned and swept out of the garden.

CHAPTER 18

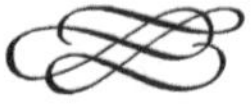

When Elinor stepped into the bedroom, the first thing she saw was the pile of newspapers that lay on her bed.

Thank goodness. She'd asked Carter earlier to arrange their collection, and now she was even more grateful than she'd expected to be. If the illusion was already beginning to show its seams, she had no time to lose. She needed to arrange a swift and permanent escape from Hathergill Hall, the very moment that Penelope's début ball came to an end.

Benedict might have blamed his eyesight once, but twice would strain anyone's credulity. And if the next person to see through the illusion was Sir John or Penelope...

She winced and sank down onto the bed cross-legged, spreading the papers all around her.

They were no longer clean and freshly-ironed, as Sir John

had already read them over breakfast, but they were still packed with closely-lined text. She pored through them as Sir Jessamyn wandered off to fall asleep on a non-crinkly area of the bed. The *Spectator* had been printed in London only two days ago, and it was full of Society gossip that she skimmed past as she hunted for advertisements.

Two titled gentlemen (referred to coyly by the writer as Lord F— and Sir G— H—) had participated in a drunken carriage race that left destruction to the tune of some £45 in their wake...the Prince Regent had ordered the commission of a new statue for his Brighton Pavilion, modeled on his favorite dragon...The celebrated Mrs D—L— was planning...

Wait. Elinor flipped back to that notice.

The celebrated Mrs. D—L— —or in other words, Mrs. De Lacey—had been planning to host a fabulous Venetian breakfast yesterday morning. According to the *Spectator*'s journalist, it would be attended by several fashionable figures and decorated with a South American theme. The *Spectator* confidently expected it to be one of the great events of the year.

And it had been held yesterday morning. Was it even possible for Mrs. De Lacey to have reached this part of Somerset by the middle of last night after spending the entire morning in London? Elinor was no expert in geography...but she had a feeling of cold certainty that the answer was *no*.

Elinor read the notice over and over again, but the tiny,

printed words never changed. How many other people had read them?

Sir John had set off so early this morning, he couldn't have had time to read the paper in any detail. He might well have missed that one small item of gossip, more focused on the larger news of the day. Penelope, on the other hand, was *only* interested in the gossip when she read a newspaper...but fortunately, she rarely did. There was a good chance that today, as she'd poured out her woes and waited for her father to hunt down her cousin, she hadn't bothered to pick up the *Spectator* for light reading.

That only left Lady Hathergill, Gavin Armitage, Miss Armitage...and every single servant who might read this paper after Elinor.

Her hands moved before she had even finished the thought, ripping off half the page and shredding the news item into dozens of tiny pieces. It was only as the last shreds fell onto her lap that she realized her mistake.

Sir John wasn't the only gentleman in the neighborhood who ordered the *Spectator*. Millie and Lucinda both came from households that subscribed to the London papers, even though their families couldn't afford London seasons for the girls. Everyone in the neighborhood would know soon enough that the famous Mrs. De Lacey had arrived at Hathergill Hall...

...And now that Elinor had ripped up the newspaper, she had just alerted every servant in the house that there was something interesting to be read in it.

Elinor stared at the shreds and felt an uncharacteristic scream of sheer frustration build up inside her, the kind that her sister Rose—or their cousin Penelope—would have unleashed without a thought.

Only fierce willpower kept it locked inside her chest.

"Too much," she said hoarsely. "This is simply *too much*."

Sir Jessamyn lifted his head off the bedcover to look up at her with lazy curiosity.

"Can't anything be easy?" she asked him. "Just for once, can't one single thing—*no*!" She slammed her mouth shut, as her mind caught up with her.

No matter how much Mr. Aubrey might snarl about fairy tales, Elinor knew exactly what happened whenever she asked for help around Sir Jessamyn.

"I just wish everyone could see me differently."

"I wish to know. What does your mother really think?

Her melodramatic impulse to scream had evaporated, replaced by cold panic. Elinor swallowed hard as she held her dragon's golden gaze. "Don't worry, Sir Jessamyn," she said steadily. "I'll be fine. Really. I'll think of something."

Carefully, she reached out to stroke the little dragon's blue-and-green head. He closed his eyes and leaned into her hand.

Elinor breathed out a sigh of relief.

The shreds of paper on her lap and on the bedcover were a reminder of just how much danger she was in...

But at least Sir Jessamyn's face hadn't gained any new markings. Not yet, anyway.

* * *

IN THE END, she found only two advertisements for a governess, and neither of them was promising. One of them requested 'a lady with a full command of the Spanish language to prepare three children for a voyage to South America,' and the other, placed by a Mrs. G. Galsworthy, offered 'a comfortable situation in which the delights of shared family life may well replace any vulgar monetary payment.'

Elinor had to read that second one twice to make certain that she hadn't misunderstood. "They won't even pay their governess a salary?!"

Sir Jessamyn, sleeping sprawled across the foot of the bed, did not respond. But after a long moment of inner conflict, Elinor gritted her teeth and made a careful note of the second advertisement's details.

Like it or not, if she didn't find anything more promising within the next few days, she would have no choice but to apply for the position and pray that 'the delights of shared family life' in Mrs. Galsworthy's household were less appalling than she suspected.

Meanwhile, her own family was waiting. By the time she had arranged her own hair and changed her gown, they had all gathered in the drawing room along with Benedict, Mr. Aubrey, and the two Armitages. Even Lady Hathergill was in attendance. With new houseguests in residence, Sir John and Penelope could hardly keep her locked up indefinitely.

When Elinor walked into the room, for the first time that she could remember, she found her aunt sitting fully upright in a hard-backed chair instead of reclining on a couch or padded armchair. With her cheeks flushed with enthusiasm and energy evident in every wave of her hand, Lady Hathergill was almost unrecognizable. She appeared to be holding the room spellbound—or at least mute with horror.

"...And of course those coverings look utterly ridiculous! *You* agree with me, don't you?" She aimed the question at Miss Armitage, who sat beside her with blue eyes dancing and one gloved hand pressed to her mouth.

Lady Hathergill sped onwards before Miss Armitage could reply. "Vulgar and overstated, to say the least. But of course once the draper had claimed they were the latest London fashion, there was nothing more to be said. Sir John has never in his life been able to resist a—"

"Look, Mama!" Penelope said. "Mrs. De Lacey has arrived!"

From the expression of joy on Penelope's face, she might have been announcing the arrival of an angel from Heaven. Sir John's face, shining with perspiration, showed the same desperate relief.

"Mrs. De Lacey!" He bounced out of his chair with alacrity and gestured sweepingly to the closest open seat. "Come in, come in, do! I hope you've enjoyed some rest? Have you—"

"It *is* good to see you, my friend." Lady Hathergill smiled at Elinor with unaffected pleasure. "I am so glad you changed your mind about visiting us, although I must say, I do think you have made a mistake. I know you were lying when you claimed a putrid sore throat in your last letter, but it was a perfectly good excuse. I can't imagine why you've decided to come after all instead of staying in London. It is deadly dull in Somerset, and particularly in our house—why, I feel as if I fell asleep years ago and have only just woken up!"

Gavin Armitage coughed loudly but didn't quite manage to disguise his laugh. His face was flushed and his brown eyes sparkling as he rose to his feet. "Mrs. De Lacey," he said. "You have missed quite a...fascinating discourse by her ladyship."

"Indeed?" Elinor raised her brows in a quelling look.

Perhaps she should have been glad that Penelope and Sir John were experiencing even a tiny fraction of the humiliation that she had suffered in their house. Perhaps she even would have been, under different circumstances. But Elinor couldn't bring herself to be a partner now to the malicious delight that sparkled in Mr. Armitage's eyes.

"Mrs. De Lacey." Benedict nodded to her, unsmiling, as he stood.

Mr. Aubrey, alone of all the gentlemen in the room, remained sitting in his armchair...and for once, Elinor couldn't blame it entirely on his book. The moment he saw her, he had scowled and lowered his head. She only just caught his muttered imprecation as he pointedly turned the page in his book.

"...blasted *fairy tales!*"

She sighed.

Sir Jessamyn craned his neck to look around hopefully. It had, after all, been nearly three hours since he had last eaten.

"Aha!" Miss Armitage said.

It was so unexpected that they all turned to look at her. Even her astonishingly well-trained dragon gave a start of surprise. She directed a look of stern reproof at him, then relaxed to smile at the rest of the company, waving one hand in graceful apology. "I do beg your pardons. I didn't mean to be uncouth. It's only that I've finally discovered the answer to a question that has been bothering me ever since we arrived. Until now, you see, I simply couldn't think of what had changed about Mrs. De Lacey."

"Mrs. De Lacey?" Gavin Armitage raised his eyebrows and turned to face Elinor. So did everyone else in the room.

Elinor swallowed, and forced her face into an expression of light interest. "Good heavens. I didn't think I could have changed so much in only four days."

"Four days?" Miss Armitage frowned at her. "I didn't see you four days ago, did I?"

Oh, dear. "But I thought—the rout that your brother mentioned, where I'd seen him last..." What had he called it? "At the Redmans?"

"The Rothershams," Gavin Armitage corrected her. She could hear the bafflement in his tone.

Elinor's heart sank. Mrs. De Lacey wouldn't have made

that mistake. How could she? "Of course," she said. "I only misspoke—I attend so very many routs, you see, it's terribly difficult to keep track." She thought about trying for a careless laugh. *Best not*. In her current state, it might come out as the squawk of a dying duck. "But I had thought—"

"I wasn't at that rout, I'm afraid," said Miss Armitage. "Gavin claimed it wouldn't be suitable for an unmarried lady, you see." Her tone was dry...and her dark blue eyes were fixed on Elinor's face with open speculation.

"Of course," Elinor repeated. "I had...forgotten."

She sat down on the first empty seat she could see, a spindly chair just to the right of Sir John. Her vision was tunneling with panic. Benedict was frowning at her from the couch, but she forced herself to ignore him and look straight into Miss Armitage's eyes.

"So," she said. "Have you come to a conclusion? What is so different about me today?"

Miss Armitage looked back at her with raised eyebrows... and all too much intelligence in her gaze.

"Oh, that was my mistake," she said. "It wasn't you who had changed, after all. It was your dragon."

CHAPTER 19

"My dragon?" Elinor repeated. She didn't look away from Miss Armitage, but she still sensed Sir John stiffening in his seat beside her and heard his bitten-off curse as he spilled sherry across his leg.

Sir Jessamyn noticed, too. Seated on Elinor's left shoulder, he was only a foot from Sir John's furious stare. He pressed himself against Elinor's neck, shivering.

Elinor put one soothing hand to Sir Jessamyn's back. "I can't think what you mean, Miss Armitage. What exactly do you think has changed about my dragon?"

"Well...everything!" Miss Armitage said. "Of course he is a completely different dragon, to begin with. Whatever happened to your last one? I thought *he* was quite an attractive creature, and he looked perfectly healthy when I saw you riding in the park with him last week."

"And at the Rothershams' rout," Gavin Armitage added. "You're right," he said to his sister, "I hadn't noticed until now, but of course it isn't the same dragon at all." He turned back to Elinor. "Your last one was a sort of reddish colour, wasn't he?"

"Like mine," Miss Armitage said helpfully, "but with pink rather than silver trimmings." She laughed, lowering her eyelashes. "You can see that I pay a good deal of attention to dragons, can't you? I confess, I find them fascinating. Far better than the ordinary run of jewelry as an accessory. I can't imagine disposing of one who was still so young and striking."

Elinor's hand tightened over Sir Jessamyn's back as, for a moment, panic mutated into anger. "Perhaps," she said, "that is because, unlike other fashionable accessories, dragons are living, breathing creatures with sensibilities."

"Oh, but they can be trained until you'd never guess it," said Miss Armitage. "Your new one is lovely, although I can see you haven't finished training him. He looks quite wild with nervousness now, doesn't he? Is he not yet accustomed to company?"

"Your *new one*," Sir John repeated, ominously. He set down his glass and leaned forward. "Mrs. De Lacey, you told me this morning, *to my face*—"

"He is *not* new," Elinor said. "He is my second dragon. Because he is not yet used to company, I haven't taken him about with me in London. But as I was coming to spend time in the countryside—"

"Of all the nerve!" Penelope's outraged gasp was almost a shriek, and it turned Sir Jessamyn's light shivers into ripples that threatened to knock him off Elinor's shoulder. He began to chitter unhappily at the back of his throat as Penelope said, "If you think just because we live in the countryside, we aren't worthy of your best dragon—!"

Elinor raised her own voice to cut across her cousin's rising fury. "I merely thought that as it would be quieter here—"

"*I* think," said Sir John, "that I have seen that bloody dragon before. That is what I think!"

He pointed a beefy finger at Sir Jessamyn.

"I think that's my daughter's blasted dragon!"

Sir Jessamyn unmistakably chuckled.

Elinor leaped to her feet. "That is quite enough!" she said. "If anyone utters one more word—"

But it was too late. Sir Jessamyn had lost control all over the back of her gown.

"Well," said Lady Hathergill brightly, "I've certainly seen that dragon before!"

Penelope fell back against the couch and began to scream. Gavin Armitage began to laugh. Sir John lunged to his feet, sputtering incoherently. Miss Armitage turned away, not quite in time to hide her amusement.

Mr. Aubrey turned the page of his book with a frown of perfect concentration and settled deeper into his armchair.

Hot dragon slime drenched the back of Elinor's gown. Her head whirled with panic. Sir Jessamyn had plastered himself so tightly against her neck, her throat was half-constricted. Even if she could have thought of what to say, she couldn't have forced the words out.

But before she could even try, Benedict Hawkins was at her side. "Won't you take my handkerchief, Mrs. De Lacey? Terrible habit these young dragons have," he added to the room at large. "I haven't met a single one that didn't do that when people made them nervous."

Penelope stopped screaming, but her breath came in short bursts as she glared at Elinor through narrowed eyes. "My dragon—*my* dragon always did that! Every day!"

"Your dragon did it too?" Benedict said. "I'm not surprised. Puppies are just the same, you know. No control when they get frightened. Wouldn't you confirm that, Miss Armitage?"

"Well..." Miss Armitage looked as if she were exerting superhuman control to hold back her laughter. "*My* dragon did it only once," she said. "It is part of the training process, you know—teaching them to be calm in all circumstances."

Sir Jessamyn let out a barely audible chitter of fear as he snaked his neck around Elinor's throat and then tucked his head so tightly underneath her chin that he nearly overbalanced her.

"Never mind," Elinor rasped to him, through her constricted throat. "You'll learn soon enough."

Miss Armitage's dragon gazed past Sir Jessamyn with cool indifference, as if the other dragon's panic was a sight far too embarrassing to even witness. Elinor gritted her teeth, held Sir Jessamyn steady with one hand, and struggled to reach around her back with the handkerchief Benedict had given her.

"Allow me." He took it from her and wiped carefully across the back of her shoulder. "Can we summon a maid to clean the rest of this up?"

"Oh, the maids won't do it anymore," said Lady Hathergill. "They utterly refuse."

His hand paused a moment in its work. "Then who—?"

"Elinor always did it, of course! But now..." Penelope's lower lip pushed out sullenly. "I didn't know that other dragons were just as bad."

Elinor bit her lip hard to repress her reaction.

Then she thought: *Why?*

Carefully, she nudged Sir Jessamyn's head clear of her neck so that she could speak more easily. She kept one soothing hand under the little dragon's chin as she looked at Penelope with all the fury she'd had to repress for six long months.

"Your dragon was not 'bad' to be afraid of you, Miss Hathergill," she said. "You heard Miss Armitage—even her dragon lost control once, when he was young. The only difference was that *she* was careful not to frighten him again as she taught him self-control. My dragon would not have panicked now, either, if he hadn't been shouted and shrieked at in an outrageous manner."

"I beg your pardon?" Penelope's voice soared upwards.

"Are you actually trying to claim that my dragon's behavior was *my fault*?"

"Penelope…" Sir John held out one hand, frowning. He turned to stare at Sir Jessamyn. "Are you quite certain that that is not my daughter's dragon?"

Elinor looked at him with every bit as much haughty contempt as the real Mrs. De Lacey could ever have summoned. "Have I not said so clearly enough?"

"My niece always did think Penelope unkind to her dragon," Lady Hathergill remarked. "It wasn't worth the effort to agree with her, of course, but I must say Penelope did shriek at him a great deal. But then, she's never had the patience for anyone else's problems but her own."

"Mother!" Penelope's lips quivered with a visible mixture of fury and hurt. "How could you? When you know how much I've suffered—"

"You see?" Lady Hathergill said, to the rest of the company. "It never seemed worth the trouble to admit the truth when Sir John would certainly support her no matter how badly she behaved. But do you know…" She smiled sunnily. "I feel quite energetic at the moment. Why, for once I'm not bothered at all by my daughter's hysterics."

"Oh!" Penelope jumped to her feet. "You are all being completely impossible. I hate you!"

She ran from the room in a whirl of sprig muslin, sobbing noisily. Sir John turned on his wife.

"Mary! What in God's name has come over you today?"

She shrugged, still smiling. "I haven't the faintest idea. It's been years and years since I last said what I truly thought. It is quite unlike me, isn't it? But I'm finding it rather liberating."

Benedict's hand stopped moving on Elinor's shoulder. For a moment, he stood perfectly still behind her. Then his warm breath rustled against her throat as he whispered, in a bare thread of sound,

"*I wish to know. What does your mother really think?*"

It was a sentence that made no sense, coming from him. Until...

Elinor's breath stopped in her throat. She knew those words. They were the ones she'd uttered that afternoon, just before Sir Jessamyn had breathed his flame and changed her aunt.

She held desperately still. Her pulse beat against her throat. She felt Benedict's hand on her shoulder, warm through the handkerchief and her slime-soaked gown. She wished she could see his face.

Sir John stared at his wife in fulminating silence for a long moment. Then he turned on his heel and walked out of the room.

"Gone after Penelope, I expect," said Lady Hathergill with a sigh. "That was why I gave up on instilling any discipline in her when she was a child. What purpose was there, when her father would only give her whatever she wanted, no matter what I said? Ah, well." She patted down her skirts. "She's pretty enough, and with such an enormous dowry, I'm certain she'll make a good match anyway and be off our hands soon enough. I expect you two gentlemen are both here for that now, aren't you?"

Benedict didn't speak.

Gavin Armitage said, "Your ladyship, your daughter's beauty and charm are—"

"Yes, yes," said Lady Hathergill. "I know. Gentlemen do tend to go foolish around girls like Penelope. Just as well, really. Her cousin, now—Elinor was a sensible girl. I always thought *she* would make a good wife, if any man was clever enough to see it. But no gentlemen would ever marry her, not after her father lost all her money—and Sir John would never allow me to sponsor her in Society, anyway. Penelope couldn't have borne it."

Elinor was glad that Benedict stood behind her. She didn't want to see his face, not now.

Miss Armitage was the one who spoke. "Lost her money? How did that happen?"

"Oh, one of those terrible fraudulent investment schemes." Lady Hathergill waved a dismissive hand. "All about the import of rare Brazilian dragons, or some such nonsense. It all sounded very promising at the time, according to my sister's letters. And the tricksters who persuaded my brother-in-law to settle all his funds on the scheme were extraordinarily persuasive. I believe they generally are."

"Tricksters?" The word emerged as a croak from Elinor's throat. "There was more than one?"

"Oh, it was a married couple," her aunt said carelessly.

"They seemed terribly respectable, you see. That must have been part of their appeal. They claimed the wife's father was in Brazil himself, directing all the operations, while the husband in England collected all of their investors. They dined with my brother-in-law and the wife charmed him, the husband was convincing..."

She sighed. "And so the money was all stolen. My sister and her husband were killed in an accident before they could come up with any salvation for the family, and the only way I could persuade Sir John to take in even one of the girls was to promise her as a sort of maid-of-all-work to Penelope." She shook her head. "But of course, without Penelope's looks, and without any dowry of her own, my niece would never have found a husband anyway. What more could she hope for than shelter in our household, even if she was treated poorly here?"

Miss Armitage's voice was warm. "I think it sounds as if you were very generous indeed, Lady Hathergill. What more could any girl expect in her situation? I do feel sorry for her, I confess, but really—what could she have been thinking to run away like that for no reason at all?"

"Indeed." Mr. Armitage's golden hair glinted in the candlelight as he shook his head regretfully. "I'm afraid she threw away her own chances there. A pity, I'm sure, but that is how life works, is it not? What do you say, Mrs. De Lacey?"

"Quite," Elinor said colourlessly. "She must have been very foolish indeed."

Behind her, Benedict Hawkins said nothing at all.

CHAPTER 20

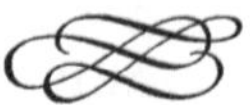

When Elinor made her excuses to the company and left before dinner could be served, she half-expected Benedict to follow her. All the way back to her room, she braced herself to be caught up with at any moment.

He knew—or at least suspected—what she and Sir Jessamyn had done to Lady Hathergill. How could he not pursue her for answers?

But she arrived at her room without being stopped, and when a knock sounded on the door twenty minutes later, it was only Sally, holding Elinor's dinner on a platter. The maid looked at Elinor's discarded gown, lying over the dressing-table chair, and nodded briskly.

"Mrs. Braithewaite said that would need cleaning. He's still up to his old tricks, is he?"

Sir Jessamyn, on Elinor's lap, looked unoffended by the comment, as well as unruffled by his earlier accident. All of his attention was on the platter that Sally set down on the bed, with its tureen of soup and full plate of pheasant, jelly, and macaroons. A glass of wine, warmly golden against its crystal glass, stood beside them, perfectly unspilled.

"Thank you," Elinor said. "I'm afraid Penelope frightened him, and—"

"Oh, *I* know," said Sally. "I wouldn't let a pet of mine anywhere near her, I wouldn't, nor a baby, for that matter." She poked at the soiled gown with one finger. "Still, I should have it ready for you by tomorrow morning."

Elinor frowned. "I thought that none of the maids would touch—"

"Not for Miss Penelope, no, not anymore," said Sally, "and Mrs. Braithewaite is behind us all the way, believe you me. She said it was too much for anyone to bear, the number of times every day we were expected to clean those messes up, especially when we all knew Miss Penelope was causing them herself. But you're an honored guest, *Mrs. De Lacey*—or at least, we're all supposed to think so. So..."

She sat down on the foot of the bed and looked expectantly at Elinor. "Tell me what happened with our Lucinda this afternoon."

"Ah." Elinor took a deep breath. Sir Jessamyn nosed the tray, and she cut off a slice of pheasant. Feeding it to him gave her a good excuse to lower her head and not meet Sally's gaze. "I emptied her reticule onto the couch—"

"That must have been a nasty shock to her," Sally said cheerfully. "How did you manage it?"

Elinor winced. "I spilled my tea all over her."

"Good." Sally reached over and scooped Elinor's wine glass off the tray with casual authority. She raised it to her lips as she asked, "And which of our little knick-knacks took her fancy today?"

"None," Elinor said. "There was nothing in her reticule that shouldn't have been there."

"What?" Sally lowered the glass so quickly, wine sloshed against the crystal rim. "Something must have distracted her. She almost always—"

"Not today," said Elinor, "and I expect she won't take anything on her next visit, either. Not now that she knows I'm watching her."

"Bloody hell." Sally shook her head. "You've torn it!"

"I did tell you I probably wouldn't be able—"

"Well, you're going to have to think of something!" Sally took a long sip of wine and slammed the glass back down onto the tray with an ominous chink. "If you imagine you can give up just because you made one little mistake—"

"I'm only here for six days!" said Elinor. "How many chances do you expect me to have? Now that she knows I suspect her, she'll be on her guard. Why would she take the risk of stealing anything this week? She isn't stupid. She'll wait until I leave before she tries anything else."

Sally raised her eyebrows. "Then you'll just have to help her along, won't you?"

Dread twisted in Elinor's stomach. "What do you mean?"

"You think she won't take anything herself? Fine. You'll just have to do it for her."

"I beg your pardon?" Elinor stared at Sally. She'd been carefully feeding slices of pheasant to Sir Jessamyn, but now her hand dropped limply to her lap, and Sir Jessamyn took over the task with enthusiasm. "You can't mean—"

"All you have to do is take something yourself and slip it into that little bag of hers," said Sally. "Who's going to take her word against the great Mrs. De Lacey—especially when everyone sees you discover the stolen goods?"

"I can't do that," said Elinor.

"Of course you can. Miss Lucinda does it all the time. Just wait until no one's looking and then—"

"That's not what I meant!" Elinor was breathing hard, the meal before her forgotten. She barely even noticed Sir Jessamyn nosing forward onto the dinner tray, golden eyes glinting with excitement, to attack the jellies on her plate. "I *will not* steal something myself and then plant it in her reticule. That would be wrong! It would be—"

"It would be exactly what she did to my sister!" Sally crossed her arms. "*She* planted all that jewelry in Daisy's room and ruined her life just to keep herself safe. Do you really think she doesn't deserve the same treatment? Just because she's a lady and we're—"

"She might deserve it," said Elinor, "but I cannot do it to her. Not without behaving just as cruelly and dishonestly as she did to your sister."

Sally's cheeks flushed with colour. For a long moment she looked at Elinor in a silence so ominous that even Sir Jessamyn stopped eating to look up questioningly.

Then she said, "Dishonest, is it? Well. If you're so worried about honesty, maybe I should go to Sir John or Miss Penelope right now. Maybe you want me to tell them exactly who you are. Because we're all just so terribly worried about *honesty* now, aren't we?"

Elinor swallowed. "If I can help Daisy in any other way—"

"You can't," Sally said flatly. "She will never get another respectable position until Miss Lucinda is revealed. And if you're too dainty to get your ladylike hands dirty, then it's never going to happen."

"There has to be another way," Elinor said. "Something that doesn't force us to sink to her level. If we—"

"You can spend the whole time you're here fretting your heart out about what's *proper*," Sally said, "but I don't have that liberty, *ma'am*. All I have is a little sister who's lost everything, and I'm watching all my hopes for her future thrown away to salve your pretty conscience!"

"Sally..."

"No!" Sally stood up and slapped down her skirts. "I'm going to Sir John right now. And I'm going to tell him—"

"*What*?" Elinor demanded. "What exactly are you going to tell him?"

It was the last of too many crises in one day. She couldn't even bring herself to be frightened. Not anymore. "You just told me that no one would take Lucinda's word against the great Mrs. De Lacey. Do you really think that Sir John will take your word against mine?"

Sally blinked rapidly. "Well, maybe not Sir John, but when I tell Miss Penelope—"

"My cousin has never had a real conversation with a servant in her life," said Elinor. "She thought that *I* was too low to be her equal, only because my parents lost our money. Do you think she'll take you any more seriously than my uncle would?"

"If they find out the truth, no matter who brings it—"

"And what evidence of it will you offer them?" Elinor asked. She turned to let Sir Jessamyn slide off her lap...and her gaze fell on the mutilated newspaper that still lay on top of the pile beside her bed. Her muscles went taut; all her momentary calm evaporated. She had to force herself to meet Sally's gaze once more, even as she realized that her own words were pure bluff: "There is no way to prove it to them."

Sally must have seen the change in Elinor's expression. Her shoulders relaxed. Her lips curved into an unpleasant smile. "Oh, there's always a way," she said. "Isn't that what you just told me, Miss Elinor, when you were dismissing my Daisy's problems as unimportant compared to being kind to the gentryfolk?"

"I am not dismissing them," Elinor said. "I'm only saying—"

"I think *you've* said quite enough, thank you." Sally

leaned over to scoop up the pile of newspapers. Before she could stop herself, Elinor gave a jerk of alarm. She couldn't tell whether Sally had noticed it...but there was a glint of satisfaction in the maid's eyes as she straightened.

"I'll find that evidence of yours," she said, "and I promise you, I'll find it before the week is up. So you'd better find that *better way* you're hoping for to expose Miss Lucinda...or else you'll be the one who gets caught out in front of the whole company by the time Miss Penelope's début ball is over...and won't that make it easy for Sir John to arrest you just as he wanted to in the first place!"

She snatched the soiled gown off the chair and stalked out of the room, leaving Elinor with an empty wineglass and a dinner tray picked perfectly clean.

Sir Jessamyn looked up at Elinor and belched.

"Oh, yes," she said fervently. "It is definitely time for bed."

* * *

SHE HAD JUST BLOWN out her candle and closed her eyes, with Sir Jessamyn curled warmly on the pillow beside her, when a soft knock sounded on the door.

Sir Jessamyn looked up alertly. His golden eyes gleamed in the shadows.

"Ignore it," Elinor whispered, and pulled her covers more tightly around herself. She didn't care who it was, or what they wanted. All *she* wanted now...

The door opened. Candlelight glowed in her cousin's hand.

"Mrs. De Lacey?" Penelope whispered. "You aren't asleep yet, are you?"

Elinor gritted her teeth and remained stubbornly silent.

Penelope stepped further into the room and closed the door behind her. "You must wake up, Mrs. De Lacey! I need to talk to you."

Inwardly, Elinor let out the kind of curse she would never allow herself to utter out loud. Resigned, she pushed herself up in bed. "What is so important that it cannot wait for the morning?"

"Well...everything!" Penelope set down her candlestick and collapsed onto Elinor's bed. In the flickering glow of the candlelight, her beautiful face was shadowed, but Elinor could still make out the signs of recent tears. "Everything's going wrong for me. You have to help!"

"Do I?" Elinor sighed. Sir Jessamyn was a still and watchful presence beside her, tense but not yet frightened. "I promised I would help you with your début, Penelope, and I will. But I've had a rather long day, and—"

"*You've* had a long day?" Penelope let out a huff of disbelief. "What about me? First my father fails to find my cousin *or* my dragon...then he announces he won't even try to hunt her down—and then my mother goes mad!"

"Lady Hathergill has not gone mad," Elinor said, trying hard not to sound guilty. "As ladies grow older, they do often tend to speak their minds more strongly, and—"

"What kind of mind would even come up with such evil things?" Penelope sniffed. "I picked those draperies in the drawing room myself! Papa and the draper *both* approved them and said how perfect my taste was. Now she decides to call them 'vulgar'? And to claim that *I* go into hysterics when anyone criticizes me—! Me? Of all the—"

"I understand," Elinor said hastily. Penelope's voice was already rising, sending Sir Jessamyn shrinking towards Elinor's side. "You were hurt by the way that your mother spoke of you in front of company."

"I was hurt by the fact that she belongs in a madhouse!" Penelope's tone was venomous. "Papa is going to summon a physician to inspect her, he promised me. *He* thinks it very likely that she may have developed some sort of mental disorder."

Elinor stared at her. "You cannot be serious."

"No one would change their entire personality so suddenly unless they had gone mad," Penelope said. "It's the only possible explanation for her behavior! But..." She drooped, her voice turning piteous. "It may already be too late. When I came back down to supper, you should have seen the way everyone looked at me. They'd all been listening to her! And Mr. Hawkins..."

Elinor stiffened. "Mr. Hawkins...?"

Penelope burst into tears. "He barely even looked at me!" She launched herself forward into Elinor's arms. "What if she's given him a disgust of me? I couldn't bear it!"

Elinor patted her cousin's back and took deep, steadying

breaths. Things could have been worse, she told herself. If anyone else had thrown their arms around her, they would have been shocked by the difference between her curvaceous appearance and the figure that they felt against them.

Penelope, on the other hand, was far too self-absorbed to take any notice.

When her cousin's sobs finally began to subside, Elinor said, "I am sure he still admires you."

"I don't believe he does." Penelope choked on her tears. "When I said that your dragon was just as horrid as all the rest, he actually looked as if he didn't care for me at all!"

Elinor couldn't halt the burst of rebellious warmth inside her chest. "Perhaps he'd eaten something that displeased him," she suggested. "He might not even have been listening to what you said."

"But that would be just as bad." Penelope drew back, her chest heaving with her final, hiccupping tears. "My mother has ruined all of my marital chances!"

"Penelope..." Elinor sighed. "You haven't even had your début yet."

"But by the time I have my season in London, she might already be in a madhouse," Penelope said. "Even if she's only kept restrained in a cottage somewhere, in the care of a nurse, people are sure to find out in the end. Then no one will *ever* want to marry me!"

Elinor cringed. "Your mother certainly does not need a nurse—much less a madhouse! And if you want to be certain to attract a good husband without any unpleasant rumours spreading around—"

"Oh, *I* know," said Penelope heavily. "There is only one thing that I can do, anymore. I simply must become betrothed by the night of my début. It's my final chance." She drew herself up, looking tragic and heroic. "Mr. Hawkins and Mr. Armitage must *both* offer for me. It's my only chance at happiness!"

"But..." Elinor blinked at her. "You can only accept one of them, you know."

"So?" said Penelope. "They *both* have to ask before I can say yes to either of them, obviously. I couldn't bear to have only one proposal of marriage. If I couldn't turn even one gentleman down...well, then, I'd be a positive laughing-stock! Don't you see?"

Elinor sighed. She did see, all too well.

She hadn't been able to save her own family, but she could still help Benedict save his...and there was only one way to do that.

"Very well," she said to her cousin. "I'll help you."

CHAPTER 21

Penelope's peacocks were shrieking outside when Elinor woke up the next morning, just as they had every morning and evening for the past six months. As soon as Elinor could force herself out of bed, she would need to wash and dress herself and find her cousin and aunt, to discover to the list of chores Penelope had chosen for her that day. Now that Penelope's début was drawing near, the list was almost certain to be unreasonable. She...

Something stepped on Elinor's legs, and her eyes flicked open.

The sun was shining through the windows of one of Hathergill Hall's best bedrooms. Sir Jessamyn had just walked over her legs on his way to the closest patch of warm sunlight...and when Elinor looked down, she saw another woman's larger hands in place of her own.

Last night's gown, freshly cleaned, lay folded on top of the chair.

Memory swamped Elinor. She pulled her covers over her head and moaned.

Then she sighed and pushed the covers off. "Well," she said. "At least I won't be doing any chores today."

It took nearly twenty minutes for her to arrange her hair as Carter had taught her, struggling to manipulate thick hanks that looked so different than they felt. By the time she'd finally succeeded, Sir Jessamyn was fast asleep again. For once, it was Elinor whose stomach was rumbling impatiently.

"Come along." She scooped the little dragon off the ground.

His eyes slitted half-open for only a moment as she set him upon her shoulder. Closing his eyes once more, he began to slide off, straight down her front.

She grabbed him just in time.

"*You're* the reason I'm so hungry," Elinor told him. "If you hadn't been so greedy with my supper last night, I would have let you sleep in!"

Sir Jessamyn, settling with relief into her arms, fell asleep with his head tucked into her left elbow. Even walking down the stairs didn't disturb his slumber. As they neared the breakfast room, though, his snout finally began to twitch.

Elinor could smell that freshly-cooked bacon, too. She wasn't surprised when one golden eye opened and then another. Sir Jessamyn's long neck rose, following the scent like an arrow.

"You see?" she said. "This wasn't such a bad idea after all, was it?"

Sir Jessamyn didn't bother with a response. He was too busy yearning towards the breakfast room.

He was perched alertly on her shoulder by the time they walked inside. *Thank goodness*, Elinor thought, as she saw Miss Armitage sitting already at the table with her dragon sitting perfectly still and composed on her shoulder.

Miss Armitage, she was certain, *never* carried her own dragon in her arms. Her dragon was so well-trained, he didn't even turn to look at them as they walked into the room.

Sir Jessamyn, on the other hand, let out a loud chirrup of glee as he spotted the well-laden sideboard.

"Mrs. De Lacey." Miss Armitage set down her knife and smiled up at her. "I see you've recovered from last night's drama."

For a moment, Elinor could only blink. How had she known—? *Oh, wait*. The *public* drama! "Perfectly." She smiled back. "Really, it was nothing."

"Really?" Miss Armitage raised her eyebrows. "*I* thought it rather an odd way to treat an honored guest. To be frank, I was surprised you didn't simply walk away when our host first began shouting—or leave the house entirely."

"Well..." Elinor was grateful for the excuse to turn her back as she took her plate to the sideboard to gather her food. "I have promised to help Penelope with her début. I could hardly leave before then."

"Very noble of you."

In the pause that followed, Elinor bent over the sideboard, spearing eggs and bacon and toast and glaring sternly at Sir Jessamyn when his nose inched too close to the platters. Soon, though, her plate was entirely covered, and she was left with no excuse to linger.

She sat down at the table, forcing a serene expression. In the bright sunlight that streamed through the windows, Miss Armitage looked well-rested, fresh, and entirely at ease, her dark hair a rich contrast to the red scales of the dragon on her shoulder. Again, Elinor was struck by the other girl's air of effortless confidence. She couldn't be more than twenty, and if her older brother had only just become known in Society, then she must have only recently made her London début as well...but she held herself with all the assurance of a matron who knew her place in society, not like a girl still searching and hoping to be chosen.

When she met Elinor's eyes, Elinor had to remind herself forcibly not to drop her gaze. The Armitages might be wealthy and charming new members of high Society, but Mrs. De Lacey was Society's reigning queen...no matter how little Elinor herself might fit that role.

"At least the food here is delicious," Miss Armitage said. "Sir John and his wife may be a rather tempestuous pair of hosts, but one can hardly fault them for their cook." Her lips twitched. "I do think your dragon may be angling for a bit of your bacon, though."

It was hard to argue, as Sir Jessamyn was now hanging off Elinor's shoulder with his mouth half-open and his golden eyes fixed on her plate. Still, Elinor couldn't stop herself from flushing under Miss Armitage's amused gaze.

"I'm afraid I—" she began, and then cut herself off. *Don't apologize.* Mrs. De Lacey set fashions rather than following them.

Elinor lifted her chin as she passed a strip of bacon to Sir Jessamyn. "I enjoy sharing meals with my dragon."

"Indeed." Miss Armitage's gaze followed the dripping oil that fell in drops onto the tablecloth as Sir Jessamyn crunched the bacon enthusiastically.

Elinor could have sworn that she glimpsed a wince of sophisticated distaste cross the perfectly symmetrical and unmarked face of Miss Armitage's own dragon. His mistress, fortunately, was too polite to say what she must have been thinking. When she spoke again, it was to change the subject.

"I take it you are a friend of Lady Hathergill, not of Sir John?"

"Yes," said Elinor. "We were close friends when we were younger."

Which meant...she frowned. In point of fact, that meant that her mother had probably known Mrs. De Lacey, too. Somehow, she had never thought of it in that way before. Her mother had never mentioned the connection herself—busy and happy with her good works in their Cornish village, with no trips to London and less than no interest in the distant world of high fashion, such matters could hardly have seemed relevant to her. It was only Elinor who had devoured all the gossip in the society pages of the newspaper, while her mother had rolled her own eyes and teased her gently over the breakfast table—*"To think of my most sensible girl letting herself be taken in by such nonsensical trivialities!"*—and her father had patted her hand reassuringly. *"Let Ellie enjoy herself, my dear. It may not be to our taste, but it harms no one, and she certainly deserves a bit of fun. She's a good girl..."*

Elinor's eyes stung with sudden tears. She blinked them rapidly away, taking a deep breath.

Happy memories shouldn't make her weep.

But she wondered, suddenly, whether her father *had* been thinking of his daughters after all when he had made those deluded investments. Had he dreamed of Elinor, Rose, and Harry entering that distant Society she had so loved to read about, with those mythical proceeds from the Brazilian scheme? If *that* had been the cause that drove him, rather than simple greed...would that make it better or worse?

And would it make what had happened to them partly her fault, too?

She barely registered the sound of Miss Armitage's voice, speaking nearby. It wasn't until Miss Armitage cleared her throat that Elinor blinked back to attention.

"I beg your pardon?"

"I merely asked..." Miss Armitage's blue eyes rested on Elinor's face with cool interest. "Had you ever met Miss

Hathergill before? I take it that it had been some years since you last saw her mother."

"Oh, years and years," Elinor agreed, and took a hasty bite of bacon to fill her mouth. Sir Jessamyn drooped with disappointment on her shoulder. Miss Armitage waited patiently, though, so Elinor was eventually forced to continue. "This has been my first meeting with Penelope."

"And yet you're whole-heartedly committed to helping her in her début no matter how rude her father might be." Miss Armitage widened her eyes. "How remarkably generous of you, ma'am."

"Well..." Elinor shrugged as well as she could without dislodging Sir Jessamyn. "Promises must be kept."

"Mm," said Miss Armitage.

Unease skittered through Elinor as she continued to eat, pretending unconcern, but all too aware of the sceptical expression on the other woman's face. Surely, Miss Armitage should have been endeavoring to ingratiate herself to Mrs. De Lacey—or, at the very least, unwilling to offend her now. If she was allowing herself to look so openly disbelieving...

"Miss Hathergill mentioned that you had sent your carriage back to London with your abigail and all of your clothing inside."

"I did." Summoning all of her inner resources, Elinor made a grand, sweeping gesture with her knife. "An amusing experiment, I thought—to see if I could survive a week in the country on my own resources. Well, and with the clothes that I found in the inn, of course."

"Of course," Miss Armitage murmured, and her gaze flickered across Elinor's high-necked, dull gray morning gown. "The poor relation's."

Elinor suppressed a wince.

Miss Armitage leaned forward, and her dragon shifted gracefully on her shoulder, arching his long, red-and-silver neck backwards for counter-balance. "Mrs. De Lacey," she said firmly, "You have nothing to fear from me."

"Miss Armitage..." Frowning, Elinor leaned forward, too. "Whyever would I?"

Before Sir Jessamyn could seize the opportunity, she set one hand between his snout and her plate. He sighed and nestled his chin against her fingers.

Miss Armitage smiled, her expression warm and understanding. "I know that you're in some distress."

"I..."

"You needn't explain anything to me," said Miss Armitage. "Five days ago, you told my brother that you would be in London for the rest of the month and had no idea of accepting any rural invitations. You were meant to be holding a great Venetian breakfast only two mornings ago. Yet you arrived in Somerset that very night, without your carriage, without your clothes, without even your abigail for company, and you informed your hosts that they must not announce your presence to the newspapers..." She shook her head gently. "And it is *quite* obvious to anyone who's ever observed you in the past that you are not yourself at the moment."

Elinor swallowed hard. “I cannot imagine what you mean by that.”

“No?” Miss Armitage raised one eyebrow. “I don’t mean to embarrass you, ma’am, but I can only imagine that something must have occurred to shake you deeply. Whatever happened in London to set you running...whomever you may be hiding from here...”

“I am not hiding from anyone, Miss Armitage.” Elinor’s voice threatened to shake, but she forced it into steadiness. “What an absurd idea.”

The other lady’s gaze never wavered. “Mrs. De Lacey,” said Miss Armitage, “I am trying to reassure you that you have nothing to fear from me. You see, I am a person who knows how to keep important secrets...and you may find me surprisingly difficult to shock.”

Elinor had to bite her lip to hold back a semi-hysterical laugh. If Miss Armitage only knew... “You might be surprised,” she said.

“I doubt it.” Footsteps sounded in the corridor outside, along with male voices, and Miss Armitage sat back in her seat. With unruffled composure, she lifted her teacup to her lips. Her eyes, above the delicate china, were uncomfortably knowing, even as her voice dropped to a thread of a whisper. “If you find that you need someone to confide in after all—or someone to assist you, ma’am—you know where to come. I can be of more support than you may imagine.”

“Thank you,” Elinor murmured, shifting back into her own seat. “I won’t forget.”

As she took a sip of her own cooling tea, though, and watched Miss Armitage smile in easy greeting to the group of male houseguests walking in the door, Elinor found herself pondering an entirely different question.

How many 'important secrets' was the other girl already keeping? And how many people had found themselves succumbing to the temptation to share them with her?

Elinor set down her teacup and took a deep breath. Like the girl across from her, she turned a welcoming smile towards the door. Inside, though, she was rapidly formulating a decision.

Miss Armitage was charming, intelligent and dangerously persuasive...and Elinor would never make the mistake of allowing herself to be trapped alone with her again.

CHAPTER 22

Two days later, though, Elinor was beginning to feel desperate.

The newspapers still hadn't provided any suitable advertisements for a governess, and she was running out of time. In one turn of shockingly good fortune, Mrs. De Lacey hadn't had a single exploit reported in London's society columns in the past two days...but Elinor couldn't help worrying that that ominous silence only meant that she would explode into more glorious activity than ever with her next feature.

Lucinda had sent a note to Penelope announcing that she had a miserable head-cold and wouldn't be able to visit her for the next few days. If she really was as cunning as Sally claimed, she wouldn't return to Hathergill Hall until she absolutely had to, on the very night of Penelope's début...the night when Sally would publicly expose Elinor's deception if Elinor didn't expose Lucinda's thievery first.

Meanwhile, Gavin Armitage, with help from his sister, was doing his charming best to sweep Penelope off her feet with stories of the glittering London life that he and his future wife would share...while constantly calling upon Elinor herself to supply more pertinent details. Even after all the society columns she'd devoured, Elinor was miserably certain that she must slip up soon, if she hadn't already—and no matter how much Elinor tried to persuade Penelope otherwise, she was becoming just as certain that she knew which choice her foolish cousin would make if both men did propose.

And worst of all, Benedict Hawkins hadn't uttered a word to her for the past two days.

Oh, he watched her. She found him watching her at the oddest moments, just when she was absorbed in conversation with someone else, or in the middle of petting Sir Jessamyn. But he always looked away the very moment their eyes met. There had been no shared smiles in these past few days, no private conversations in the gardens or her room.

...Which was hardly the point of his visit, Elinor reminded herself, grinding her teeth as she walked down the stairs with Sir Jessamyn on her shoulder.

Of course there was no reason for Benedict to seek out her company. But if he wanted to have any chance of beating out Gavin Armitage, he would do well to start acting more like himself. For the past two days, he had been so strangely reserved—polite but barely attentive in company, even to Penelope when he sat beside her—it was no wonder that Penelope was falling under Mr. Armitage's practiced spell. Elinor might find the other man's ruthless charm as insubstantial as false gold, but Benedict was barely even trying to rival it.

Perhaps if she took him aside to warn him...

No. That was a pitiful excuse.

She stalked off the bottom step with a swish of her aunt's best riding habit. The house party was going on a picnic today, and as Elinor's own collection of clothing hadn't included a habit, Lady Hathergill had offered hers.

"I haven't ridden in years. Why would I want to spend the afternoon on a horse listening to everyone natter on about tedious things? I hear enough of that at home, and at least here, there's tea for comfort. You may as well borrow it, just as I borrowed so many gowns from you in our début season."

This riding habit might be five years out of fashion and far from a perfect fit, but it was also a satisfyingly deep and dangerous crimson that matched Elinor's current mood... especially as she opened her reticule to take out the folded letter she had finally been forced to write.

To Mrs. Galsworthy, it read. *The Oaks, Halstead, Hamps.*

There had been no suitable governessing advertisements, so Elinor had been forced to apply for this one, after all.

"Better to go without a salary than without a home," she whispered to Sir Jessamyn. She tried, without much luck, to find some comfort in the words.

The salver on the front table already held four letters written in Miss Armitage's elegant hand. Elinor took a quick look around the hall to ensure her privacy, then lifted the other letter up by its corner. If she slipped her letter carefully underneath…

"Mrs. De Lacey," Benedict said, directly behind her.

Elinor dropped her letter and almost dropped Sir Jessamyn, too. He clenched his claws into her shoulder as he slipped halfway off, cheeping frantically, and she gasped with pain as she re-settled him.

"Oh, your claws are sharp! Oh…*oh*," she finished, in a different tone entirely.

Benedict had stooped to pick up her letter.

He looked down at it for a long moment, his eyes shaded by a fallen lock of thick brown hair. Then he looked back up and met her gaze. "Mrs. Galsworthy," he said. "Would that be Mrs. G. Galsworthy?"

"Well…yes," Elinor said. "Do you know her?"

"No," said Benedict, and dropped the letter onto the salver, just on top of Miss Armitage's missive. She gave an instinctive jerk of protest, and he looked questioningly at her. "You did want to post this, didn't you?"

"Yes," she said, "I only…" She forced herself to pull back her hand. "Thank you. It was nothing."

There was no reason to worry about other people seeing it, she told herself. No one would think anything of it.

…Except, perhaps, for Benedict Hawkins, who was giving her exactly the kind of disconcertingly probing look that she had surprised upon his face all too often in the last two days.

"How do you know of Mrs. Galsworthy?" she asked him.

He raised his eyebrows. "How do you?"

She was silent for a moment, weighing possibilities. He smiled ruefully and reached out to scratch Sir Jessamyn behind the ears. Sir Jessamyn leaned into his hand; Elinor forced herself not to step closer and seek his warmth, too.

"*There* you both are!" Penelope swept into the hall, resplendent in a bright blue riding habit that matched her eyes perfectly. The feather on her bonnet curled fetchingly against her cheek; her smile turned jubilant as Gavin Armitage, his sister, and a wide-eyed, giggling Millie all followed in her wake. "Now we can finally leave. I hate waiting!"

So do I, Elinor thought grimly.

In three days, she would leave Hathergill Hall and never see Benedict Hawkins again. *The sooner the better*. Every day that she allowed herself to watch the shifting expressions on his face, to listen for his voice and his rich laugh, and to wonder hopelessly what he might think of her, only intensified the unwilling attraction that she felt...and the pain of its impossibility.

She was too sensible for such foolishness, so she swept past him to the front door without looking back.

Somehow, though, she found him at her side again only ten minutes later, as they rode across the fields on the way to a picturesque set of ruins that Penelope often visited with her friends. They had begun the trip in a close cluster of horses, but Elinor struck off as soon as she could, grateful for the opportunity to escape Penelope's high-pitched laughter —aimed equally at both gentlemen—and Gavin Armitage's mocking wit. She could even forget Miss Armitage's watchful —and coolly assessing—gaze as she urged her mare forward, away from all of them.

It was the first time she'd been on horseback in over a year, and it felt like pure freedom. Lady Hathergill's mare, Buttercup, was sweet-hearted and clearly anxious for a good gallop. The wind against Elinor's face swept away every worry that plagued her. Even Sir Jessamyn, harnessed tightly against her lap, lifted his head to luxuriate in the sensation.

When she heard approaching hoofbeats, she bit back a groan. It would be Miss Armitage, no doubt, ready to press more offers of friendship...and even more of her sleuthing, which had become more and more blatant over the past two days. Elinor readied a neutral expression, marshaled her inner resources, turned...

And Benedict smiled at her, only a few feet away. "I couldn't resist," he said. "It's the first time I've ever seen you truly happy."

His words felt, ridiculously, like the sun breaking through the clouds. Elinor tried and failed to look reproving. "You shouldn't be here," she told him, even as she nudged Buttercup to match his pace. "You're leaving Penelope to Gavin Armitage."

He shrugged. "She was riding between him and his sister anyway."

"Only because you didn't make an effort to push yourself forward."

"I didn't want to," he said. "I wanted to be with you."

Elinor had no good response to make. Luckily, he didn't seem to expect any. He tipped his face back to soak in the sunlight, and they rode side by side in silence for a few minutes. Laughter from the others floated through the air as if from very far away, mixing with the soft hum of insects and the low mooing of cows at the other end of the field.

In their own perfect bubble of companionship, they were alone.

Together, they jumped their horses over a low hedge. It felt like flying through the air. Laughter bubbled up in Elinor's throat for the first time in days. She looked across at Benedict and found him grinning at her, his intelligent hazel eyes warm with pleasure.

For the first time in days, he looked the way he had when they'd first met: open and relaxed and effortlessly charming, with none of the tension that had gripped him ever since. It must have been the pressure of battling Gavin Armitage to woo Penelope that had made him so tense and grim these past few days. But how could he possibly forget that worry with Gavin and Penelope laughing together only half a field behind them? Unless...

All the pleasure that had been radiating through her

body suddenly coalesced into a tight, spiky ball of sickness in her chest. She nearly choked on it.

Unless he thought that he had found a new marital prospect to replace Penelope...an even wealthier one.

"What is it?" Benedict's grin had disappeared; he was frowning at her. "What's amiss?"

"Nothing." Elinor swallowed hard. "Nothing of importance. Let us race to the end of the next field." She urged Buttercup on before he could respond. Any answer that he might have made was lost in the wind as she galloped across the field, her heartbeat thumping loudly in her ears.

Mrs. De Lacey was at least fifteen years older than Benedict...but older women married younger men often enough when those women were wealthy. And with Gavin Armitage so clearly charming Penelope, who could blame Benedict for fixing on a new prospect for his family's salvation?

Elinor wanted to be sick. But when Benedict caught up with her, and their horses stood panting at the end of the race, she only gave him an imperiously dismissive smile. "I think we'd better let the others catch up with us, don't you?"

He looked at her steadily. His cheeks were flushed with colour from the race; his brown hair was tousled by the wind. "Is that what you wish?"

"Of course," she said, and turned away from him. "Why wouldn't it be?"

They arrived at the ruins half an hour later, in company with the rest of the party. The servants had come much earlier, of course, so a picnic lay spread out and waiting for them near the remains of a medieval manor house. The roof had crumbled long ago, along with half of the outer walls, but the skeleton of the old stone house still remained, rambling along the side of a broad brown river.

"Oh, how perfectly delightful!" said Miss Armitage. "Gavin, you must build a set of ruins at Stanton Court. I absolutely insist upon it."

"Oh, yes," Millie breathed. "Just think, Mr. Armitage, you could have Roman ruins of your very own! Or even an abandoned abbey. Just think of all those ghosts!"

"Oh, I *would* love ghosts," Penelope said. "Just think how everyone would talk about them!" She smiled into Gavin Armitage's eyes as he set his hands firmly around her waist and swung her down off her horse.

Elinor rolled her own eyes as she slid down off her horse, too quickly for Benedict to assist her. The last thing she needed—for the sake of both the illusion and her own peace of mind—was for him to put his hands around her waist right now.

"I am almost entirely certain," she said, "that ghosts only haunt real, abandoned ruins."

"Nonsense," Gavin Armitage said gaily. "Any ruins I build will be quite convincing enough for ghosts, I promise you. If Miss Hathergill desires ghosts, then ghosts she shall have."

"You may trust my brother on that," said Miss Armitage. "Gavin can persuade anyone of anything, I assure you. Ghosts would have no chance whatsoever of resisting his blandishments."

He bowed, grinning. "You see? The matter is settled. Now the only question left is which era the ruins should hearken from." His lip curled into a sneer as he looked across at Benedict. "What about you, Hawkins? Can you advise us? How many ruins have you built upon your great estate?"

"Oddly enough," said Benedict, "I haven't even been tempted." He looked the other man in the eye with open disdain. "I like real ruins, like this one, but I don't care much for wasting an estate's funds on a pretense of past glory."

Elinor winced and stepped away from Benedict. As she brushed down the skirts of her aunt's riding habit, she watched Mrs. De Lacey's hands perform the task. Just how much pretense had gone into her disguise in the past few days?

"A noble principle," said Gavin Armitage. It wasn't just his lip curling now; his nostrils flared too, until he looked like an angry horse. "It's a pity your father didn't share it."

Benedict's jaw set. He stepped forward. "I beg your pardon?"

"He—"

"Oh, Gavin." Laughing, Miss Armitage placed a hand on her brother's arm. "Honestly, *gentlemen*. Only let them outside on a nice sunny day and they turn into territorial animals, don't they?" She shot commiserating glances at all the women in the circle.

Benedict was still glaring at Gavin. "What exactly did you mean to say about my father?"

A long look passed between Gavin Armitage and his

sister. He shook off her arm and stepped back. "Nothing at all. Only a moment of confusion. Because we all know..." He raked Benedict up and down with a contemptuous gaze. "*You* would certainly never pretend to be anything other than what you are, would you? Even to impress..." His gaze slid idly across Penelope's frowning face. "...*anyone*?"

"I..."

"Of course not," Miss Armitage said warmly, before Benedict could continue. "Mr. Hawkins doesn't believe in putting on any pretense of false glory. So I am certain he is to be trusted."

Benedict stayed stonily silent, while Penelope looked back and forth between them with narrowing eyes. It was left to Millie to say, with a half-giggle, "I don't understand a word that any of you just said. What *are* you all gossiping about?"

"Nothing relevant," said Mr. Armitage. "At least—it won't be relevant as long as Mr. Hawkins doesn't break our trust."

With a charming smile, he offered Penelope one arm, and Millie the other. "Shall we enjoy a little stroll before we picnic? I do like to work up an appetite."

CHAPTER 23

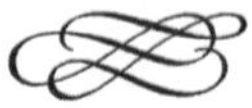

"They know," Elinor said.

Two hours after their arrival at the ruins, the party had set off back for home. This time, she and Benedict had struck off together from the beginning, without needing to exchange a word in advance. As soon as they were safely out of hearing distance of the others, she slowed Buttercup and nudged her closer to Benedict's mount for ease of conversation. "They both know, I mean. Mr. Armitage and his sister."

"Of course they know," said Benedict. "You heard them—if I 'break their trust,' they'll tell everyone what my father did...and exactly how close I am to losing my estate."

"'Breaking their trust'..." Elinor's hands clenched around the reins; she had to force herself to loosen them and soothe her horse. "I suppose *that* means proposing to Penelope."

"What else? He clearly wants to marry her himself...and now he's made it impossible for me to even try."

"Damn it!" Elinor heard the words escape her mouth with a feeling of shock. She never, ever swore out loud. *Rose* swore, when she was in a passion; even Harry swore occasionally, when a particularly tricky intellectual problem was resisting solutions for too long. But Elinor only ever swore inside her head, where no one else could hear her.

Until now.

"How could they have found out?" she demanded. "You said you'd kept it secret. Did your father tell anybody?"

"When my father realized what he'd done..." Benedict's lips tightened; he shook his head, releasing his breath in a whoosh. "No. He never told anyone but me. Even my brothers didn't know until I told them, and *they* certainly wouldn't have spread the word. They know exactly what it will mean to us if the news reaches our creditors before I can find a way to mend our fortunes."

"You'll lose the estate," Elinor said flatly.

And with the estate...

She had fought so hard to keep her own family together, those long six months after their parents had died. How dare the Armitages rip Benedict's family apart now, just when he had a real chance to save them?

"There has to be a way around this," she said. "Perhaps if you tell Penelope before he can..." Her words trailed off as she imagined the scene.

Benedict laughed. "Oh, yes, I can certainly imagine how

that would go. I don't see Miss Hathergill throwing the world away for love, do you?"

"Well..." Elinor bit her lip.

If only she was the real Mrs. De Lacey. If only...

Benedict shook his head. "If you want to know the truth..." He drew his horse to a halt as they reached the top of a low hill. The green landscape spread out before them, tidy fields covered by cows and sheep and sliced by streams and hedges. A rook cawed as it flew overhead, and Sir Jessamyn nestled more tightly into his harness.

"It feels like a relief," said Benedict.

"I beg your pardon?" Elinor stared at him. "But—"

He gazed at the fields spread out before them, his brows drawn into a frown. "I wasn't lying, earlier," he said. "I don't like pretense. I don't want to pretend to be someone I'm not. And you were right, the very first day we arrived. It was a terrible thing to think of doing to Miss Hathergill. You know as well as I do that, no matter how hard I might try, she would be miserable buried on a country estate."

Elinor said, "With Penelope's dowry, she might be able to visit London even after your estate was saved."

"Perhaps," said Benedict. "But that isn't exactly the glorious lifestyle she's been dreaming of, is it?" He shrugged and turned to her with a rueful half-smile. "From halfway across the country, it was all too easy to ignore the feelings of a future-fiancée. But I can't imagine myself making Miss Hathergill happy as a husband. And..." He took a breath. "Now the Armitages have done me a favour, in a way, though I can't quite bring myself to thank them for it."

"A favour!" Elinor let out a disbelieving huff of air. "They—"

His smile twisted. "They've made it impossible for Miss Hathergill to make me utterly miserable as my wife. If it weren't for my brothers and my niece, I think I might even be grateful to them for it."

Elinor was silent. Her emotions were too tangled to allow her any speech.

Benedict looked down at the view before them. "I wish I could show you Kennington Park," he said. "I think you'd like it. You'd like to ride across it, anyway. There's a waterfall built into the rocks, only a quarter mile from the house. My brothers and I had a secret fort there, when I was younger. And the woods..."

"You love it," Elinor said.

"I do. I would have done anything to save it, and my family. But I don't have that choice anymore."

"But you do!" Elinor leaned forward. "You must. There has to be a way, if we think hard enough!"

He didn't seem to hear her. His eyes were still fixed on the fields before them. "I only hope that whoever buys the estate will take care of it. The workers—"

"Stop!" Deeply daring, Elinor reached out to brush her fingers against the thick cloth of his blue coat sleeve, to drag his attention back to her. "You cannot give up so easily. We *won't* give up. And...oh!" She gasped and grabbed his sleeve outright as she suddenly remembered. "Penelope is absolutely not going to accept Mr. Armitage until you propose to her yourself!"

"I beg your pardon?" Frowning, he turned back to her. "I don't think I can have heard you—"

"She told me," said Elinor. "She's determined to be betrothed by the night of her début, but she won't accept either of you until both have proposed. She thinks anything less would be beneath her dignity."

He stared at her. "Good God. You really are serious, aren't you?" At her nod, he began to laugh helplessly. "Good God," he repeated. "Poor Armitage. Little did he know he was ruining his own chances by scuppering mine. If he'd only realized..."

"The point is," said Elinor, "you still have a chance. And I would wager anything that the Armitages have just as much to hide as you do. Miss Armitage is altogether too fond of ferreting out other people's disreputable secrets."

"Oh?" He stopped laughing and narrowed his eyes at her. "What secrets has she discovered about you?"

Elinor felt her cheeks heat. "None at all," she said...and finally realized that she was still clutching the sleeve of his coat. She released it with a wince, hoping that her cheeks weren't as pink as she feared. Perhaps the illusion would hide her blush.

"She tried, though, didn't she?" Benedict reached out to take her hand even as she withdrew it; with a quick movement, she jerked her fingers away just before he could touch them. He frowned harder and leaned closer. "What did she do?"

"Nothing," said Elinor. His closeness was beginning to make her feel very strange. Her skin was prickling as if with great cold or heat, and her voice sounded odd in her own ears. She cleared her throat and leaned discreetly backward, away from his disconcerting warmth. "She only asked insinuating questions, which I chose not to answer."

"Hmm." Benedict's hazel gaze rested speculatively on her face. "Are you quite sure that's all?"

"Why wouldn't it be?" Elinor finally, belatedly, remembered exactly who she was supposed to be. She straightened, stiffening her back and lifting her chin. "I hope you don't imagine that *I* have anything to hide, Mr. Hawkins."

He opened his mouth as if to speak—then shook his head with a rueful half-smile. "When you look that way," he said, "I wouldn't dare. I'll wager you stared Miss Armitage down like a queen."

"Your faith overwhelms me," Elinor said dryly.

"Good." Benedict settled back in his saddle and nudged his horse forward into an easy canter...but his words floated back to her and stopped her breath. "...Because my faith in you is limitless."

The sigh of relief that Elinor had been about to expel froze in her throat. From her lap, Sir Jessamyn cocked his head and looked up at her with an all-too-knowing golden gaze.

Elinor stared at Benedict's back as he rode away from her,

down the hill towards Hathergill Hall. His broad shoulders were outlined in his tight blue coat; his final words rang in her ears.

Be Mrs. De Lacey.

She swallowed hard and followed him.

They didn't speak for the rest of the journey, but Elinor's head buzzed with so many contradictory instructions, they nearly deafened her. She had to find out more about the Armitages and what they might be hiding, themselves... She had to speak to Penelope and persuade her that money wasn't necessary in a suitor—

—Had Benedict really said—?

Don't think of that now!

...She still had to find a way to expose Lucinda at the ball before Sally could fulfill her own threat to expose her...

She barely noticed the unfamiliar carriage that was pulling up in front of Hathergill Hall as they arrived, nor did the tall, thin man being ushered out of it seize her attention. It was only the look of hard satisfaction upon Sir John's face as he stood and watched the carriage roll away that finally set belated warning bells ringing.

He looked up as they approached, and his expression eased into a false, jovial smile. "Nice trip, eh? A pretty set of ruins, ain't they? I'd pull 'em down completely if it was up to me, but the ladies always like such fripperies. Don't they, Mrs. De Lacey?"

Elinor raised her eyebrows and looked quellingly down her nose at him. As unimaginable as it would have felt only three days ago, it was surprisingly easy from horseback. Height really did give an advantage.

So did her illusion. Mrs. De Lacey couldn't have cared less about civility.

"Who was the gentleman in the carriage?" she asked.

"Him?" Sir John shrugged, his smile turning fixed. "Oh, just an acquaintance. Here to see m'wife, you know."

"Oh?" Elinor arched her brows even higher. In the corner of her vision, she could see Benedict watching her with an appreciative quirk of his lips. It made her jittery, and her hands tightened on her reins. Buttercup shifted her feet, and Sir Jessamyn, who had just begun to fall asleep, opened his eyes with a cheep of complaint.

"Your dragon will be wanting to get down, won't he?" Sir John strode forward with obvious relief. "Here, allow me." His meaty hands reached for Sir Jessamyn, who recoiled.

"I'll do it myself," Elinor said hastily. "Mr. Hawkins, if you wouldn't mind..." She lifted Sir Jessamyn out of his harness and passed him carefully to Benedict. Their fingertips almost brushed; she let go quickly, and the little dragon settled against Benedict's chest with a look of alert interest.

She slid down the side of her own mount with inelegant speed, waving off both Sir John and the footman who'd stepped forward to aid her. When she'd brushed down her skirts, she looked up and found Benedict idly stroking Sir Jessamyn's back while the little dragon preened with satisfaction. She held out her hands...but Sir Jessamyn stayed exactly where he was, half-closing his eyes and leaning his head against Benedict's chest.

"Well, really!" Elinor stared. "Are you hiding food in your coat, by any chance?"

Benedict laughed. "If only I'd thought of it...but no, it's only my famous charm holding him here."

"Hmm," said Elinor, expressively.

The footman had already retreated, and Sir John moved away, too, waving to the others as they approached. Elinor crossed her arms as she gazed up at her traitorous dragon and tried not to let her mouth twitch. "You're going to have to come back now, whether you like it or not," she told him. "I'm the one who feeds you, remember?"

Benedict grinned. "You can leave him a moment, if you like. I think...yes." He swung his leg over his horse and jumped down with Sir Jessamyn still tucked against his chest. "Here we are. I don't mind holding him for a while. Let's just hope history doesn't repeat itself, eh?"

"I beg your pardon?" He was standing very close now, grinning down at her. Elinor felt her heartbeat speed up and her thoughts scatter. She reached desperately for her fleeing wits.

"The first time I met him," Benedict said. "Don't you remember what happened?" He heaved a mock-tragic sigh. "My poor waistcoat..."

Dizzy and tingling, it took Elinor a moment. Then she remembered, and groaned. "That was only because he was frightened! If you hadn't..."

Wait!

She slammed her mouth shut. Benedict was looking down at her from only half a foot away. She said, "Isn't that what you told me? You said that the first time you met Miss Tregarth and her dragon..."

"I told you that she'd fallen in the mud," Benedict said. "I don't recall telling you what her dragon did next."

"Well, it was obvious, wasn't it?" Elinor said. "I mean, we all know how Sir Jessamyn reacts to frightening situations."

"Do we?" His grin had widened, but it wasn't a triumphant smirk; instead, it felt oddly intimate. He looked as if they were sharing a private joke. His voice softened. "Last time we spoke about it, you were still denying that he *was* Sir Jessamyn. Remember?"

"I..." Elinor took a jerky step backward, breathing quickly. She needed air, and space to think. Being close to him was too dangerous. It made her brain stop working.

Before she could say anything, though, either to save herself or to dig herself deeper, he looked past her and breathed a quick warning.

"Careful!"

A rattle of hoofbeats swept up behind her, and the others arrived in a happy rush. Mr. Armitage swung himself down first, and then lifted down a bright-eyed Penelope. She tipped her head back and laughed with pleasure, while Miss Armitage watched with a fond smile and Millie stared in blatant envy.

"Oh, Papa, it was wonderful!" Penelope cried, as Mr. Armitage turned to help his sister.

"I'm glad, puss." Sir John chucked her under her chin affectionately as he moved past her to assist Millie. Sir John's next words might have been meant as a whisper, but his voice was trained to boom; Elinor heard the words clearly. "And you'll be very pleased with what I did while you were out."

Elinor swung around, all of her confusion dropping away. Every instinct she had was shrieking a warning.

"What *did* you do while we were away, Sir John?" she asked.

"Oh, well..." He wouldn't meet her eyes. "It's nothing you'd be interested in, ma'am, only—"

"Did it have to do with your visitor?" she said. "The gentleman who left just as we arrived?"

"Well—"

"Papa!" Penelope breathed. She seized his arm with a glowing face before he could reach Millie's horse. "It was him, wasn't it? The physician from London!"

"Physician?" Miss Armitage said. "Is someone ill, sir?"

"I wouldn't exactly say—"

"You did it." Elinor shook her head. Shock and horror mingled so strongly that for a moment, her whole body felt numb. "You really did it," she said to both of them together, her uncle and her cousin, standing side by side. "I can't believe it. You actually summoned that physician to declare Lady Hathergill mad."

CHAPTER 24

"Shh!" Sir John hissed.

But it was too late.

"Good heavens!" Miss Armitage hurried forward to clasp Penelope's free hand. "What a terrible thing for your family. You have suffered so much!" Warm sympathy infused her voice as she drew Penelope close. "You must tell me all about it immediately."

"It has been quite dreadful," Penelope agreed happily. "You mustn't tell anyone else, of course, but the things she's said and done since it happened—"

"—Are blunt," Elinor said through gritted teeth, "and honest. Never mad!"

"Mrs. De Lacey." Sir John cleared his throat heavily. "I understand you're an old friend of my wife's, so you can't be best pleased by this news, but I think you'll agree that the opinion of a trained physician—"

"One hired by you," said Elinor, "to give the diagnosis you prefer. Do not treat me like an idiot, Sir John!"

"Then don't treat me like a servant, ma'am," he snapped. "This is my household, and I'll run it as I see fit. I made that clear to Mary when we first wed. If she can't tolerate that anymore, then she'll just have to deal with the consequences!"

Elinor's fists clenched at her side. How many times had she had to stand silently by in the last six months, while he made stupid, brutal decisions about her and everyone else? But she wasn't a poor relation anymore, and she *would not* let him do this to her aunt.

She couldn't. Not when it was her own foolish, careless wish that had brought it all about in the first place.

"You may run this household, Sir John," she said, "but when word spreads throughout fashionable Society that you and your daughter, between you, have had your wife locked up for selfish reasons, Penelope's reputation will be ruined along with your own."

Sir John's face reddened. "By God, ma'am—"

"Oh, come now, Mrs. De Lacey," Miss Armitage said, her voice as smooth as silk. "Do you really think the word would spread? Who among us would spread it, may I ask?"

Elinor kept her eyes locked on her uncle's furious face. "I would," she said, "and I think you all understand what *my* word is worth in Society. Is that truly a risk you wish to run,

Sir John? Because I will not stand by and allow my oldest friend to be abused."

"Abused!" Penelope gasped. "How can you say such a horrible thing? As if anyone would ever abuse my mother! All we want is to keep her in a cozy little cottage where no one has to hear her ravings. It's what she'd prefer, I'm sure, if she were more herself. We'll get her an attendant who knows just how to properly look after her. Papa told me! She'll have all the comforts she could ever want, I am sure. What could there possibly be in that to complain about? It is only to keep her safe, you know."

"To keep *you* safe, you mean," said Elinor. "Just because she doesn't give in to you on everything anymore—"

Benedict cleared his throat warningly. But it was Sir John whose bellow cut her off.

"That's enough!" He strode towards her, bull-like shoulders thrust forward and big hands knotted into fists. "From the moment you first arrived, ma'am, it has been one demand after another. But when it comes to threatening my daughter's reputation..."

"You won't let her do it, Papa," Penelope said. "You couldn't let her...oh, everything goes wrong for me nowadays! You're all against me." She burst into tears.

"Now, now," Miss Armitage murmured. She tucked Penelope's head into her shoulder, and Gavin Armitage moved to shelter the two of them protectively...but both Armitage gazes remained locked with keen appreciation upon the scene in front of them.

They were only gnats on the verge of Elinor's consciousness, though, as Sir John bore down on her. She lifted her chin as high as it would go and stood her ground. "You are the one threatening your daughter's reputation," she said. "All you need do to remove all danger to Penelope is simply to forget this cruel scheme you've concocted."

"Oh, is that all I need to do?" He spat the words, and spittle flew out from his mouth, one wet drop landing against Elinor's cheek. "You take an eager interest in all of my family, don't you, ma'am? First you make demands about my nieces, and now..."

"Nieces?" Miss Armitage murmured. "Which nieces are those?"

"I'll tell you this, Mrs. De Lacey," said Sir John. "If you still care so much about those nieces of mine, you'll do well to forget your concern about my wife."

Elinor froze. "What do you mean?"

"Purely to satisfy *your* whim," he snarled, "I promised not to pursue Elinor Tregarth despite her theft from my daughter. Only to make *you* happy, I promised not even to warn those poor innocents sheltering her sisters of the danger they're in from those serpents."

Elinor's voice came out thin and strained. "I told you, if you want me to attend and help Penelope's début..."

"And how much help do you imagine you'll be if you're busy spreading lies about my daughter?"

Her aunt...

Her *sisters*...

She couldn't let him hurt Rose and Harry. She *couldn't*.

Sir John smiled. It was not a pleasant expression. "I see you've grasped the situation, madam."

Elinor didn't speak. He turned and beckoned to Penelope. "Come along, puss. You've had some packages arrive from the dressmakers. You'll want to see those, I expect."

"Oh, Papa..." Penelope detached herself from Miss Armitage's embrace. Wiping away tears, she shot a defiant look at Elinor.

"If you're going to help," she said, "I want *real* help from now on. And no lectures!"

She flounced into the house with Millie running after her. Gavin Armitage only laughed as he looked from Elinor to Penelope, and followed at a more leisurely stroll. Miss Armitage, though, stayed to give Elinor a long, considering look.

"So," she murmured, "you've chosen the welfare of Penelope's cousins—whom you've never met—over that of Lady Hathergill herself." She raised her eyebrows. "Interesting."

She glided away.

Benedict stirred beside Elinor. As the front door finally closed behind Miss Armitage, he began, "If I can help..."

Tears blurred Elinor's vision. She snatched Sir Jessamyn out of his arms without meeting his gaze.

"It's too late," she said. "I've already ruined everything."

* * *

She ran until her legs stopped moving, and when she finally stopped she found herself in the Hathergill's enclosed wilderness.

How appropriate, she thought bitterly.

Sir Jessamyn was watching her with large, worried eyes from her arms. She choked down a sob as she leaned down to nuzzle him.

"I'm sorry," she whispered. "I shouldn't have run with you. It wasn't fair. It probably frightened you."

For a wonder, though, he hadn't chuckled yet. She stroked her hands soothingly over his back even as she choked down a sob.

Ahead of her stood the same boulder Sir Jessamyn had sunned himself upon three days earlier, when she'd come here with Benedict. She forced herself forward those last few steps, then simply allowed her legs to give out. She landed on the boulder with a thump that sent pain shooting up her spine, and gathered up Sir Jessamyn against her chest as tears streamed down her cheeks.

"How did I get here?"

Of all of her sisters, she had always been the sensible one. The one who always kept a level head, no matter how angry or frightened she felt inside. The one who never, ever let herself lose control

...Because she couldn't. She was the oldest. It was her role to be sensible, her role to pay attention to the practicalities of life, while Rose threw herself headlong into one passion after another and Harry lost herself in the beautiful maze of her own intellect. As a triangle, they had worked. They had functioned perfectly for seventeen years, even after their parents' death.

But now her sisters were gone, Elinor was alone, and she didn't even know who she was anymore. Would Rose and Harry recognize her if they saw her now?

Well… "Probably not," she said out loud, and found herself hiccupping a laugh.

Who was she trying to fool? She was magically disguised as the foremost lady of London fashion. *No one* would recognize her right now.

"Miss Tregarth?" said a voice behind her.

Without looking up, Elinor murmured, "Yes?"

And then every inch of her body went cold.

She lunged to her feet so swiftly that Sir Jessamyn protested, digging his claws into her skin to keep his balance. She barely noticed.

Benedict stood three feet away from her on the shaded path that led through the wilderness.

For a long moment, the hum of insects buzzing over the pond nearby was the only sound in the enclosed garden. Then Elinor said, "I mean—that is, of course, I didn't—"

"*I know.*" Benedict took a step forward. His eyes were wide and filled with intense emotion. "I've known ever since that first morning here, when I touched your hand and saw you. *Really* saw you. I told myself that I'd imagined it, but I already knew better in my heart, even then."

Elinor moistened her lips. "You can't have known," she

said. "We haven't touched even once since then. When you look at me—"

"I see you," he said. "Elinor Tregarth. Brave and witty and caring and strong—the strongest person I've ever met. Oh, the appearance is wrong most of the time nowadays, but..." He shook his head and took another step. Then he reached out as if to touch her face—but his fingers hovered an inch away, as if waiting for permission. "It's *you*," he repeated softly.

Elinor couldn't breathe. His fingers were so close; his eyes so intent on hers. And his expression...

"I thought I'd lost you," he whispered. "I thought I'd met you just long enough to regret you forever."

She was crying again. But she was moving, too.

Elinor stepped forward, into his arms.

CHAPTER 25

Sir Jessamyn, of course, protested. But it took only a moment to set him down on the boulder, and he never minded stretching out to sun himself at leisure on a warm day.

As for Elinor... It was no wonder people tossed aside everything for love, she thought dizzily. Who needed food or drink, compared to this?

She could have kissed Benedict forever in the wilderness. The trees and plants around them rustled in the soft, warm breeze, and sunlight caressed her skin as Elinor wrapped herself around him, discovering a wholly unexpected core of wildness inside herself. Benedict's kiss was more intoxicating than any wine she'd ever sipped; his thick hair softer against her hands than she had imagined; his arms warm and strong around her.

And Benedict himself...

He drew back, panting and laughing, and cupped her cheek in one big hand while he wrapped his other arm around her waist. "It really *is* you," he said. "No flickering between different faces anymore. Just you, and me."

"Just us together," Elinor said, and felt wonder nearly break her open. "You really wanted it to be me?"

"Are you actually jesting, at such a moment?" He shook her lightly, his eyes sparkling. "Look at me, Elinor Tregarth. Do you think there's any chance in the world that I am feeling *disappointed* right now?"

"No." Elinor laughed breathlessly. "I only..." A bird squawked raucously overhead, making her jump. It was a great black crow, settling onto one of the long, knobbled branches of the tree nearby, and Elinor sucked in a breath at the reminder. *Crow...* The word even sounded in her head with Penelope's contemptuous intonation, repeated so many times with such vicious precision. *You look just like a crow. You're such a crow. You...*

She looked up at Benedict grinning down at her, and with an effort of willpower, she set the words aside—for good, she hoped. "No," said Elinor, and shook her head. "You're not disappointed."

"I should say not." He kissed her again, as if he couldn't help himself. She couldn't help herself either as she melted against him. He tasted like salt and sweetness and everything that she had ever wanted but known she couldn't have.

She couldn't have... The words took shape and resonated with horrible force inside her. She shoved them aside.

He rested his forehead against hers. Their noses bumped companionably. "Anyway," he murmured, "I shouldn't dare be disappointed in the great Mrs. De Lacey, should I? I've seen you stare down enough challengers, these past few days. Utterly terrifying!"

He was laughing as he said it—but it broke the spell. She pulled back, fighting to catch her breath. "Wait," she said. "Wait."

"For what? I've been waiting three days already. No, four days—ever since we met. Ever since that first moment when I saw you walk towards me covered in mud and holding your chin up like an empress. I'm so grateful Aubrey wasn't clever enough to get out of the carriage himself and fall under your spell." He leaned back in, his breath warm against her lips—but she pushed him back.

"Wait!" She stepped back herself, forcing her hands to let go of him. Her palms felt cold, parted from his warmth. "We cannot do this!"

"Whyever not?" Frowning at her, he shifted closer. "I'm not actually betrothed to Penelope, remember? I'm not even trying to betroth myself to Penelope. Thank God, the Armitages made that impossible. I take back everything I said before. I'd shake Gavin Armitage's hand to thank him if he were here. The only person in the world I want to marry is—"

"Stop!" Elinor's voice broke on the word. She wrapped

her arms around her chest and turned away. She couldn't look at his face while she said this. She didn't want to say it. She didn't want it to be true.

But it seemed that a lifetime of common sense couldn't be thrown away so easily after all…not even for love.

"We cannot marry," she said, "and you know it. I have no dowry. Soon, you'll have no income and no home, either. How could we possibly marry?"

"We'll think of something." Benedict's voice was quieter and more subdued than before, but he didn't move away. "We have to think of something. If I—"

"And what of your brothers?" Elinor said. "Not to mention your five-year-old niece? What will *they* do, while we think of something for ourselves? Do you truly think you can forget them?"

"I don't want to forget them," Benedict said. "For God's sake—!" He cut himself off with a jerk and spun around to glare at the ivy-covered stone wall of the wilderness.

Elinor waited through his silence. She wouldn't cry. Not anymore.

But inside her chest, she felt as if she were breaking.

When Benedict turned back to her, his face was grim. "I don't know how we'll manage," he said. "You're right about that. But I do know we can't just shrug our shoulders and walk away from each other as if this had never happened. Could *you* do that, now? Truly?"

Elinor bit her lip hard and forced her voice to steady. "We have to face the facts. If you don't find some promise of income within the next few weeks, whether it's from Penelope or someone else—"

"Good God!" He stared at her. "Are you actually trying to persuade me, *now*, to pursue another Penelope Hathergill?"

"It's the only thing that makes sense," Elinor said miserably. "Your—"

"I am not marrying any other woman, any more than *you* are going to voluntarily enslave yourself to Mrs. G. Galsworthy without even getting any salary in return!" Benedict held his body rigidly still, but his voice lashed out like a whip. "I read the newspapers, too, you know, *including* the advertisements. That one was absurd, and so is your plan for me."

"But how else can you save your estate, and your family, in time?" Tears blurred Elinor's vision, but she blinked them away and clenched her jaw to keep more from escaping. "Of course I don't want you to marry anyone else. But—"

"Then stop trying to throw me away!" Benedict glared at her. "Damn it, I'm not a handkerchief or a—a bloody pincushion to be given away to one of your friends when you don't want it anymore. I'm in love with you!"

Despite everything, Elinor felt the tightness in her chest melt at his words. Her treacherous lips softened; the cold, hard words she'd been about to speak faded out of her grasp.

Relief lightened Benedict's expression. He stepped forward, his lips curving gently, and ran one hand over her hair. "What?" he said. "You don't want to tell me all the practical reasons why I can't be in love with you? Logically, rationally?"

Elinor shook her head against his hand. "That wouldn't be sensible at all," she said, "because I'm in love with you, too."

His lips were just as soft this time, his shoulders every bit as warm and solid against her hands. But when she drew back and rested her cheek against his broad chest, she heard his heart beating as rapidly as if he'd just run a race.

"I don't have any perfect answers," he whispered. "All I know is..." His voice dropped to a low rumble against her hair. "In the last few years, I've lost too many people. I can't lose you, too."

Elinor tightened her arms around him as the pain in his voice resonated through her own chest. Grief and loss might be too well hidden under his easy charm for most observers to ever guess at, but she *knew* Benedict Hawkins. And she had known, from that very first night when they had traded their stories, how much lay underneath his lighthearted exterior.

"I don't want to lose you either," she said, "but—"

"There has to be a way," said Benedict. "That's what you told me earlier, wasn't it, when we were talking about my problems? So, how about this astonishing dragon of yours?" He turned her towards Sir Jessamyn, who had sprawled across the boulder in an attitude of pure bliss, eyes closed and scales glittering. "He's already performed two miracles, hasn't he? How about a third?"

Elinor winced. "I don't think I would call them 'miracles.' More like horrible accidents." Memory flooded in upon her, sickeningly. "My poor aunt..."

"What did Aubrey say, when you asked him about it?"

"He didn't," Elinor said bitterly. "He thought I was playing a practical joke on him. And then *you* interrupted us and accused me of trying to trick him into marriage."

"Ah. Yes." Benedict's lips twitched. "Perhaps you could forget that part? It was a long time ago, you know. Days and days."

"I have an excellent memory," Elinor told him.

"That is a pity," Benedict said. "You'll have to fix it before we're married." He laughed when she rolled her eyes at him, and grabbed her hand. "That's the first thing we should do, then. Come along! Aubrey may have brushed you aside, but he won't dismiss me so easily, I promise you. I have years of experience in badgering him. That was how we both survived school."

"Wait!" Elinor dug her heels into the path as he tried to drag her forward. "We can't just go rushing in on him like this. What if he's in company with Sir John and the others? What if—?"

Benedict stared at her. "Aubrey?" he said. "Voluntarily in company? Involved in social conversation with our host? My dear Elinor, have you lost all of your wits?"

Elinor sighed and scooped up Sir Jessamyn from the boulder. His eyes fluttered open; he muttered grumpily but nestled into her chest almost at once. "Very well," she said.

"But if Mr. Aubrey starts shouting about fairy tales again, Sir Jessamyn isn't the only one who might lose control."

She had to drop Benedict's hand, of course, as soon as they left the wilderness. Neither of them knew who might be standing at the windows of Hathergill Hall, hidden by the sunlight striking against the glass. But it was only as they approached one of the back doors a few minutes later that Benedict sucked in a harsh breath.

"What is it?" Elinor asked. She spun around, searching the horizon. "What did you see?"

"Mrs. De Lacey." He gave her a twisted smile. "She's back." He gestured to her face.

Elinor put one hand to her cheek. "You mean—?"

"It's been too long since we touched...but never mind." He reached for the door handle. "That just gives us one more reason to talk to Aubrey at once. This illusion may have served a purpose in the beginning, but I think it's high time to be rid of it."

Mr. Aubrey wasn't in the library, where they first looked, but Benedict walked past the drawing room without a pause, ignoring the hum of voices rising behind the door. Instead, he led Elinor up the staircase to the second-floor wing of the house where the bachelors were quartered. While Elinor looked guiltily around the empty hallway for observers, he knocked sharply on the fourth door to the right, then turned the door handle and walked inside without waiting for a reply.

"Leave your books for a moment, Aubrey! We need your help."

Elinor whisked in and closed the door quickly, before anyone could catch sight of her. She was the only one who seemed worried about the proprieties, though...and the room she walked into bore little resemblance to anything she had ever imagined as a dangerous bachelor's bedroom.

Much like the carriage they had traveled in, Aubrey's bedroom was entirely carpeted with papers and books. He sat on the floor in the center of it all—indeed, there would have been no space to sit on the bed—and his hair looked wildly rumpled. as if he'd been dragging his fingers through it.

But actually, Elinor corrected herself, it must have been his pen that had done that rumpling. There were several distinct spots of blue ink scattered among the wild blond tufts.

"It's all very well to say 'leave your books,'" Aubrey muttered, "but it isn't as simple as all that. I've had another letter from my friend in Wales, and if he's right, there's a devilish complicated situation springing up that needs my urgent attention. If I can just figure the probable length of a wingtip when—"

"You will," Benedict said, "but have a heart, Aubrey. I'm in urgent trouble of my own right now."

"Again?" Mr. Aubrey sighed and took off his glasses. "This isn't to do with your marriage scheme, is it? I must say, I don't care for your future fiancée. If she knows a single word of Latin, I'd be surprised."

"Ah..." Benedict's lips twitched as he looked at Elinor. "Miss Tregarth?"

She couldn't help the smile that tugged at her own lips. "My sister Harry knows Latin very well," she offered. "I suppose she could teach to me by post if required."

"Only for Aubrey's wife," Benedict assured her. "Never my own."

"Hmph," said Mr. Aubrey. "More fool you. How could you ever have an interesting conversation with anyone who can't even debate a Latin manuscript?"

"Some of us find a way," said Benedict. "But I think you will find this interesting, even though it's not in Latin. I have a question for you about dragons."

"Oh?" Mr. Aubrey put his glasses back on. Then he looked at Elinor and his eyes widened. "Oh. Oh, no. This is Mrs. De Lacey, isn't it? Hawkins, if you dare tell me you've joined in that offensively foolish practical joke she tried to play on me when we first arrived—"

"I'm deadly serious," said Benedict, "and so is she. There was never any joking involved."

Mr. Aubrey looked at him for a long moment. Then, without a word, he rose to his feet. His hands had clenched about his pen and his open book; his face was pale with fury.

"If the two of you will excuse me," he said with icy courtesy, "I'm afraid I need to pack. I am leaving Hathergill Hall immediately."

CHAPTER 26

"Aubrey!" Benedict started forward. "For God's sake, man, just listen—"

"Listen?" Mr. Aubrey stormed across the room, gathering up heaps of papers with every step. "You want me to listen to you, Hawkins? Why, do you need some fresh entertainment? You've grown bored and decided to start laughing at me with your new friends?"

"No!" Benedict said. "It's not like that."

"Is it not?" Mr. Aubrey snatched up a traveling case and threw it onto the teetering pile of books that covered the bed. The case popped open at the impact, and he began stuffing papers into it with furious concentration. "I may not pay attention to the trivialities of fashionable life, but I am *not* witless. Or perhaps I am, as I actually thought us good friends!"

"We are!" Benedict said. "I—"

"I am almost a week late to an important visit, only because I wished to do a favor for you!" said Mr. Aubrey. "I have been suffocated in this illiterate household for days and days, forced to listen to vapid laughter and inanities at every hour of day and night. And now you want to play me for a laughingstock?"

"No!" Benedict strode across the room and slammed the case closed. "Damn it, Aubrey, if you'll only hear me out—"

Mr. Aubrey grabbed the lid of the case to force it open. Benedict held it shut. In a moment, they would start brawling. Elinor gritted her teeth, set Sir Jessamyn down, and hurried across the room, aware that she was trampling important papers with every footstep.

"Mr. Aubrey!" she said sharply. "Look at me!"

"If you think I have time for idle banter, Madam..." He shot her an irritated, sidelong look as he continued to grapple over the traveling case.

Seizing her chance, Elinor stripped off her right glove and placed her bare hand on his face.

It was an act of startling impropriety, as even Mr. Aubrey clearly realized. He fell back, so startled that his hands dropped to his sides...and then his eyes widened behind his spectacles, and he leaned forward.

"Wait," he said. "Wait! Your face—it's changed somehow, hasn't it? There's something different—"

"You see?" Benedict was breathing hard as he leant over

the bed, still holding the traveling case shut. "This isn't a practical joke, Aubrey. This is real. Dragons can do magic."

* * *

FIVE MINUTES LATER, Mr. Aubrey was still sputtering. They all sat on the floor now, even Elinor. There was simply nowhere else to go. She could only hope that her newly-outspoken aunt wouldn't be too horrified by the state of her riding habit when it was returned.

Benedict reached across to brush his hand across Elinor's cheek, and she blinked. "I beg your pardon? Did I miss something?"

"No," he said, and gave her a rueful half-smile. "I just missed you, that was all. It seemed too unfair that Aubrey could see your true face and I couldn't."

"So the illusion is tied into touch." Mr. Aubrey was staring at Sir Jessamyn, not at Elinor. Adapting to circumstances, the little dragon had built himself a nest of papers and was settled comfortably in the center of their triangle, watching the humans around him with bright golden interest.

"Does nothing else ever shatter the illusion?" Mr. Aubrey asked.

"I don't think so," Elinor said. "One of the housemaids knows who I am, but she worked that out by logic, not by sight."

"By logic?" He snorted. "There's nothing logical about magic. Any reputable scholar could inform you—"

"Any reputable scholar would be wrong," said Benedict. "You're all too shackled by academic theory, old man. This dragon in front of us doesn't care about what should or shouldn't be possible for him. He just *is*."

Sir Jessamyn preened under the attention.

Elinor rolled her eyes. She would have scooped him into her lap, but he was all too clearly enjoying himself where he was. As Mr. Aubrey leaned closer, Sir Jessamyn stretched back his long, glittering neck to show off every blue-and-green scale.

"Tell me exactly what happened to create the illusion," Mr. Aubrey ordered.

Elinor took a deep breath. "The first time was the night we met. After I came back from supper. I was..." She felt Benedict watching her, and chose her words carefully. "...a bit anxious and unhappy. I think Sir Jessamyn was worried about me."

"You acted so cheerful at supper," Benedict said. "Why didn't you ask us for help?"

"Stick to the point," said Mr. Aubrey. He was studying the golden whorls that curled beneath Sir Jessamyn's chin. "Tell us exactly what happened between you and your dragon."

"I was talking to Sir Jessamyn—he was comforting me, really. And I told him..." Elinor stopped, looking again at Benedict. "Do you think you could leave the room for just a moment?"

"No," said Benedict. "Keep going." He reached out to lace his fingers with hers.

She held his hand tightly, but kept her gaze turned away from him. "I suppose I was wishing that I looked different. That I *was* different, as a person. That I was someone people would take notice of. I was thinking of Mrs. De Lacey, because I've read and heard so much about her. So I told Sir Jessamyn that I wished..." She closed her eyes, searching for the exact words. "I wished that people could see me differently—more like her."

"And what did your dragon do next, exactly?"

"He breathed fire on me."

Aubrey's head snapped up. Panic shone in his eyes and on his suddenly haggard face. "Please," he begged. "Please tell me there was no fire involved. Not that, at least. *Please* tell me you imagined it."

"I didn't. I saw it clearly. What's wrong?" Elinor leaned forward. "Is it a disaster? Does it mean something terrible?"

Mr. Aubrey let out a groan of pure despair. "It means that those bloody damned fairy tales were right. *Again*! Oh, God, Hawkins, stretch out your leg. I need to kick something."

"Kick one of your books," Benedict said. "You have more of them to spare."

"Why not?" Mr. Aubrey stuck his fingers into his hair and tugged frantically, eyes wild. "They're all useless now, aren't they? Everything we've all been working on, everything—"

"Oh, come now," said Benedict, and grinned maliciously.

"Not every book is useless, old chap. What about all those fairy tales?"

From the look on his face, Mr. Aubrey was about to commit an act of violence. Elinor cleared her throat hastily to distract him.

"What about those illustrations you told me of?" she said. "You said there had been drawings of other dragons in South America with similar markings to Sir Jessamyn."

"Yes," Mr. Aubrey said. "Yes. Indeed. The new, golden markings." His breathing steadied as he turned back to Sir Jessamyn. "Of all the hundreds of drawings that I've studied, only three of them have ever shown any similar patterns, along with that single stuffed specimen I mentioned. I've never before seen them on any living specimens of this captive breed, so there's one saving grace—at least this madness can't be common. You say the markings arrived only after the...events?"

"The first ones appeared at the same time as my illusion." Elinor reached out to stroke the swirling golden lines that spread along Sir Jessamyn's left cheek, and he leaned into her hand, eyes drifting halfway shut.

"I can tell you exactly when those markings on his neck appeared," said Benedict. "It was just after Elinor wished for Lady Hathergill to speak her mind. Sir Jessamyn breathed fire onto her and frightened me half-out of my wits."

"As if *that* means much," said Mr. Aubrey gloomily. "What few wits you still bother to keep around, now that you've left Cambridge..." His voice trailed off. Horror crept across his features. "Wait. Did you say 'wish?'"

Elinor frowned. "Well...that was what I said to Sir Jessamyn the first time," she said. "And I suppose I may have used the word 'wish' again the second time, but—"

"'I wish to know: what does your mother truly think,'" Benedict quoted. "Sorry, old man. It was definitely a wish."

"Bloody hell," said Mr. Aubrey. He lowered his head into his hands, the very picture of a broken man. "Bloody, bloody, bloody—"

"Mr. Aubrey!" Elinor stared. "It can't be that bad."

"Why are you even bothering to sit here talking to me?" Mr. Aubrey moaned into his hands. "What do I know about dragons, anyway? Obviously, you should be consulting a book of fairy tales instead."

"Buck up, Aubrey." Benedict clapped one hand against his friend's shoulder. "Just think: you'll be the one to inform the scientific community of the most amazing discovery of our era. That's something, isn't it?"

"Oh, it might be," said Mr. Aubrey bitterly, "if there was any chance of them believing me. But as there certainly isn't..."

Elinor was frowning down at Sir Jessamyn. "You really think he was granting wishes?" she said to Benedict. "Like in a..." She swallowed back her final words, with a guilty look at Mr. Aubrey.

Benedict nodded. "And that's not all," he said. "It may have been a long time since my nursemaid used to tell me fairy tales at night, but there is one thing I do remember. How many wishes does everybody get?"

"That is absurd!" The words burst out of Mr. Aubrey. He jerked upright, glaring. "No, Hawkins, I will not go that far. It's one thing to admit that there may be some tiny shred of validity to the occasional detail included in a fairy story, but—"

"Tell me," Benedict said to his friend, "in those few similar pictures you saw of other dragons, did any of them have more than three sets of golden markings?"

Mr. Aubrey clamped his mouth shut. His expression was intent with concentration...and then despair. "That could be mere coincidence," he said. "You can hardly call it scientific evidence."

"Perhaps not," said Benedict, "but all the rules of fairy tales started somewhere. Look here—her first wish brought this clever set to the left side of his face, the second set leads down and around his throat, and I'll wager anything you like that the third wish will complete the pattern on the right. Scientific evidence or not, would you really wager against me?"

"It hardly matters," said Elinor. "There isn't going to be a third wish. Every time I make one—"

"Of course there has to be a third," said Benedict. "How else are you to break the illusion?" He raised his eyebrows at her. "Don't you remember all the old stories? Every time anyone is ever granted three wishes, they always end up using the third wish to break all of the earlier ones."

"I always hated that," Mr. Aubrey muttered. "What a waste of time and energy! If they'd only used their wits and thought through all of their wishes in the first place..."

Benedict's gaze rested on Elinor with a tenderness that warmed her even from two feet away. "Make your third wish," he said. "Here. Now. With us. Or we can pack our bags and leave first, if you like, so you're safely away from your relatives before the transformation happens."

"No. I can't." Elinor pulled her hand away from Sir Jessamyn as if he were a loaded pistol. "I have to stay for Penelope's début."

"Oh, good God. If we're going to start talking about *dances* now—!" Mr. Aubrey let out a heartfelt groan.

Benedict frowned. "But why—? Oh, yes. Your sisters?"

"That was the bargain I made with Sir John." Elinor knotted her fingers together. "I have to—that is, *Mrs. De Lacey* has to be present for the début, to raise Penelope's social standing, or else he'll attack my younger sisters in revenge for what I did. I can't run away and let that happen."

"Of course not." Benedict sighed. "Well, we'll simply have to wait a few days longer, then." His smile looked forced. "Anyway, it's probably for the best. Why not stay and enjoy some truly excellent, free food for a few more days while we think up a brilliant plan to find an income to be married with?"

"Why not?" Elinor doubted that her own smile was any more convincing than his.

She couldn't wish away her first two wishes until she was

safely distant from Hathergill Hall, or she'd be arrested for theft and Sir Jessamyn doomed to a life of misery and fear. But that might already be too late to save her aunt from a life of seclusion and despair...and she would never have enough spare wishes to save Benedict's estate and let them marry.

He might be enough of a dreamer to believe in miracles, but Elinor knew exactly what she had just learned.

Even with all the help that Sir Jessamyn's magic could give her, there would be no happy ending for their fairy tale.

CHAPTER 27

The day of Penelope's début dawned gray, grim, and drizzling with fat and sulky rain drops. Elinor's sister Rose might have taken it as an omen. Unfortunately, Elinor was far too busy with Penelope to think about anything else at all.

The final two young men of fortune that Sir John had invited from London had been expected to arrive that morning. Unfortunately, all that had arrived in their stead had been two beautifully-written letters full of apologies and excuses that rang false even to Elinor's ears. They had been the final straw.

"Why can't anything ever go right for me?" Penelope wailed, for at least the tenth time since breakfast. She and Elinor were overseeing the decorations of the ballroom together, and the room was full of footmen on ladders, hanging swags of flowers and billowing pink silk, while housemaids scrubbed the chandelier to sparkling perfection. Penelope flopped deeper into her chair, a vision of perfect misery. "Just you wait. By suppertime we'll have thunderstorms, and then no one will come at all. No one! My début will be *canceled*." Her face crumpled. "I can't bear it!"

"No one expects any thunderstorms." Elinor should have been paying more attention to the white roses she was arranging in a purple stand; as she spoke, a thorn pricked the flesh between her right thumb and forefinger, drawing blood. Hissing out a breath, she counted to ten, then continued, in a tone of deliberate calm, "Remember what Mr. Hitchens said when your father summoned him to ask his opinion, Penelope. The clouds should part by mid-afternoon."

"Oh, well if *Mr. Hitchens* says so—!" Penelope snorted. "For heaven's sake, Mr. Hitchens is only a farmer on Papa's estate. He's not even a gentleman. Why should I trust his opinion on anything?"

"Well, when it comes to the weather...oh, never mind." Elinor abandoned the argument in favor of a far more important point. "Have you decided yet whether your mother is to attend the ball tonight?"

Penelope scowled. "Papa says she must, or too many awkward questions would be asked in the neighborhood. I think it's absurd. Why shouldn't the guests believe she has a headache if we say so?"

"Perhaps because tonight is her only daughter's début?" Elinor jabbed a sixth rose into the stand with more force than absolutely necessary. "What mother would miss it for a mere headache?"

"That's what Papa said." Penelope crossed her arms. "*I* said we could always claim that she had smallpox, but he said that no one would come to the house if that were true. So we have to pretend everything is normal and just pray she can be stopped from saying anything too dreadful before she's taken away at the end of the night."

Elinor squeezed her eyes so tightly shut, her forehead throbbed with pain. But when she opened her eyes again, Penelope was still there, looking sulky and disconsolate. This wasn't just a bad dream, after all. So she would have to try another approach.

"I have another idea," Elinor said brightly. "Why don't you just tell all your guests that she's gone mad? It *is* what you and your father truly believe, after all...or so you say. So you shouldn't be ashamed to admit to your neighbors exactly what the two of you are doing to her."

"Don't be absurd." Penelope stared at her. "I'm not ashamed of *us*. I'm ashamed of her! If we let the world know what she's become, it will ruin my social chances before I'm even betrothed."

"If you truly wanted to keep it a secret," said Elinor, "then Mr. Armitage and his sister are the last people you should have confided in."

"Mrs. De Lacey, I am deeply hurt." Miss Armitage's rich voice was laced with amusement as she spoke behind them.

"Of course our dear Miss Hathergill knows that she can trust us."

With her dragon posed like a statue on her shoulder, she sauntered forward, elegant as always in a deep burgundy morning gown. Society might dictate that unmarried maidens ought to wear only soft pastels, but even Elinor couldn't fault her taste. The rich colours she favored suited her remarkably well.

"In fact, I've come to offer my support. With so many lovely flowers to arrange, you must need another friend to help. Mrs. De Lacey..." Miss Armitage smiled warmly and gestured to the empty flower stand at the far end of the room. "Won't you show me the trick of doing them?"

Elinor raised her eyebrows and met the other woman's eyes measuringly. They were as enigmatic as ever. At any other moment, she would have found an excuse to avoid a private conversation. But just now...

She slid a glance at Penelope, and sighed. Slippery and untrustworthy as Miss Armitage might be, at least a moment or two alone with her might save Elinor from murdering her cousin.

She scooped Sir Jessamyn up from the chair he'd sat on, five careful feet away from Penelope. He perched happily in her arms, twisting his head around to follow every bustling movement of the servants around them as she and Miss Armitage crossed the busy, crowded room. Ladders swung through the air, brooms and sponges were wielded with fervor, and Sir John bellowed over all of it as he stepped into the doorway:

"For God's sake, is no one in this household available to bring me a cup of tea when I ring for it? Have I hired you all to do *nothing*?"

Mrs. Braithewaite, the housekeeper, hurried across the room to soothe him, while another housemaid followed Elinor and Miss Armitage to carry the prickling mass of roses and greenery for them.

"Thank you," Elinor said to the maid as they reached the stand. The maid only curtseyed in response, head lowered, but Elinor felt Sally's accusing gaze on her back, and she drew a deep breath. The other girl stood only a few feet away, scrubbing the sideboard to a vicious gleam, and Elinor could feel her rage burning through the air. She had to force herself not to move away or hunch her shoulders in guilt.

No matter what Sally thought, Elinor wasn't like Penelope. She did care about injustice, even if she hadn't managed to prove it yet.

Lucinda hadn't appeared at Hathergill Hall since Elinor's first day, but as one of Penelope's best friends, she had no choice but to attend the ball tonight. Penelope would accept no excuses. All that Elinor had to do was think of some clever way to unmask her there...before Sally could decide that she had waited long enough.

Miss Armitage knelt gracefully to choose among the pile of flowers, and her dragon balanced on her shoulder as beautifully as a dancer. "You *are* kind to show me how to do this."

"I doubt that you need any help," said Elinor. She shifted Sir Jessamyn to her shoulder—there were no chairs for him here, and if she set him down on the clean sideboard, Sally really might lose all control. "What is it that you want from me, Miss Armitage?"

"My, such refreshing directness." Miss Armitage smiled as she straightened, holding an armful of roses. "If only more people believed in honesty, how much easier all conversations would become."

Elinor felt her cheeks heat, but she didn't lower her gaze. She might not have any evidence to prove it, but she was absolutely certain that Miss Armitage was far more versed in deceit than herself. "What did you bring me here to tell me, then?" she said. "As we are being so honest with each other."

Miss Armitage raised one perfect eyebrow as she set the first of her roses into the stand. "You," she said, "are very much in the confidence of Miss Hathergill, despite your blatant disapproval of her actions."

"And?" said Elinor, without moving to help.

"And..." Miss Armitage pursed her lips consideringly as she set a delicate fern to one side of the rose, and adjusted their positions half an inch in each direction. "I very much hope that you may be able to enlighten me. Why exactly would Miss Hathergill turn away an advantageous offer of marriage just when one might imagine she would be in most urgent need of it?"

The tension in Elinor's shoulders eased, and she let out her breath, curling her lips into a half-smile. "Are you telling me that she's refused your brother?"

"I did not say that," said Miss Armitage. "'Turn away' was the phrase I used—it was a refusal to give an answer...*yet*. So perhaps you can tell me, Mrs. De Lacey...what exactly is your young cousin waiting for?"

"Miss Armitage," said Elinor, "I could hardly answer for Miss Hathergill's whims. Perhaps she wishes to make her début first, before making any decision. After all, she might meet a young man tonight who sweeps her off her feet."

"Tonight?" Miss Armitage raised both eyebrows this time. "This is a small country ball, ma'am, as you and I both know. My brother and Mr. Hawkins and his odd scholarly friend are the only gentlemen outside Miss Hathergill's usual circle of acquaintances. All the other young men in attendance must have known her since birth. They can hardly surprise her at this point."

Elinor frowned. "It was an odd coincidence, those other two young men from London both canceling their attendance at the last moment, wasn't it?" She'd been so busy this morning, and so distracted by her own worries, she'd only been annoyed by the news as it had impacted Penelope's temper, without thinking more about it. But now that she did...

"Very distressing," Miss Armitage agreed calmly. "It was almost as if they had come into some disturbing knowledge of the family."

Elinor's eyes narrowed. "I have noticed you writing a great many letters since you arrived at Hathergill Hall."

"Have I?" Miss Armitage smiled serenely. "My goodness, I am flattered that you noticed...especially when you were so busy writing them yourself. Although not to your usual sort of correspondent, I don't think."

Elinor blinked. She'd only sent one letter.

One letter...

She remembered Benedict setting it atop the pile of letters in Miss Armitage's hand. She hadn't had the chance to hide it deeper in the pile before the others arrived, and she hadn't been with them when they'd returned to Hathergill Hall. She'd been in the wilderness with Benedict. But still...

"I wonder," Miss Armitage said dreamily, "how exactly would Sir John react if he knew you were writing letters on his niece's behalf? Seeking her out a comfortable new position *and* using his daughter's own stolen dragon as an inducement for them to hire her?"

"You opened the letter," Elinor said blankly. "You stole a private letter and you read it—and you don't even feel ashamed to admit it."

"I?" Miss Armitage laughed gently. "I am not the one who would feel shame if confronted with the truth, Mrs. De Lacey. Sir John is a magistrate, is he not? And—correct me if I am wrong, but—it is a legal crime, is it not, to knowingly aid and shelter a thief?"

Elinor pressed her lips together. They felt oddly numb.

The room seemed to be narrowing around her, until she could barely breathe.

Sir John stood in the doorway, haranguing the housekeeper. Sally stood five feet behind from her, glaring at her back. Miss Armitage smiled with false kindness.

There were no escape routes, no matter where she ran. Even her one chance at governessing had been taken away.

"What is it that you want from me?" Elinor said, for the second time in minutes. But this time, she heard despair in her voice.

Miss Armitage must have heard it, too. She smiled as she set a final fern among her roses. "I want only the best for my brother," she said, "so I want him officially and publicly betrothed to Miss Hathergill by the time her début ball is over, with no doubts in anyone's head as to their binding."

Perhaps it was the overpowering smell of the roses, or the fact that Elinor hadn't slept well in days, or that she was just being blackmailed by one too many people. But she found her mind stuttering, as if it couldn't take in this one last demand.

"Why?" she said. "Why should it matter so much to you? Those other gentlemen were frightened away by the stories of madness—stories that you spread, to drive them off. Why haven't they driven you off, too?"

"Oh, Mrs. De Lacey." Miss Armitage shook her head reprovingly. "You know just as well as I that Lady Hathergill is not mad. If all I have to fear from Miss Hathergill's bloodline is a bit of plain speaking in middle age...well, my brother is not so cowardly as to mind that."

"But why is it so important to you?" Elinor studied Miss Hathergill's elegant figure, bent over the flower stand. "Why can't your brother wait any longer to persuade Penelope to accept his offer? In fact, why should it matter so much whether she accepts him at all? Everyone knows about his fortune...and you cannot pretend that he's actually in love with her."

"You have a great many questions, Mrs. De Lacey. And you are, of course, admirably intelligent. Unfortunately..." Miss Armitage straightened and dusted off her hands. "You are in no position to demand any answers. I have your letter, and I am fully prepared to pass it to Sir John, with my deepest horror and outrage on his behalf, if my brother is not betrothed to Miss Hathergill by ten o'clock tonight. Do we understand each other?"

The flower arrangement in the vase was, of course, perfect. Miss Armitage's smile glinted with satisfaction.

Elinor hadn't thought that she could dread tonight's ball any more than she already did...but of course, she had been wrong.

"Perfectly," she said, and walked away with both of her blackmailers' gazes on her back.

CHAPTER 28

At six o'clock that evening, the first round of guests—a carefully selected half-dozen local families—arrived for a private supper with the Hathergills. As the butler announced the last few names to the small crowd milling around the salon, Elinor felt her pulse beating hard against her throat.

Lucinda's and Millie's mothers clustered on one side of her, begging for her predictions of next Season's fashions and cooing together over a nervous Sir Jessamyn, who hunched closer to her neck with every sweeping gesture of their be-ringed hands. The vicar and his wife hovered on her other side, frowning uneasily at her dragon and wanting her opinion of the Regent's latest scandalous escapade. Elinor could barely take in a single word, let alone make up any coherent answers. Her whole body was taut with panic.

Penelope had refused to descend from her room until all of the supper guests had gathered. Even Miss Armitage hadn't been allowed into her dressing room beforehand. Only Elinor had been allowed to advise her on her appearance—because only the great Mrs. De Lacey's opinion was trustworthy enough on the matter of fashion.

Sir John's voice cut across the chatter that filled the room. He beamed at the assembled company. "Well, then. Is everybody ready? Shall I fetch the lady of the hour?"

It was the moment of truth. Elinor's fingers tightened around the stem of her glass until it threatened to snap.

She'd managed to persuade Penelope and her friends of the brilliance of her plan, but she knew perfectly well how absurd it truly was for them to trust her. No matter what she looked like, she was no leader of fashion. She'd never been to London in her life.

If Penelope's grand entrance was a disaster—a disaster of Elinor's making—then everything she had worked for all week would be lost. If anyone in the room looked at Penelope and recognized how ridiculous Elinor's idea was...if one single person laughed in Penelope or Sir John's presence...

"And here she is!" Sir John announced, from the doorway.

Gasps sounded throughout the room. There was a moment of dumbstruck silence.

Then Miss Armitage stepped forward, past all the staring local gentry. "Good heavens." She shook her head in open wonder. "How in the world did you ever come up with it?"

She brushed one finger against the curling peacock feather that had been pinned against Penelope's shoulder exactly where a dragon might have sat. Her lips curved into the first genuine smile Elinor had ever seen on her face.

"Simply and utterly brilliant," she said. "I'll wager anything you like that within two weeks of your London début, half the ladies in London will have tossed aside their dragons to follow your brilliant example."

Oh, no. Horrified, Elinor set one hand on Sir Jessamyn's warm back as if she could protect every dragon in London with her gesture. On Miss Armitage's own shoulder, her dragon posed as still as a statue, as usual...but Elinor thought she'd glimpsed a flicker of discomfort cross even his normally impassive face at his mistress's words.

Everyone else in the room was moving forward in a tidal wave of congratulation and envy. Despite herself, Elinor found her shoulders relaxing as she saw Penelope basking in the group's admiration. This evening might yet bring disaster and ruin, but so far, her sisters were still safe.

Benedict moved up behind her, his fingers brushing—as if by accident—against her bare arm. "Bravo," he murmured. "You're a genius."

"Shh." Tingles swept across her skin in response to his touch, but Elinor kept her face serene, under the scrutiny of so many of Penelope's guests. On her shoulder, Sir Jessamyn had perked up for the first time in half an hour and was stretching his neck as far as it would go, tilting his head and putting on all his best tricks to entice Benedict into a petting session. Elinor bit back a smile, maintaining her own dignity despite her dragon's display. "I was just trying to stop her from tormenting any more dragons."

Benedict leaned over to pet the sensitive area underneath Sir Jessamyn's chin. As the little dragon's eyes slitted half-shut with pleasure, Benedict dropped his voice to a whisper, his warm breath tickling her ear. "Perhaps the real Mrs. De Lacey can hire you as her fashion adviser and pay for our wedding in gratitude."

She raised her fan to shield her face as she rolled her eyes at him. "Perhaps," she agreed. "It does sound likely, doesn't it?"

And yet it still sounded likelier than any of the other plans they'd come up with in the last two days.

Elinor bit her lip. Benedict was smiling down at her from less than half a foot away as he petted Sir Jessamyn, looking amused and affectionate and close enough to touch, if only so many other people hadn't been watching. He was so certain they would succeed. It made her chest hurt.

She would have to be the one who made the hard decision, in the end. It would be so soon, now. All she had to do tonight was avoid discovery and imprisonment. They would leave Hathergill Hall tomorrow morning, And then...

Sir Jessamyn made a low, clicking sound of pleasure deep in his throat as he leaned into Benedict's petting hand, his scaly body relaxed against Elinor's shoulder for the first time since the guests had arrived and surrounded them. She wished she could toss aside convention and show her own inclinations just as openly.

She had to be strong, for Benedict's sake. But she couldn't bear for him ever to think she hadn't wanted this—wanted them together, forever—as much as he had.

"Benedict," she began, in an urgent whisper.

"Ah, there you are," said Sir John. His voice was jovial, for the sake of their company; his eyes, though, were hard as obsidian with dislike. "Won't you allow me to escort you into supper, ma'am?"

Even if it hadn't been the law of social custom, she couldn't have refused. Her bargain had been to do everything she could to help with Penelope's début, no matter how much it burned.

She laid her gloved fingers as lightly as possible against his coat-sleeve, careful not to brush against any bare skin. She smiled brilliantly even as they passed Lady Hathergill, who fell into place behind them under the escort of Lucinda's bewildered father.

Her aunt's voice carried to her ears as they passed. "...But of course *I* didn't have anything to do with that. For goodness's sake, I'm a lady, not a cow—we hire wetnurses for such matters!"

Lucinda's father uttered a choking sound—either muffled laughter or outrage—and Sir John's arm stiffened under Elinor's hand. Crimson swept across his face in a wave.

Elinor only wished she could take any pleasure in his

humiliation. But she had seen the physician's black carriage draw up outside the house that afternoon. It was waiting now behind the stables, where none of the guests would notice it or wonder.

Guests were smiling and nodding at her now, blatantly angling for her attention: leaders of the local gentry who had never had a kind word to spare for her a week ago, when she had been Penelope's despised companion. She forced herself to return their nods as graciously as a visiting queen. If it hadn't been for Sir Jessamyn's claws digging into her shoulder through her aunt's second-best lavender silk evening gown, she would have thought herself in a dream.

Even as she smiled for the sake of their observers, though, she spoke in a whisper only her uncle could hear.

"Please," she whispered. "Wait a few more days before you send her away. Lady Hathergill may well return to her old self in a day or two. This may be only a passing change. If you can only put off your decision until next week—"

"Enough," Sir John snarled, and yanked out her chair from the table. He glowered at her menacingly as she sat down in the place of honor on his right, and he leaned in to whisper: "From now on, you will hold your tongue on the subject of my wife, madam. Do you understand me?"

Shivers swept Sir Jessamyn from his nose all the way down his tail. Elinor lifted her chin and glared back at her uncle with all the haughty disdain of an empress.

"You," she said, "are irritating my dragon. Good-bye."

And she turned away to smile graciously at Millie's father, seated beside her.

Like Millie herself, Mr. Staverton was essentially harmless, a good-humoured man who was only too happy to be asked questions about his hunting dogs and then allowed to run free with anecdotes about them for hours. She shifted Sir Jessamyn to her right shoulder—"That's a demmed fine little dragon you have there, Mrs. De Lacey, if you don't mind me saying so! Have you ever tried him on a hunt?"—and let her neighbor ramble on for the rest of supper, grateful for the respite and the chance to think.

Benedict sat across from her, between Lucinda and Penelope. Penelope, as radiant in her pale blue ballgown as a fairy princess, leaned in close to him as they spoke, laughing encouragingly and sliding him meaningful looks beneath her lashes. He cheerfully ignored them, focusing on his meal, while Lucinda conversed with Sir John. Elinor couldn't help the warm glow of relief in her chest...but she knew that look of gathering storm on her cousin's face. The weather outside might have cleared since that morning, but the tightness pinching Penelope's pretty face promised thunderstorms ahead, even as Mr. Armitage, on her other side, devoted all his attention to charming her.

Miss Armitage watched the byplay with narrowed eyes from the other end of the table.

Meanwhile, half a table away, Mr. Aubrey was seated next to Millie and listening to her with an attitude of bewildered despair. He had been bundled into proper evening attire and forced to leave behind all his books, and as Millie rattled on happily, his shoulders sagged lower and lower and his head drooped over his plate.

Poor man, Elinor thought, but really—he didn't realize how fortunate he was. He could have been seated next to Millie's mother instead. *Her* whole life was devoted to hunting down a husband for her daughter, and as an eligible bachelor with a vast fortune, he would have made the perfect prey. Like it or not, he would have found himself betrothed by the end of supper.

Speaking of which...

As Elinor glanced down the table, she met Miss Armitage's steely gaze. The other girl looked pointedly to the tall clock in the corner of the room as it chimed the hour, a deep, resonant sound.

Seven o'clock. Only three hours until her deadline. Elinor swallowed down a suddenly-flavourless slice of smoked pheasant and fed the next two pieces to Sir Jessamyn. She had lost her appetite.

At half past seven, the ladies retired to the second-floor sitting room, which had been set up for the night as a private retiring room, complete with mirrors, maids, and discreetly screened chamber pots for their convenience. Elinor drew Penelope aside before Carter could even begin her ministrations.

"You look lovely," she said, "but Penelope—"

"You really think so?" Penelope slid a glance back at the

closest mirror, where Carter was smoothing Lucinda's hair back into place with practiced hands. "I'm not sure. I—"

"Of course," Elinor said, "but Penelope..." She drew a deep breath, searching for the right words. "Isn't there anything you want to share with me?"

Penelope blinked. "I beg your pardon?"

"About your plan?" Elinor prompted. "To be betrothed by the end of this evening?"

"Oh!" Penelope's lips quivered. "Oh, Mrs. De Lacey, I don't know what's gone wrong! I could have sworn it would happen by tonight. Perhaps this gown wasn't right, after all. Perhaps—"

"Surely Mr. Armitage has proposed by now."

"Well, of course he has." Penelope scowled. "But that's the problem! I can't accept him yet, can I? Mr. Hawkins hasn't yet proposed. If he doesn't hurry up and do it, I'll end up an old maid!"

Elinor forced herself not to roll her eyes. "There is a simpler solution, you know."

"There is?" Penelope narrowed her eyes. "Do you think I ought to trick him into a compromising situation? So that he *has* to propose, like it or not?"

"No!" Elinor stared at her. "For heaven's sake, of course you shouldn't. I *meant,* you can simply accept Mr. Armitage! He is the one you want to marry, isn't he?"

"I'm not so certain anymore." Penelope's lips pouched out into a pout. "I did think so, at first...but I don't see why Mr. Hawkins wouldn't want to marry me. What does he have to be so picky about, after all? He may be very handsome, but he can't expect to find anyone prettier than me! Can he?"

Elinor sighed. "You find Mr. Armitage handsome, too, don't you? And you certainly want to share the life he leads. All those London soirees, fancy house parties..."

"I suppose so. But..." Penelope scowled. "Why shouldn't Benedict Hawkins want me? He's barely even looked at me for the past few days. From the way he's been acting, if I didn't know better, I'd think he was in love with you!"

Heat crept up Elinor's face. "Penelope..."

"Oh, don't worry. I know he isn't really," Penelope said. "You're far too old. But it's the principle of the thing, don't you see? He has to want *me*."

Elinor gritted her teeth. "You are sending your mother away *tonight*, Penelope. The news is bound to spread, no matter how hard you and your father work to keep it quiet. In fact, the news has probably"—*definitely*, she amended silently, as she thought of Miss Armitage's busy pen—"already spread to London, even if your neighbors haven't yet found out. If you wish to find a fiancé before the gossip goes wild, you haven't any time to lose."

"You're right." Penelope nodded firmly. She straightened her shoulders and tossed her hair, making the golden curls bounce on either side of her determined face. "It has to be tonight. There isn't any way around it."

"Good," Elinor said, and let out her breath with a whoosh of pure relief. "That's good. As soon as we go downstairs, you can tell Mr. Armitage—"

"First," said Penelope, "I'll get my proposal from Mr. Hawkins...whether he wishes to make it or not."

And, with a sweep of her skirts, she was off, pushing her way to the front of the closest mirror while Elinor stared after her with a sick feeling of mounting dread.

CHAPTER 29

There was no time for Elinor to warn Benedict before the ball began. As the great Mrs. De Lacey and the most honoured guest anyone in the neighborhood had ever known, she was required to stand in the receiving line between Lady Hathergill and Sir John to greet the long stream of lesser guests whose carriages rattled up outside Hathergill Hall at eight o'clock.

Two more hours...

Elinor's skin twitched with impatience as she touched her gloved fingers to hand after hand, nodding to each new guest with a smile that felt more forced with every passing minute. At least Penelope was trapped in this receiving line as well; that was her only consolation. As long as Elinor found Benedict the very moment the ball began, to warn him of what her cousin had in mind...

Penelope leaned up to whisper in Sir John's ear, with an imploring look, just as old Mr. Adams from the next village clasped Elinor's gloved hand.

"Enchanting, enchanting," mumbled Mr. Adams. "Now when *I* was a lad, and went to London..."

Beside her, Lady Hathergill said loudly to Mr. Adams's granddaughter, "Good God, but I pity the bird who died to make your hat!"

But Elinor still caught Sir John's words to his daughter. "Of course you can, puss. Take all the time you need."

Penelope curtseyed prettily to the line of remaining guests, and hurried away with a determined bounce to her step. A moment later, she was lost in the crowd.

"I beg your pardon," Elinor said to Mr. Adams, "but if you'll excuse me—"

"Nonsense," said Sir John, overhearing. "You won't abandon us at the post, will you, Mrs. De Lacey?"

The guests around them might have missed the warning in his tone. Elinor did not. She gritted her teeth.

The queue had to end soon. There weren't that many people in this entire county, for heaven's sake. All she had to do was wait a few more minutes.

"Of course not," she said, and smiled fixedly at Mr. Adams's granddaughter as the receiving line moved forward.

As usual, nowadays, her aunt had been perfectly correct: the huge, goggle-eyed stuffed pheasant that weighed down the girl's bonnet looked as if it wanted to weep with outrage at its own indignity.

Sir Jessamyn, however, had the opposite reaction. He leaned forward, golden eyes fixing hungrily upon the bonnet. His tongue darted out from his mouth. The muscles in his legs bunched as he prepared to leap.

"What a pretty dragon!" Miss Adams said. "May I pet it, please?"

"It would be wiser not to." Elinor put a steadying hand on Sir Jessamyn's neck before he could lose all control, lunge forward and snatch himself an after-supper snack.

"Never mind," she whispered to him consolingly, as Miss Adams moved forward in the line. "It was old and rotten anyway."

Sir Jessamyn subsided, grumbling.

Fortunately, there were no more dead animals on the headpieces of the remaining guests. Only ten more minutes passed before the last guest had been greeted, and Elinor was free. She started forward through the crowd.

"Oh, Mrs. De Lacey—"

"Mrs. De Lacey, if I may—"

"Excuse me," she said, and then raised her voice as her uncle's neighbors clustered closer. "Pardon me!"

"Oh, but Mrs. De Lacey, if I could have one quick word—"

"Just a moment for my daughter's sake, if you please..."

There was no way to push past the gathering circle of local matrons and their husbands without risking the touch of bare skin. Elinor could have screamed with frustration.

She hung onto her patience with every ounce of self-control she still possessed.

Then she remembered: for this one last night of her life, she was still Mrs. De Lacey. Why on earth should she bother with self-control?

"Will everyone please move out of my way?" she bellowed.

There was a moment of frozen silence. Then the local gentry scattered before her, bowing and scraping and apologizing in agonized embarrassment.

"*Much* better." Elinor unfurled her aunt's second-best black evening fan to cool her face as she sailed forward. Sir Jessamyn sat up alertly on her shoulder, his golden gaze sweeping the room.

"Benedict," she murmured to him. "Look for Benedict, not for food. We need to find—"

She was cut off by a sudden fanfare of flutes and horns. Sir John stood before the orchestra in the corner of the room, looking ready to burst with pride as the guests paused in their conversations and turned to listen.

"Ladies and gentlemen," he said. "We've gathered in honor of the prettiest girl in England tonight. And now, ready to lead off the first set of the evening...my daughter!"

He pointed to the center of the room, where Penelope stood next to a politely smiling Benedict. His gaze searched through the crowd and met Elinor's; his smile turned rueful. He gave an infinitesimal shrug.

She tried to give him a reassuring smile in return, but his face was lost to her within seconds as other young ladies and their partners surrounded him, taking their places for the dance.

At least Penelope couldn't do anything in front of so many people, Elinor told herself. Her cousin would have to trick Benedict into taking her out of the ballroom if she wished to create a compromising situation. All that Elinor had to do was intercept him the moment that the first set of dances ended, and he would be perfectly safe.

"Mrs. De Lacey." Gavin Armitage bowed before her. His evening coat emphasized his broad shoulders, and gold thread glittered on his waistcoat, picking out a pattern studded with tiny jewels. "May I have this dance?"

She smiled thinly. "Thank you, but I do not dance tonight."

"Oh, but you must. Don't forget, I've seen you dance before, in London, so you can't pretend to be too old and staid. How can you possibly refuse me?"

"With great ease." Elinor turned pointedly away from him. She couldn't dance with anyone, of course; there was too great a risk of bare skin brushing in the turns of the dance. But with Gavin Armitage, of all people, she felt no need to pretend regret. Surely blackmail removed any need for courtesy between them?

She would have walked away without looking back, but Sir Jessamyn let out a warning chirrup. She turned just in time: Mr. Armitage's bare hand had been about to close around her bare arm, in the dangerous gap between her cap sleeves and her glove.

"I beg your pardon!" She snapped her fan out between them like a shield.

His blue eyes were glittering with anger, his social mask dropped for the first time since she'd met him. "So you should," he said. "Why is Miss Hathergill dancing with Benedict Hawkins, may I ask?"

"She must have promised him this dance," Elinor said coldly. "Now if you'll excuse me—"

"She promised it to me," said Mr. Armitage. "Now she's shifted my dance to the second set. What have you been telling her, Mrs. De Lacey?"

"To marry you, of course," she snapped. "Much good may it do either of you."

She was horrified to realize that she was trembling, an involuntary response to the menace that suddenly thickened the air. She took a shallow breath, and forced herself not to step back. They were standing in a crowded ballroom, for heaven's sake. There was nothing he could do to her. But as Elinor looked into Gavin Armitage's eyes, she suddenly had no doubt whatsoever that he *would* physically hurt her, if need be, to get what he desired.

He might even enjoy it.

Good God. She fought not to let the horrifying realization show on her face. *I can't let him marry Penelope after all.*

Her cousin was many things, almost all of them horrid.

But even Penelope didn't deserve to be wed to Gavin Armitage.

Damn it, damn it, damn it!

Elinor lifted her chin. "If you will recall," she said coldly, "I have until ten o'clock to secure your future happiness."

Slowly, reluctantly, Gavin Armitage stepped back. "Until ten o'clock."

She turned her back on him and walked away. But the quivering tension in her muscles didn't relax until the crowd had closed between them, and he could no longer see her.

Then she closed her eyes and let out a long, shuddering breath. She would have gladly collapsed if there had been a chair at hand to fall into. As it was, though, she was being watched by far too many people, not to mention Sir Jessamyn, who was nuzzling her cheek with deep concern.

She had to find her courage, and her spine.

Elinor opened her eyes and found at least ten of Sir John's neighbors watching her with open fascination. She bared her teeth, and they turned hastily away. *Good.* Later, she might feel guilty for how badly she'd behaved, but right now, she didn't have time to make sparkling conversation about London life and high society. Muffled under the cheerful tones of the orchestra's quadrille, the clock in the corner was chiming a warning that resonated through her bones. It was a quarter to nine, and she had no time left to lose.

If she wanted to save herself—and, maddeningly, Penelope—from the Armitages, she only had one choice. She had to find out what was making them so desperate to secure the betrothal now, tonight. There was only one person who could help her.

Elinor took a deep breath and struck out through the crowd. It was time to deal with the problem of Lucinda.

IT WASN'T difficult to find Penelope's friends. At this ball, like so many country balls, there were too many young ladies and not nearly enough gentlemen, so Lucinda and Millie were both waiting this set out, standing together by the refreshment table. Millie watched the dancers with open envy. As her eyes followed Penelope, her hand fluttered unconsciously to her left shoulder; it would not be long, Elinor thought, before she started wearing a peacock feather of her own. If it hadn't been for Lucinda's cooler head and guidance, Millie probably would have given in to temptation and worn one tonight, earning Penelope's eternal ire.

Lucinda, though...her lips might have been smiling as she chatted to her friend, but her gaze moved ceaselessly about the room, sharp and searching, taking in every detail. Who could she possibly be looking for? Elinor frowned as she glanced around the ballroom. The shifting patterns of the dance filled the center of the floor, while the older gentlemen, matrons and wallflowers flowed about the sides of the room. She squinted, taking it all in, and for one dazzling moment they all blurred into a whirl of colour and sparkles.

That's it. Elinor sucked in a breath at the realization. Lucinda wasn't looking for any one person—or any person at all. She was looking at all the sparkling *things* that filled the room. All the gentry of the county had flocked to Hathergill Hall tonight, wearing their finest attire…and accessories. There wasn't a woman there, apart from Elinor herself, whose throat, ears, and wrists didn't glitter with her most expensive jewelry.

Lucinda would never be able to resist.

How was she to be caught in the act, though? Elinor worried at her bottom lip as she puzzled it through. It had to be soon, before the music could stop and Lucinda could be swept up into the patterns of the next dance. And it couldn't be Elinor herself who set the trap. Lucinda knew not to trust her.

But who else could possibly be asked? Benedict was still trapped in the dance. Mr. Aubrey was sitting the quadrille out, of course, crossing his arms and glowering at the triviality of the dance, but he wore no jewelry to provide a temptation—not even a gold watchfob of the type many gentlemen favored.

That left only one dangerously unpredictable possibility.

"…And I was sick for days!" Lady Hathergill said cheerfully behind her. "I puked like a pig. Disgusting!"

The vicar's wife made a muffled sound of horror and fled as Elinor turned. Her aunt shrugged philosophically as she watched the other woman run away. "Ah, well," she said. "Horrible woman. Her husband only married her for her dowry, you know. He was actually in love with her sister, but *she* ran away with their footman ten days before they were meant to be wed. A ridiculous way to escape, if you ask me. She should have at least held out for a butler, don't you think?"

"I—well, I suppose..." Elinor blinked. Then she put the story aside to be wondered at later. "Aunt—I mean, my old friend. I need to ask a favor of you."

"You can always ask," Lady Hathergill said. "But I may or may not say yes. I used to agree to everything, you know, only because it seemed so much easier not to argue. Nowadays, though, I feel quite invigorated. Almost like a different person!"

"I know." Elinor winced. "But I need to expose a thief—one who's ruined a young girl's life only to save her own reputation and standing. Will you help me?"

A smile spread across Lady Hathergill's face. She leaned towards Elinor and tapped Sir Jessamyn approvingly on his snout. "Do you know," she said, "I'd actually believed that this whole evening would be a crashing bore. How glad I am to know I was mistaken!"

CHAPTER 30

For the first time that evening, Elinor was grateful for the shifting masses of the crowd that filled the Hathergills' over-stuffed ballroom. They allowed her to hang back, safely hidden, while her aunt sailed forward to the refreshment table.

Safely hidden...but close enough to overhear. It might be good to have a partner, but Elinor couldn't imagine any more dangerous co-conspirator than Lady Hathergill, unleashed. If her aunt announced to Lucinda and Millie what she was doing, their entire enterprise would be shattered.

But her first words were fairly innocuous, by recent standards. "Ah, there's the punch-bowl at last. I certainly need it in a tedious crush like this. I'm positively *reeking* with sweat. Repulsive!"

Millie tittered nervously, raising one hand to her mouth,

but Lucinda only said politely, "May I fill your cup for you, Lady Hathergill?"

"No need for that," said Lady Hathergill. "I want Millie to do something for me. Will you fetch my lavender shawl?"

"But..." Millie blinked at her. "I thought you were too hot?"

"It's an excuse, girl!" Lady Hathergill barked, and Elinor closed her eyes in pure anguish.

She should have known better than to ever make such a doomed attempt.

But before she could even begin to form new plans, Millie breathed, "Ohhhh. You mean, you said you were hot because you wanted an excuse to drink more punch. *I* see! My cousin Agatha does that sometimes, too, although she does act very silly afterwards. My mama says it's always wisest for ladies to stick to lemonade when not in the safety of their own chambers." And with a warning shake of her head, Millie hurried off through the crowd to fulfill her errand...leaving Elinor to wonder what exactly Mrs. Staverton *did* drink in the safety of her bedchamber.

Still: *Thank goodness*, Elinor thought, and let her head drop for a moment against the warmth of Sir Jessamyn's shoulder. That had been a too-close escape.

Taking a deep breath, Elinor eased closer to peer through the throng. Her aunt was leaning over the tall crystal punch bowl, while Lucinda stood beside her, sipping her own punch and looking faintly bored. As Lady Hathergill muttered to herself, words that Elinor couldn't catch, Lucinda's lips curled into an expression of pure contempt. It melted away only a moment later to be replaced by a politely expectant look as Lady Hathergill straightened, but Elinor's breath had already caught and her eyes narrowed.

The last remaining traces of her own guilt melted away. Lucinda *deserved* to be trapped, and to pay for what she had done to Sally's sister. Her actual thefts might have been forgiven, but Sally was right: no inner compulsion could excuse the way that she had treated other people...and the way she would continue to treat others if she wasn't stopped now.

Lady Hathergill took a long sip of her punch...and the glittering diamond bracelet on her wrist slipped off her arm. It slid down her gown and landed just beneath the table.

Lucinda's face sharpened, like a hunting dog on point.

Lady Hathergill said, "Do you know, I never thought you were a good friend for my daughter, although you *were* always good at flattering her. I must say I wasn't at all surprised when—"

"Lady Hathergill!" Elinor broke through the crowd to stop her. "Won't you come give me your opinion on something?"

Her aunt shrugged and tossed down a sip of punch. "I'm always happy to give my opinion nowadays."

Lucinda's eyes darted back and forth between Lady Hathergill and the table.

Elinor sent her a dismissive smile. "You won't mind my stealing her away from you, will you?"

"Not at all," said Lucinda. Her cheeks were flushed. She looked down into her punch glass, lowering her eyelashes, as if she were suffering from shyness in Mrs. De Lacey's presence...but Elinor caught the motion in the corner of her eye as Lucinda reached out with one slippered foot and nudged the bracelet another careful three inches underneath the table.

Elinor took her aunt's arm in her gloved hand and drew her away.

As soon as they were hidden from Lucinda's view, though, she spun around. "Can you see the bracelet?" She stood on her tiptoes, but she couldn't see under the table past the cluster of matrons who stood between them, feathered turbans and headdresses bobbing.

"I shan't mind if I lose that bracelet," Lady Hathergill said. "I always thought the stones were tastelessly large. But then, Sir John has never consulted me in the jewelry that he buys for display."

"Of course not," Elinor agreed automatically, as she peered past shoulders and waving fans. She would have to wait at least a minute or two to be certain; Lucinda, after all, would surely wait a minute to be safe before she took the risk of scooping up the bracelet.

If Lucinda was only holding it in her hands when she was caught, there would be no proof of her wrongdoing; she might well claim she had only picked it up to return to Lady Hathergill. She would have to hide it in her reticule or on her person to look incriminating. But if Elinor didn't see where she hid it…

"Sir John has never listened to me about anything," Lady Hathergill said, "but he did used to talk at me a great deal, back when I was too tired to disagree with him. Now that I'm able to share my own opinions, it's remarkable how little he wants to see me at all. I must say, that really has been one of the pleasantest side effects of the great *change*." She accented the word meaningfully.

"The great…what?" Elinor blinked, distracted for a moment from her search. Then her mouth dropped open. Heat spread across her face as she struggled for words. "I'm not sure…I don't think you're undergoing *the change*," she finally managed. "I mean, I don't think this is a physical issue. That is…"

"What else could it be?" her aunt asked. "Come now, Sophia, it may be some years since we knew each other *well,* but even when you were a girl yourself, you never used to blush at discussing such matters. Surely you remember your own mother telling us about the change that happens in mid-life."

"Well…" Elinor didn't, actually—her own mother had been only thirty-eight when she'd died, and the subject hadn't arisen between them. Elinor had heard only the vaguest of old wives' tales about what happened to older women. Still, she was certain that none of those whispered changes were brought about by dragon wishes.

And she was suddenly miserably certain of something

else, too: if she let her aunt go on thinking that this change in herself was natural, all the way to the doors of her confinement, she would be no better than Sir John himself. He might be the one who paid to send her to that cottage...but Elinor was the one who was at fault.

She stared at her aunt, caught in helpless silence. She couldn't tell her the truth now, in the middle of the crowded ball—the news would spread like fire across the room, just like every other thought that entered Lady Hathergill's head nowadays. But she couldn't let her walk unknowingly into the trap that Sir John had set, either.

She reached out and laid the tips of her gloved fingers on her aunt's arm. "There is something I have to tell you," she said. Her mouth felt suddenly dry. She swallowed hard, trying to moisten it, but there was no way to soften the words she had to say. "Sir John thinks you've gone mad."

"Oh, I know that." Lady Hathergill snorted. "He would, wouldn't he? As far as my husband is concerned, any woman or servant who doesn't hop to his bidding must be entirely perverse. He was never in love with me, you know, even in the beginning. You were right when you warned me against the marriage. I should have listened instead of thinking you blinded by jealousy. I'm sorry for that. *He* only wanted a pretty ornament for the grand new estate he was building... but then, I married him for his money, so I suppose it's only fair. I always did envy my younger sister marrying for love, even if she did have to bury herself in the wilds of Cornwall for it. But then, you and I would never have been allowed—"

"None of that matters right now!" Elinor shook her head, shaking away the paralyzing grief that wanted to snake out and trap her with the memory of her parents. "You have to listen to me. That physician who came—Sir John has paid him to declare you insane. He'll be taking you to a cottage in the middle of nowhere, tonight, with a nurse to keep you solitary and hidden from everyone. His carriage is waiting behind the stables now. You haven't any time to lose."

For the first time in days, Lady Hathergill was silent. For a long moment she only stared.

Then she said, "Well, I should have expected it. This is exactly why I gave up all those years ago, you know. But I don't care. I'm glad I had this week. I'm glad I finally told my husband exactly what I thought of him." She downed the rest of her punch with a fierce swallow.

"He deserved it," Elinor said, "but you don't. You have to do something."

"Do something?" Lady Hathergill let out a crack of laughter. "Easy for you to say, my friend! You're a widow, with the right to your own money and decisions. Sir John is my owner in the eyes of the law. Even if he wanted to send me to the worst sort of madhouse, there would no one with a legal right to stop him, not even you or your fine London friends." Snorting, she turned to walk away.

"There's *you*," Elinor said, and tightened her hand around her aunt's arm, forcing her to stay. "And there are all of your neighbors, too. You know how much Sir John cares for his reputation. I can't tell them myself—I had to promise to hold my tongue tonight. But you can tell anyone you want. You can make as much of a fuss as you want! You *must*. Make such a spectacle he can't hide it. Embarrass him so much that he can't stand it. Only, please..."

She knew it was hopeless, but she had to try, for her sisters' sake: "Please don't tell anyone how you found out the truth, I beg you. Let Sir John think you spotted the physician's carriage yourself, or heard the servants gossiping. Please."

Lady Hathergill's eyes narrowed. Confusion crept across her face as she leaned forward. "There's something about your voice...for a moment, you sounded exactly like..."

Elinor let go of her aunt's arm as if she'd been burned. But it was too late. Her aunt seized her hand, and their bare arms brushed against each other.

Lady Hathergill's jaw dropped. "Elinor?!"

Elinor jerked away so quickly that Sir Jessamyn almost slipped off her shoulder. Her mind whirled. She opened her mouth to speak. There had to be a solution, if she could only think fast enough to find one.

Then she met her aunt's gaze and realized the truth: there was no escape. No matter what Lady Hathergill might think or want, she couldn't keep a secret anymore—not even to save her own life. After a week of illusions and reprieve, Elinor's time had run out.

She looked into her aunt's shocked face and said the only thing she could: "Forgive me."

Then she turned and hurried away through the crowd without waiting for a response.

Sir Jessamyn's claws burned into her shoulder as she ducked and slid through openings to avoid any more telltale brushes of bare skin. Guests' voices roared in her ears, but she couldn't take them in. Her vision narrowed to a tunnel before her. She had to find Benedict. She could not run without saying farewell to him first. She might have failed her sisters and her aunt, but she had promised not to abandon him.

She'd *promised.*

She had almost reached the center of the room before it hit her: the music of the quadrille had stopped. It must have stopped a few minutes ago, in fact—the dancers had abandoned the patterns and were forming a new set. *Good.* Penelope would be busy with Mr. Armitage, and Elinor could safely draw Benedict aside.

Perhaps he could even convince Mr. Aubrey to drive her away in his carriage, to escape. That would give her an hour or two's head start before Sir John could leave the ball and come after her. But no—that would require abandoning all of Mr. Aubrey's books and papers. He would never agree to it.

Where *was* Benedict? She drew to a halt, panting, and stood on her tiptoes to peer around. People were looking at her wonderingly, but she didn't care anymore. All she wanted...

Mr. Armitage's voice spoke in her ear, as sharp as a blade, and as sudden. "Devil take you, where has she gone?"

Elinor fell back, gasping. "What do you mean? Who?"

Then she saw his furious face, and her heart sank.

"Penelope," snarled Gavin Armitage. "She's supposed to be dancing this set with me...but she and your precious Mr. Hawkins have disappeared."

CHAPTER 31

Elinor stumbled back. She almost fell. Gavin Armitage's hand swung out to catch her, but she caught herself just in time to wave him back.

"Wait here," she said urgently. "I'll go and find them."

"Oh, will you?" He sneered at her, his handsome face twisting. "How much of a fool do you take me for, Mrs. De Lacey? You've been manoeuvering on Hawkins's behalf all along. I should have guessed that you two would hatch this scheme in the end. He's compromising her right now, isn't he?"

"No!" Elinor gritted her teeth as Sir Jessamyn hunched on her shoulder, glaring at Mr. Armitage with slitted golden eyes. "But if I don't hurry—"

"If you don't hurry up and publicly discover them, then it won't work, will it?" Gavin Armitage stepped closer to loom over her, fists clenched at his sides. "Do you think I can't see for myself how you've planned it? You'll be *shocked* and *horrified* to discover the two of them alone together. Then Sir John won't have a choice in the matter. He'll be forced to let them marry—to *insist* that they marry—no matter what Hawkins's fortune might be!"

"Mr. Armitage—"

"I should have revealed everything days ago. Hawkins would have been tossed out on his ear, as he should have been from the beginning. He may be pretending to fortune and respectability, but if Sir John had any idea what his father had done—"

"Well, then, why didn't you simply tell him?" Elinor tilted her neck back to glare up at him. "I am growing weary of your theatrics, Mr. Armitage. Don't bother pretending that you were motivated by kindness or generosity to hold your silence until now."

His face worked. He didn't answer.

"We haven't time to waste in arguing. I'll be back as soon as I can. If you're wise—"

"What is going on here?" Miss Armitage's voice was lowered, but irritation snapped through it as she stepped between them. Her dragon looked down his snout at Sir Jessamyn with open disdain; Miss Armitage's own expression mirrored his as she looked at Elinor. "The two of you are drawing far too much attention with your argument. What can you be thinking?"

"Blame your brother," Elinor snapped, "and keep him

under control. I'm going to find Penelope before she can cause any more damage."

She stalked off before they could stop her, and Sir Jessamyn, for the first time ever, let out an unmistakable hiss of warning as he glared back at them over her shoulder.

"Brave dragon," she whispered, patting his back. "Good dragon."

Elinor knew she didn't have long before they would follow. Miss Armitage might insist on some subtlety and discretion, but once she understood exactly what had happened, she would be every bit as determined as her brother. Neither of them would ever trust her to manage the situation on her own.

If she wasn't fast enough, someone else would find them first.

Panic pulsed against Elinor's throat. She hurried out of the ballroom, desperately trying to think herself into her cousin's mindset. Penelope would want—no, would need—to be discovered, and as quickly as possible, before Benedict could safely extract himself from the situation...but she had to have tricked him into someplace private, someplace with a door that she could close, a setting that couldn't be seen as innocuous.

It had to be nearby. But where?

A row of doors, at least half of them closed, met her eyes as she stepped out of the ballroom. A scattering of guests sauntered up and down the long corridor, laughing and talking. Elinor looked at Sir Jessamyn; he looked back at her, wide-eyed.

"Your magic isn't going to help us right now, is it?" she whispered. "Not without a wish."

Her shoulders slumped as she contemplated the task ahead. She could work her way up and down the corridor, opening every single door...or she could use her wits. *How* would Penelope have tricked Benedict out of the ballroom?

A headache would have required fresh air—but the garden was too private for Penelope's purposes. A chill would have required a shawl, but Benedict would never have agreed to escort her to the privacy—and impropriety—of her bedroom. A strained ankle would only have required a chair, and there were plenty of those in the ballroom. If she had dropped or forgotten something in a public room, though, and wanted his escort as she fetched it, it would have been unpardonably rude to refuse her.

The dining room. It stood at the end of the corridor. As she watched, the door eased shut—from the inside.

"Hold on, Sir Jessamyn." Elinor picked up her skirts and ran.

She was lucky: the small groups of guests that she passed moved out of her way. But as her hand closed over the doorknob, she suddenly realized that she had a new problem, and this one was of her own creation: they were all staring expectantly after her now. Just as Miss Armitage had warned, she had drawn exactly the wrong kind of attention.

Even if she hurried Penelope and Benedict out of the

dining room before anyone else could walk in and discover them, every guest who lingered curiously in the corridor would see her emerging with the two of them and realize what had happened. *Damnation.*

Elinor paused for a long moment with her hand on the doorhandle, fighting to think clearly through her panic. Perhaps if she moved on, pretended she'd been looking for something else, then doubled back...

She heard Benedict's voice through the door. "I don't see your fan here, Miss Hathergill. Are you certain this is where you left it?"

Out of the corner of her eye, she glimpsed Miss Armitage emerging from the ballroom.

Elinor gritted her teeth and eased the door very slightly open. She turned to one side to slip through it, praying that no one could see past her and Sir Jessamyn into the room beyond. She had no idea how she would explain things in five minutes...but she had no time to waste in attempting complex plans. Not anymore.

A crash sounded in the dining room the very moment she turned the doorhandle. Penelope let out a breathy shriek. Quick footsteps sounded across the room.

"Are you hurt?" Benedict said, as Elinor eased through the partially-open door. "Let me take your arm. Is it your ankle?"

"No," Elinor answered for her cousin, as she closed the door behind her...

...and Penelope threw her arms around Benedict's neck, lunging upwards to kiss his mouth.

Benedict staggered back. "Miss Hathergill—!"

"Too late!" Penelope beamed up at him. "We've been discovered."

"What?" Benedict's gaze went to the closed door, and he blanched. "When was that shut? I thought—"

Elinor crossed her arms. "It's no use, Penelope," she snapped. "I'm the only one who's seen. And I am not convinced."

"What?" Penelope let go of Benedict. "Of course you're convinced! We planned this together, didn't we?"

"You did *what*?" Benedict backed away from both of them, staring at Elinor as if he'd never seen her before.

Only the memory of the guests waiting outside the room gave Elinor the strength not to scream.

"We," she said to Penelope, "did *not* plan this together."

"Of course we did! Don't you remember? You said he wasn't going to propose otherwise, so—"

"I never said that you should do this! I said you should accept Gavin Armitage. Although," Elinor added hastily, "I don't actually think that you should do that, either, now."

"Will you please make up your mind?" Penelope crossed her arms, glaring at her through slitted blue eyes. "You're not making any sense! You know I have to be betrothed by the end of tonight. If you don't want me marrying Mr. Armitage, then—"

"Why didn't you warn me?" Benedict asked Elinor. "If you knew she was going to attempt this—"

"I tried!" Elinor gritted her teeth. "We can discuss all of this later." *I hope*. "But in the meantime, I have to leave immediately, and—"

"Leave?" Benedict started towards her. "What do you mean? What's happened?"

"No one is going anywhere until you both agree that I've been compromised!" Penelope announced. "I *am* going to marry Mr. Hawkins, whether or not you think that it's a good idea."

"You will not." Elinor's gaze fastened on the door half-hidden in the opposite wall; relief soaked through her body. It was the servants' door, and it was exactly the escape route that she and Benedict needed. "You," she said to Penelope, "are going to walk out of this room by yourself. Mr. Hawkins will leave from a different direction. And as I'm the only one who's seen the two of you alone together..."

The door handle turned behind her. The door swung open and hit her hard on her back, knocking her off her feet. She slammed forward onto her hands and knees, hairpins scattering around her. A long hank of hair fell over her eyes, obscuring her vision. Sir Jessamyn fell off her shoulder and tumbled onto the floor with a desperate, low chuckle of fear.

"What the devil is going on here?" said Sir John.

Sir Jessamyn lost control on the glossy wooden floor.

Benedict let out a whispered curse that Elinor had never

heard before. Penelope raced to his side and flung her arms around him, pinning his arms to his sides.

"Papa, I am betrothed!—And compromised," she added hastily. "So we haven't any choice about it."

"What?!"

"She is *not* compromised," said Elinor, "and not betrothed, either!" She pushed herself up, gathering up Sir Jessamyn in a protective embrace. Her hair had come half-undone; she was panting, and she could feel a new bruise forming on the same area of her back that had been injured in her fall a week ago. Still, she raised her head and met Sir John's gaze squarely as the unmistakable stench of dragon slime filled the room. "Your daughter attempted to trick Mr. Hawkins into a compromising situation. Fortunately, I arrived in time to save them both."

Sir John's face was puce with fury. His murderous gaze fastened onto Benedict, who was trying to politely detach himself from Penelope's embrace. "I was told by at least three different people that Mrs. De Lacey had gone tearing from the ballroom into this room by herself. No one else has entered the room in the meantime, and the door has been closed the entire time. How do you explain that, sirrah, except by the fact that you have compromised *my* innocent daughter?"

"But they weren't alone," said Miss Armitage calmly, behind him.

As everyone else turned to stare at her, she glided into the room, composed as always, and closed the door behind her.

"Oh, dear. Has there been a misunderstanding? I was with them the entire time until well after dear Mrs. De Lacey arrived." She shot Elinor a look of pure venom. "Didn't she think to mention that?"

"But..." Sir John scowled. "Where did you go in the meantime, may I ask?"

"Oh, I left by the servant's entrance." Miss Armitage shrugged delicately. "I had torn a bit of lace on my dress. I didn't want anyone else to see me until it was pinned. But as they were safely chaperoned by Mrs. De Lacey when I left—"

"She's lying, Papa!" gasped Penelope. "That isn't what happened at all. She wasn't anywhere near us until now!"

"No," Sir John agreed. "I know she wasn't. Good friends may do their best to save you from an unwanted marriage, pet, but I saw her in the ballroom not five minutes ago, talking to her brother. No one else will believe her, either." He turned on Benedict, shoulders squaring like a bull's. "You, sir, have publicly besmirched my daughter's honor, and you *will* pay the price, whether you care for it or not."

"He did not!" Elinor protested. "Nothing happened between them. I can swear to it!"

"You know as well as I that that makes no difference in the eyes of society." Sir John glared at Benedict. "Well, Mr. Hawkins? Are you ready to come with me back to the ballroom, to make the announcement together to our guests?"

Benedict straightened his shoulders. He squared his chin. "No," he said. "I'm afraid that is not possible. I cannot marry Miss Hathergill, because I am already betrothed."

"What?" Penelope's jaw dropped. She fell back, her arms finally dropping away from him. "You can't be!"

"Already betrothed?" Sir John snapped. "Balderdash. To whom?"

"Benedict…" Elinor whispered.

His eyes met hers, rueful and resigned. One strong shoulder lifted in a shrug.

"To Elinor Tregarth," he said. "Your niece."

CHAPTER 32

Pinpricks of panic raced up and down Elinor's skin. She opened her mouth. No sound emerged.

"My *niece*?" Sir John's words came out as a roar of disbelief. "What the devil—?"

"Elinor?" Penelope shook her head wildly. "But that's not possible!"

"You think not?" Miss Armitage's vivid blue eyes were alight with speculation as they darted back and forth between Benedict and Penelope. "They did meet at an inn the night before he arrived here, didn't they? It must have been a memorable meeting indeed, to bring about such a swift betrothal. Perhaps she has more personal attractions than you'd realized."

Penelope's face was rapidly turning pink with fury. "She

must have tricked him into it! There is *no* other reason any gentleman would *ever*—"

"You mean as you tried to trick me into marriage tonight?" Benedict's voice was sharper-edged than Elinor had ever heard it. "Is that the sort of underhanded, dishonourable trick to which you're referring, Miss Hathergill?"

She stared up at him. "Why—well—that is hardly the same! Anyone would marry me!"

"Not anyone," said Benedict. He looked back at Elinor, his gaze warm and intent. "Not me."

But Penelope's father had already seized upon Miss Armitage's statement. "By God, you're right. I thought it a mere coincidence. But if Hawkins has been in cahoots with my niece all along—good God, we'll have to check his room, see if he's stolen anything himself!"

"Oh, for heaven's sake!" said Elinor, finding her voice at last. "Mr. Hawkins is no thief. If you would simply calm down for a moment, Sir John—"

"Calm down?" Sir John roared. "My daughter has been compromised, her seducer is in league with the wretch who stole from us—and you think I should calm down, ma'am?!"

He kept on roaring, but Elinor had stopped listening. A movement had caught her eye in the corner of her vision: the servants' door cracking open. It slid half an inch back from the wall, then stopped: just far enough to listen, without being seen. *Servants know everything.*

Elinor had a feeling that she knew exactly which servant had come to find out what she was doing now. She took a deep breath. Within the next ten minutes, depending on how well she managed her negotiations, she would either be exposed and imprisoned or else in desperate flight. She had no remaining chance to protect her sisters or her aunt.

But perhaps she did have one last chance, after all, to see one piece of justice done. And at least, this way, she would have fulfilled a promise.

Elinor aimed her voice directly at that crack in the wall. "If you want a real thief, look for Lucinda Grace. I saw her steal your wife's diamond bracelet not half an hour ago."

The door quivered, as if whoever was holding it had given a start of surprise.

Sir John stopped bellowing at Benedict to stare at her.

Penelope said, "Don't be absurd! Lucinda would never—"

"She's done it in the past," Elinor said, "and blamed innocent servants to save herself from being caught. But this time you can all see it for yourself. She'll have hidden the bracelet on her person somewhere. Why don't you go and find out if I'm telling the truth? Lady Hathergill knows; she'll help you do it."

"This is all irrelevant nonsense!" snapped Sir John. "You're trying to distract us, ma'am, and I won't have it. Do you understand me?"

But the servants' door shut, and Elinor knew that her message had been received. She had done her part, as much as she could; now, Sally would have to find a way to finish it herself.

Miss Armitage sighed and moved forward to take control

of the room. "This is all perfectly fascinating, I am sure. But now, if we could all turn our minds to saving Miss Hathergill's reputation, I'm sure my brother would be only too happy to—"

"That won't be necessary," Elinor said. "Mr. Hawkins can leave by the servants' entrance. No one outside this room will ever know that he and Penelope were alone together."

"Excellent plan," Benedict said. His face was solemn, but his eyes were full of mischief as he looked at her. "May I hope that you will accompany me, Mrs. De Lacey?"

Sir John snorted. "Don't be ridiculous. My daughter's début hasn't finished. If you think you can waltz off with our guest of honor after what you've done—"

"I'm afraid you haven't any choice in the matter, Sir John." Elinor drew herself up as proudly as an empress. She set one hand on Sir Jessamyn's glittering scales and felt a surge of pride as he straightened, too, looking brave and astonishingly noble despite the smell of dragon slime that still permeated the room.

Back in the ballroom, her aunt was no doubt telling everyone around her exactly what she had seen. At any moment, the gossip would spread along the corridor. But for these last few moments, Elinor would *be* Mrs. De Lacey for all that she was worth and snatch her only chance to escape.

"If you think I am going to stay for even one more moment in this house..." she began.

But her words were cut off by a sudden commotion in the corridor outside. Guests' voices rose in a muffled roar of shock and horror—then fell silent as one loud, imperious, and utterly unfamiliar voice spoke over all the rest:

"What exactly is going on here, and why are you all staring at me like nincompoops? I know rural society can be vulgar, but really—!"

"Who the devil is that?" Sir John snarled. He started towards the door.

It opened before he could reach it, revealing a footman who looked as if he were about to be sick. As he closed the door behind him, his gaze slid to Elinor, then to Sir John, and back again. He stared at Elinor with as much fascinated revulsion as if she had developed a second head.

She fought the urge to take a step backward. *Be Mrs. De Lacey*, she ordered herself. *Show no fear*.

She lifted her chin to look down her nose at the entire room. *Be Mrs. De Lacey...*

"Well?" Sir John snarled. "What's happened now? Who's set off all that commotion out there?"

"I beg your pardon, Sir John," the footman said. He must have been at least nineteen, but his voice cracked like a boy's as he finally tore his gaze away from Elinor's face. "I had to come and tell you, sir, as quickly as I could. Mrs. De Lacey has arrived."

"OH, BLOODY HELL." Benedict's whisper was only a thread of sound, but it carried perfectly through the room. He started towards Elinor, but she shook her head at him infinitesimally and flicked out her fingers to wave him back as discreetly as she could.

Panic had clouded her head, earlier, when she'd still had time to run. Now, she felt shot through with bleak clarity. She had lost her gamble and her freedom...but she *would not* let him suffer with her.

Sir John didn't spare him a glance. "What are you babbling about?" he asked the footman. "Mrs. De Lacey is *here*. Can't you see that?"

"Yes, sir. But, sir..." The footman swallowed visibly, his Adam's apple bobbing up and down his long throat. "She's out there, too. I saw her myself."

"Don't be absurd! If you're trying to tell me—"

The door opened behind the footman before Sir John could finish.

"Has everyone in this house gone mad? Or does *anyone* remember how to properly greet a guest?"

Mrs. De Lacey swept into the room like a hurricane, sending the footman lurching to one side to get out of her way. Everyone else in the dining room froze in a tableau of shock, even Elinor herself.

It was, of course, the real Mrs. De Lacey. Elinor had seen that nose, that hair, those dark eyes in her mirror every day for nearly a week. They were as familiar as her own features, now. And yet...

"Good God," said Mrs. De Lacey. "Who *are* you?" Even the dragon on her neck—rose-and-purple-scaled, with a long snout and a comfortably round belly—was craning its neck with open fascination. Mrs. De Lacey stroked its neck with absent-minded affection as she said, "I never thought until today that I might have a sister."

They weren't quite the same, after all. Energy vibrated through every one of Mrs. De Lacey's moves and gave vibrant character to her face. Her dark eyes—fixed now on Elinor's face—looked nothing like they had when Elinor had stared hopelessly at her reflection in the mirror.

Her illusion had been only a pale imitation of Mrs. De Lacey's reality.

Crow, her cousin's remembered voice whispered tauntingly through her ears.

Everyone in the room was waiting for her to speak. She looked at the real Mrs. De Lacey. A faint, desperate hope circled inside her.

Sister, she thought. *"I never thought I had a sister..."*

Was it worth a try? If nothing else, it would sound far more plausible than the truth. Elinor moistened her lips. "Well..."

"Ah, there you all are." Lady Hathergill walked in, and did a double-take as she saw Mrs. De Lacey. "Good heavens. So the real one has arrived now, too, eh? Good evening, Sophia. I thought you weren't coming. Putrid sore throat, wasn't it? Or had you decided on a different excuse?"

"I changed my mind at the last moment," said Mrs. De Lacey. She leaned forward for a perfunctory exchange of cheek-kisses with Lady Hathergill, still frowning. "I had heard the most disturbing gossip, you see, and I felt it was my duty to investigate."

"But if you're the real Mrs. De Lacey," said Sir John, "then who the devil is this?"

Lady Hathergill opened her mouth to answer, but Elinor spoke first. Her eyes rested on Benedict, for strength, for reassurance—but most of all, to stop him before he could do anything rash.

"It's Elinor," she said. "I am sorry for the deception, Uncle...but not for anything else."

"Bravo." Ignoring her warning look, Benedict strode forward and took her hand firmly in his.

"No!" Elinor tried to push him away. "You mustn't—"

"Don't even try to send me away." Benedict wrapped his fingers tightly around hers and turned to stand by her side, shoulder-to-shoulder. "I will not abandon you."

"But I don't understand!" Penelope wailed. "That's not Elinor. It can't be! Her hair—her face—they don't look anything alike!"

"You can see the real Elinor when you touch her," Lady Hathergill explained with cheerful matter-of-factness. "Quite the shock it was, too, when I first saw her—I nearly tossed my punch all over myself. Now *that* would have been embarrassing!"

Sir John set his jaw. "You have to touch her to see it, eh?"

"*No.*" Benedict stepped in front of her. "You shall not lay a hand upon her, Sir John."

"You don't have to." Elinor looked around the room, at

her family, at Mrs. De Lacey, at Miss Armitage—who was, of course, watching everything with calculating interest—and at Benedict. Tears pricked her eyes, but she held her head high as she turned to meet her dragon's golden gaze. "I wish," she said clearly, "with all of my heart for *both* of my wishes to be undone."

Sir Jessamyn opened his mouth. Tingling flames rushed across her face, momentarily blinding her. She staggered. She heard her aunt made a loud sound of surprise. She felt someone—Benedict—catch her by her arms. Penelope was letting out a series of gasping shrieks. The entire room was in an uproar.

When her vision cleared, Benedict was all that she could see. He held her close—far closer than was proper—and he was smiling down at her. His hazel eyes were clear; his big hands were warm on her bare upper arms. With every breath, she could feel the closeness of his body, only inches away from hers.

"There you are," he said softly. "It's you, again. Really you. Elinor Tregarth."

"*Elinor Tregarth*," her uncle growled. "By God, you will regret what you've done! As magistrate of this county, I'm placing you under arrest. You'll spend the rest of tonight in gaol...and I'll see you transported for your crimes if it's the last thing I do."

CHAPTER 33

"Not," said Mrs. De Lacey firmly, "until someone explains to me what's going on."

Penelope said, "*She* stole my dragon and lied to us *and* took my fiancé!"

Gritting her teeth, Elinor nudged Benedict out of her way. "He was never your fiancé."

"Not even a future fiancé," Benedict whispered into her ear. He had let go of one of her arms, but he held the other firmly tucked against his side.

"But who is she?" Mrs. De Lacey demanded. She tapped one strong finger against her dragon's side. "Elinor Tregarth...Mary's little sister married a man called Tregarth, didn't she? I hadn't seen her for years by then, of course, but I heard he'd lost his money and then got them both killed. He left their daughters destitute, didn't he?"

"Very sad," Miss Armitage murmured, "but if you'll all excuse me now..."

"No," said Elinor. "Wait!" She moved forward, pulling Benedict with her, to stand between Miss Armitage and the door. Disaster, it seemed, was a state well beyond panic. Once everything had already been lost, there was nothing left to fear...so her brain could finally begin to function properly again. "*I* want to hear about the gossip that brought Mrs. De Lacey here. Those disturbing rumours."

"Isn't it obvious?" Miss Armitage said. "She must have heard that she was known to be here. Why wouldn't she come running to investigate?"

"I don't think that was it," Elinor said. "*She* said it was a matter of duty. I think she was referring to those rumours that you spread in your own letters—the rumours that Sir John was having his own wife declared to be mad."

Penelope let out a squeak of horror. "You *told* people? How could you?"

"The question is," said Mrs. De Lacey coldly, "is it true?"

Sir John's face had moved beyond puce to a mottled medley of colours. "Will everyone stop interfering?" he bellowed. "*I* am the head of this household! I make my own decisions. I—"

"It is perfectly true," said Lady Hathergill. "My husband is a selfish, stupid man who cannot bear to be contradicted, and he is declaring me mad only for his and our daughter's convenience." She blinked. "Good heavens. Nothing was driving me to say any of that...but I said it anyway. And it felt delightful!"

"You will soon feel even better," said Mrs. De Lacey grimly. "Sir John is about to re-consider his scheme."

"The devil I will!" Sir John stomped towards her, bullish shoulders squared. "I have had quite enough of being ordered around by you, ma'am, one way or another, across this past week! If you think you can tell me how to manage my own wife—"

"I can tell you," Mrs. De Lacey said, raising her right hand in warning, "that I have the ears of every hostess in London. I couldn't stop my dearest friend from marrying you all those years ago, but now, at least, I have the power to protect her from your abuse. If you make any move to confine her against her will, I will see your daughter black-balled and a social outcast. She won't even be allowed to glance at the front door of Almack's."

Penelope let out a scream of horror. "Papa! You won't—you can't let her—"

"There is," said Miss Armitage, "another solution." She stepped into the center of the room and waited for all eyes to turn to her before she continued. "My brother, as you all know, is passionately in love with Miss Hathergill. He would be more than happy to announce their betrothal now, tonight, at her début ball. As a matron of substance, she will be far safer from the social tyranny of Mrs. De Lacey, and you, Sir John, will be quite free to do as you like in your own household. As you should be." She smiled, dark eyelashes drifting down to conceal her eyes.

"You really are a despicable creature," Lady Hathergill said.

Even in the midst of fury, Elinor felt a moment of true admiration. Her aunt, it seemed, had not lost her ability to tell the truth or to stand up to injustice anymore.

Sir John frowned thoughtfully. "Penelope does like him—"

"I can't be an outcast," Penelope breathed. "I just can't!"

Sir John nodded. "In that case..."

Elinor stared at Miss Armitage with open loathing. A smile was playing at the corners of the other girl's mouth. She looked, of course, as unlike her brother as two people could look, but their danger felt exactly equal. And...

Wait.

Elinor felt her pulse speed up against her throat. She swallowed hard as an impossible idea blossomed inside her.

"Wait," she breathed. "*Wait.*"

"What is it?" Benedict said.

"She and her brother *knew* from the beginning," said Elinor. "They knew *exactly* what had happened to your father, even though you had kept it so carefully secret. But they *didn't tell Sir John*. There was never any reason for them to keep their silence on that, especially when they were so desperate to betroth Mr. Armitage to Penelope—unless *they* were too afraid to risk bringing up the topic."

Miss Armitage's eyes flared open. "You're speaking

nonsense. And as you're no more than a penniless hanger-on who is about to be transported—"

"No one had heard of them in London until this past year," said Elinor. "They appeared out of nowhere, complete with wealth and a newly-purchased estate. No one had even heard of their whole *family* before."

"That is true," Mrs. De Lacey agreed judiciously, "although we must remember that many wealthy families newly-arrived in Society do prefer to make a mystery of their background. Take Sir John, for instance, who likes to pretend that he does *not* come from a background of low trade."

Sir John scowled. "Look here, ma'am—"

"*And* she looks nothing like her brother," Elinor added. "But we do all know of another charming couple who are also exceptionally persuasive...and good at keeping secrets."

Realization dawned in Benedict's eyes. "You don't really think—"

"She *can't* think!" Miss Armitage snapped. "None of you should listen to her. You all know exactly who she is! You told me about her, remember, Penelope? How useless, how pathetic, how utterly plain and unwanted by anybody—"

"I may be all of those things," Elinor said, "but I am *right*."

Knowledge surged through her with the force of true power. She pulled her arm free from Benedict's support and stepped forward to glare at Miss Armitage, eye-to-eye. "You," she said. "Armitage is *not* your name. And that man you arrived with is not your brother!"

"What are you talking about?" Penelope demanded. "What would *you* know about fashionable people or society?"

"I read the society columns," said Elinor, "and I remember the stories I've been told. So *I* believe that Mr. 'Armitage' is actually her husband. His betrothal to you would be illegal, and *you* would be attempting bigamy with it. He and his so-called sister are the same pair of fraudsters who came up with a so-called investment scheme and stole all of the money from my and Benedict's fathers, among other unfortunates."

Penelope collapsed onto a chair. "*Bigamy*?"

Miss Armitage said, "I am not going to stand here listening to this libel from a nobody. I'm leaving!"

"I don't think so." Benedict moved to bar the door, his face white with rage. "I've wanted to catch the fraudsters who ruined my father's life for over a year now. I, for one, will *not* let you go."

"But why does he even want to marry Penelope, if he's already married?" Lady Hathergill inquired.

"Quite!" said Miss Armitage. "An excellent point. Thank you, Lady Hathergill."

"Oh, don't thank me." Lady Hathergill's nostrils flared with disdain. "*You* want to see me locked up for my husband's convenience. I'm only asking my niece a question, because I want to hear *her* answer."

"He doesn't want to marry her," said Elinor. "He only wants an official betrothal. It has to be because of her famous fortune." All of the pieces were snapping into place, now. She'd spent the last week worrying so much about her own disguise, she'd barely noticed all of the clues that the other two had dropped. Now they all came back to her in a rush. "They arrived unexpectedly early because they'd canceled a different visit. They took care to frighten away all of her other male visitors by spreading false rumours of her mother's madness. Now they're desperate to have a public announcement of the betrothal by the end of tonight."

"They're in a hurry," Benedict said. "In other words, they've been found out."

"*Exactly*. Someone must have discovered their secret." Elinor crossed her arms. "I may be a nobody," she told Miss Armitage. "I may be just as penniless and as powerless as you and your husband both *made* me when you tricked my father into handing over everything. But I still have my common sense. So *I* think you're planning to blackmail a fortune out of Sir John the very moment that Penelope publicly and undeniably commits herself to your husband...a fortune that the two of you can carry with you when you flee the country afterwards."

"*Because*," Benedict finished with unmistakable relish, "you can't carry your grand new estate with you, can you? That's the estate, of course, that you bought with *our* parents' money, as your introduction to Society."

Sir John, for once, said nothing at all. He had staggered back a step and was staring at Miss Armitage as if she were a poisonous snake. Mrs. De Lacey, though, took a step closer, and regarded her with dark eyebrows raised disdainfully.

"I never cared for you *or* your so-called brother," she said finally. "An untrustworthy, slippery pair, the two of you. Born blackmailers, I always thought. I am not at all surprised."

Lady Hathergill kept her own mouth shut and—for once, lately—did not speak. But she did smile with perfect satisfaction.

Miss Armitage's lips curled as she looked around the room. "You have no proof," she said, "and you cannot hold me here without it. Sir John—and the *real* Mrs. De Lacey—I bid you both goodnight."

An unexpected voice spoke from the other end of the room.

"Miss Tregarth might not have proof," said Sally as she stepped through the servants' door, "but I do."

* * *

LADY HATHERGILL SAID, "Is that one of our maids?"

"Sally." Elinor took a step forward, trying to read the other girl's face. Was this revenge, or something completely different? "I'm sorry I haven't—"

"Oh, yes, you have," said Sally, and her smile was fierce. "Poor Miss Lucinda had the misfortune of bumping into a maid carrying a whole tray of champagne glasses, not twenty minutes ago. What do you think came falling out of her gown right in front of everyone—including that very lady whose fan she'd tried to steal last month? Lady Hathergill's diamond bracelet, *that's* what! There's no covering up for her thievery anymore—and everybody knows, now, that she must have been behind those earlier thefts, too."

"Thank goodness," Elinor said. "Your sister is safe."

"What the devil are you two talking about? And why is one of our maids talking at all?" Sir John roared.

Sally bobbed a curtsey. "Beg pardon, sir, but I couldn't help overhearing, and I thought I should mention what I found in Miss Armitage's room."

Servants know everything, Elinor thought. A smile spread across her own face, to match Sally's wide grin.

Miss Armitage's face had paled. "If you are all going to start listening to a *maid* now—"

"Oh, I didn't think anyone ever would," said Sally, "but Miss Tregarth has done me a true favor, so I thought that I should do her one in return."

She reached into the pocket of her apron and withdrew a sheaf of papers. Miss Armitage made a muffled sound of protest as she saw them, and Sally's eyes widened in innocent surprise.

"I've only brought your marriage lines for you, ma'am. Aren't you glad? You forgot to lock your box this morning, you see, so I thought I'd better keep them safe for you. I brought the deed to your husband's estate, too—I must say, I thought it more than odd that he was carrying *that* with him. Not the usual sort of thing you'd bring along for a week-long jaunt to a house party."

"You are *brilliant*," said Elinor. "Oh, Sally. Thank you!"

Sally's face was flushed as she met Elinor's gaze, but she held her chin high. "I gathered other things, too," she said to Elinor, "in case I needed them. But you proved me wrong, miss, and helped me even when you didn't need to anymore. I won't do any less in return. I did listen to what you said last week, you know. But I couldn't hold back when Daisy needed protecting."

"I understand," Elinor said. She looked at Benedict, standing before the door, strong and true and on her side forever, and she thought of her sisters. "I would have done the same."

There was a sudden flutter of skirts—Miss Armitage making a dash for the open door to the servants' passageway. Benedict and Sir John both started forward.

But it was Sally who stuck out a foot and tripped her neatly, sending the other girl sprawling on the floor.

"Oops." Sally smiled at Elinor. "Two accidents in one evening. How clumsy I'm becoming!"

CHAPTER 34

Three footmen marched Miss Armitage away, while another four were ordered to apprehend her 'brother.' Still, once they had left, Sir John sagged into a chair as if he were the one who had lost after all.

"I would have betrothed my own daughter to that rascal," he said heavily. "Good God. If that came out...if anyone knew how close we had come to catastrophe..."

"It's a good thing that Elinor saved you, then" said Benedict. He crossed his arms. "Now tell me, Sir John: how exactly do you plan to show your niece your gratitude?"

Penelope leaped up from her own chair, her face infused with sudden panic. "Papa, you cannot send Mama away. Not anymore! If Mr. Hawkins is betrothed, and Mr. Armitage is married—"

"That's right," Elinor said. "There is no one left for you to engage yourself to before your London season."

Penelope worried at her lower lip. "Perhaps that Mr. Aubrey...?"

Elinor rolled her eyes, but Benedict was the one who answered. "You are not tricking Aubrey into a betrothal. I won't allow it."

"Everyone is against me. No one cares how I feel!" Penelope's lower lip wobbled. "Papa, please..."

He sighed and turned to meet his wife's eyes. "Will you swear to behave yourself and hold your tongue from now on?"

"No," said Lady Hathergill tartly, "I shall not. I've held my tongue for the past twenty years, and it's nearly suffocated me. I won't do it for even one more day!"

"You won't need to," said Mrs. De Lacey. "You can come and stay with me in London, join my new club for ladies, and flaunt all of your adventures in your husband's face. We may not have *quite* the relationship we once did, but I think it has finally been enough years for both of us to forgive that old break and form a new kind of friendship. I do like people who speak their minds. I like it even more when I can mend fences *and* irritate a man I've always loathed."

She smiled sharply at Sir John. "You won't spread any more rumours about your wife's sanity, now, will you? I can promise that neither you nor your daughter would care for the results."

"No," Sir John muttered. "No. But..." Breathing heavily, he

swung on Elinor. "But as for you, young lady, you will hand back my daughter's dragon immediately!"

Elinor flung a protective hand across Sir Jessamyn, but Penelope was the one who let out a gasp of protest. "Oh, no! I'm not letting that horrible creature anywhere near me!"

Sir Jessamyn hunched onto Elinor's shoulder, glaring at his former mistress. Penelope's finger shook as she pointed at him.

"Didn't you see what he did? Shooting flame all over Elinor's face? Tricking us all? He's a monster!" She shuddered. "I wouldn't trust him for an instant. I'm not allowing any dragons onto my shoulder ever again."

Elinor opened her mouth, a hot retort burning on her tongue—but Benedict shook his head at her. *Careful*, he mouthed.

She took a steadying breath. Benedict was right. The last thing she needed was to persuade Penelope *not* to fear Sir Jessamyn after all.

But she looked at the little dragon on her shoulder, who had sat there proudly and without fear through all the shouting and commotion of the past hour, and she let all of her love and admiration shine in her expression.

He nuzzled her face. She stroked his neck, admiring the brand-new golden markings that had spread along his left side, completing the pattern.

His magic had led them to triumph, and they both knew it.

"Fine," Sir John said heavily. "Fine. You may all leave, and the devil take every one of you! But what am I to do about that couple of serpents who are locked away upstairs? If I have them arrested and they go to trial, they'll embarrass the whole family with their revelations. But I can't just let them go merrily on their way after what they've done."

"But you have to arrest them," Benedict said. "They are criminals. What they did to my family—and to Elinor's—"

"I," said Sir John, drawing himself up, "am still the magistrate in this county. *I* make those decisions, not you, young man. And I can still decide to arrest your fiancée for theft if I so choose! Don't make me regret my generosity."

Benedict pressed his lips tightly shut, but Elinor saw the struggle still working on his face. She shared it.

To let them go free, after all that they had done...

She thought of her sisters, scattered across Britain. Of Benedict's own family, about to lose their estate.

Their estate...

"Don't," she said. Her voice sounded half-strangled, and wholly unlike herself. She had to clear her throat to speak. "Don't let them go on their way as they please. They wanted to flee the country with a fortune blackmailed from you *and* with the deed to their estate, too, so that they could sell it. Don't let them."

Sir John glowered at her. "I just told Hawkins—"

"What perfect justice." A smile hovered at the edges of Mrs. De Lacey's mouth. "I believe I approve of you, young Elinor. It's no wonder you managed to pass yourself off as me for so long. You have a sense of style."

"Elinor?" Penelope snorted. "*What* style?"

"A flair for justice," said Mrs. De Lacey. "That is what you intend, isn't it, Elinor? They meant to sell their estate once they were safely distant from England. But the estate wasn't bought with their money. It was bought with yours."

"And Benedict's," Elinor said. "If Mr. Armitage signs the deed over to him, in exchange for his freedom..."

"...Then I can sell it to save my own estate—the one he ruined." There was colour in Benedict's cheeks again and a half-wild look in his eyes. "My brothers...my niece... but even more than that. Everyone's been talking about how grand his estate is. It must be worth ten times more than Kennington Park! That means we'll have plenty of money left over to share with the other families they hurt."

Elinor nodded. "We'll track down all of the others that he and his wife tricked. We can help to save them, too."

"You won't make all the money back," Mrs. De Lacey warned them. "The amount that he and his wife must have spent on their clothes alone during this past Season, not to mention all those theater tickets, champagne soirées and so on..."

"But we can do *something*," Elinor said, and swallowed hard. She was trying to rein in the tears of mingled relief and wonder that wanted to escape before them all. She had to remember her common sense and not allow exhilaration to carry her away too soon.

It would take time to sell the Armitages' estate—weeks, if

not months. By the time all of the legal and financial wrangles were sorted, it might be autumn or even winter.

But she *would* see her sisters again, after all. Once everything was cleared, she could offer them a home to share. And for the first time in a year, she, Elinor Tregarth, was no longer helpless. She could be a true force for good, as her own mother had been.

Sir John scowled. "I don't know..."

"Do you not?" said Mrs. De Lacey. She raised her eyebrows. "The other option, of course, is that I could begin to catch up on my correspondence. I'm sure that everyone I know in London would be *most* interested to learn what happened here, tonight, in every—single—detail."

Penelope had already moved on. "But if Mama is going to live with *you*, Mrs. De Lacey..." She frowned. "...Then she will be more fashionable than me, won't she? That doesn't make any sense!"

Lady Hathergill sighed and looked at her daughter with a decidedly jaundiced eye. "In that case," she said, "you will have to think very hard about becoming a respectful daughter from now on, won't you? Perhaps there is hope for you yet."

Penelope looked horrified.

Sally bobbed a curtsey and backed away from the family group, leaving her sheaf of papers on the long dining room table. Among them, Elinor recognized a familiar package of letters, wrapped together in ribbon. She didn't have to look any closer to recognize her sisters' handwriting.

She caught Sally's eye. Sally closed one eye in a wink.

We're even, she mouthed, and left through the servants' door.

* * *

Two hours later, Elinor left Hathergill Hall for good...for the second time that week. This time, she walked out through the front door rather than skulking out a back entrance. Benedict walked on one side and Mr. Aubrey on the other. Sir Jessamyn sat tall and proud upon her shoulder, glancing about at the remaining guests with regal condescension. His gold markings glittered magnificently about his mouth and chin in the candlelight.

Mrs. De Lacey and Lady Hathergill would be staying the night, but Elinor couldn't wait any longer to escape—and as neither she nor Benedict was willing to wait long for their wedding to take place, there was little left to fear about the impropriety of it.

"Back to the inn again, I'm afraid," Benedict said cheerfully, as he helped her into Aubrey's carriage. It was already stacked with books and papers, which had taken nearly an hour to pack. "I do hope they have the same private dining room available. I have good memories of that room."

Aubrey was still glowering even as a footman closed the door, stuffing the last few papers into the footwell. As the coachman cracked his whip and the horses set off into the moonlight, he said, "I cannot believe that you wasted your last wish! Of all the worst nonsense in fairy tales, to spend your last wish un-wishing the first two..."

"How would you have spent it?" asked Elinor, with genuine curiosity.

"Yes, do tell us, Aubrey." Beside her, Benedict stretched out his legs. They pressed companionably against Elinor's, sending tingles of warm promise up her skin. She could only just glimpse his smile in the shadows of the carriage. "You've obviously spent a deal of time thinking through these matters, for someone who *claims* to hate fairy tales so much."

"I despise them," said Aubrey coldly, "and I always have. But *if* I ever had the chance myself..."

"Oh, you must." Elinor leaned forward. "You've spent so many years studying dragons, Mr. Aubrey. Why shouldn't you have one of your own as a companion?"

"An excellent point," Benedict agreed. "Come, Aubrey, you know now how misguided your theoretical research has been. Why not get a dragon of your own and find out the real truth? Or are you too afraid of getting mixed up in irrational magic yourself?"

"I am not afraid of anything," Mr. Aubrey said with dignity. "But you know I must go to Wales first. I am already a full week overdue. And fortunately, it is quite clear that the irrational, *magical* sort of dragon is not common."

"Not common at all." Elinor ran an admiring hand along Sir Jessamyn's back, and he stretched luxuriantly in her lap, letting out a noisy belch. He had eaten so many canapés in the past hour, as they had waited to leave, that it was a wonder he could even move at all. "Greedy pig," she said fondly. Then she leaned closer and whispered into one pointed ear, "My hero."

"Dragons certainly are more interesting than *I'd* ever realized before this week," said Benedict. "But you know, Aubrey, they're not the only kind of magic in the world. You might want to make an attempt, after all, at getting yourself some of the other sort, too."

Elinor looked up, frowning. "What do you mean?"

Grinning, Benedict leaned closer, running one finger across the back of her hand.

"Oh, for God's sake, Hawkins," Mr. Aubrey moaned. "If you're going to get all lovey-dovey just because you've finally found a girl to marry, I'm not even going to talk to you any longer. I'll read a book instead."

An irrepressible giggle built up in the back of Elinor's throat as she peered through the shadows between her fiancé and the friend who sat across from them. "It is rather dark," she pointed out meekly. "It may be difficult to read."

"All the same," said Mr. Aubrey, "it's far better than listening to him babble. *That's* the danger of romantic love, you see. It completely ruins a good man's intellect."

He picked up a book and held it pointedly in front of his face, where it remained as a shield for the rest of their journey.

So Elinor spent the rest of the carriage ride dreaming

with Benedict about their future, hands interlaced, while her dragon snored in her lap across the miles with perfectly undignified satisfaction.

WHAT COMES NEXT

Thank you so much to everyone who's read this first Regency Dragons rom-com! All three Tregarth sisters will have their own dragon-influenced romantic adventures, and Rose has her turn next, with *Claws and Contrivances,* a fake betrothal, and a most unexpected romantic hero (whom you've already met) coming in July 2023. Snap it up!

Also, make sure to sign up to my newsletter to get all the updates on this and my other upcoming books:

www.stephanieburgis.com/newsletter

In the meantime, though, if you'd like to read a very different kind of Regency fantasy rom-com, why not check out my Harwood Spellbook series? In that version of nineteenth-century England, Boudicca successfully expelled the Romans long ago. Now a powerful Boudiccate of practical, hard-headed ladies rules the nation of *Angland*. For centuries, they've left the whole realm of magic to the more 'naturally' emotional and irrational gentlemen...but no one wants to follow the rules forever, do they? ;)

Dive in with *Snowspelled* (Volume I) and then enjoy the full series, which is packed with romantic gentlemen, ambitious ladies, dangerous elves, giant trolls, pining ex-lovers, underwater balls, and magical fey shenanigans!

Or, for a spookier kind of rom-com, preorder *Good Neighbors*, my collection of cozy fantasy rom-com stories and novellas charting the romance of a grumpy inventor and her outrageous neighbor in the big black castle down the road.

You can find out more (and read excerpts from all of my novels and novellas) on my website:

www.stephanieburgis.com

To stay up to date with *all* of my new releases (and get the chance to win advance reading copies of my new books), sign up for my newsletter:

www.stephanieburgis.com/newsletter

To get early copies of all of my independently-published ebooks *and* take part in my monthly Dragons' Book Club, sign up to my Patreon (where *Scales and Sensibility* was first published as a weekly serial across 2021):

www.patreon.com/stephanieburgis

And most of all, if you have the time and energy to review *Scales and Sensibility* online, I would be incredibly grateful. Word-of-mouth makes a huge difference, especially with a new series. Thank you!

AN EXCERPT FROM SNOWSPELLED

CHAPTER ONE

Of course, a sensible woman would never have accepted the invitation in the first place.

To attend a week-long house party filled with bickering gentleman magicians, ruthlessly cutthroat lady politicians, and worst of all, my own infuriating ex-fiancé? Scarcely two months after I had scandalized all of our most intimate friends by jilting him?

Utter madness. And anyone would have seen that immediately...except for my incurably romantic sister-in-law.

Unfortunately, Amy saw the invitation pop into mid-air beside me as we sat *en famille* at the breakfast table that morning. She watched with bright interest as I crumpled it up a moment later in disgust...and then she dashed around the table, with surprising agility despite her interesting condition, to snatch the ball of paper from my hands before I could toss it into the blazing fire where it belonged.

Naturally, I lunged to retrieve it. But I was too late.

The moment she smoothed it out enough to read the details, her eyes lit up with near-fanatical ardor. "Oh, *yes*, Cassandra, we *must* go! Just think: you will finally see Wrexham again!"

"I know," I said through gritted teeth. "That is exactly why we are going to refuse it!"

"Now, love..." Her eyes widened, and she gave me her most innocent look...which put me on guard immediately.

Kind-hearted, loyal, and *adorable* are all phrases that may apply very well to my brother's wife; *innocent* is not one of them, and never has been.

She had, after all, been my mother's final and most promising political protégée.

"I should think," she said now, as if idly, "that you would wish to show everyone how little notice you take of any gossip. After all, if we refuse this invitation, you know everyone will say it was because you were too afraid to see Wrexham again."

My teeth ground together. "I am *not* afraid of seeing Wrexham."

"Well, *I* know that," Amy said, looking as smug as a cat licking up fresh cream. "But does *he*?"

Well. It isn't that I don't know when I'm being managed. But there are some possibilities that cannot be borne. And the thought of my ex-fiancé's dark eyebrows rising in his most fiendishly supercilious look at the news of my cowardly refusal...

I drummed my fingers against the table, searching for a way out.

Behind my brother's outspread newspaper, an apparently disembodied voice spoke. "Better leave early," my brother said. "It's meant to snow next week, according to the weather wizards."

Amy sat back, smiling and resting her hands on her rounded belly...

And that was how the three of us ended up rattling through the elven dales in mid-winter, with the first flakes of snow falling around our carriage.

Find out what happens next in *Snowspelled*, Volume I of The Harwood Spellbook

ACKNOWLEDGMENTS

Thank you so much to the beta-readers who cheered on my first draft of this book all the way back in 2010 and then kept on reminding me about it over the years, arguing for me to keep my faith in this story as I waited for the market to shift: Jenn Reese, Patrick Samphire, Tricia Sullivan, Tiffany Trent, and Karen Healey. I appreciate all of you so much!

Thank you to everyone who took the time to critique this book for me, whether in its original form or in its 2021 re-conception: Patrick Samphire, Jenn Reese, Marissa Lingen, Claire Fayers, Mette Ivie Harrison, and Barry Goldblatt. All of your thoughtful feedback made a big difference!

Thank you so much to the sharp-eyed readers who helped me catch typos and other mistakes along the way as I first posted these chapters on Patreon: Jenn Greiving, Karen Kisner, Fiona Morton, TheSFReader, Katrina Middelburg, Elisa Wiik, Julia Knowles, and Risa Bobroff Myers. You made this book better for everyone!

Thank you to Ravven for designing the utterly gorgeous front cover of this book and to Patrick Samphire for designing the spine and back cover of the paperback edition.

Thank you to my wonderful agent, Molly Ker Hawn, for selling the audio rights for me and being a fierce advocate every time I needed you (and reminding me to *rest* when I needed that, too).

And thank you so much to all of my patrons, who kept me such fabulous company as I serialized this novel over the course of 2021! I absolutely loved reading your comments and conversations about every new chapter along the way.

Specifically, thank you to Abigail Gawith, A. C. Bauer, Alexis, Ali Baker, Amanda Taylor-Chaisson, Amber Alexander, Amy K., Anna M., Anne Nesbet, Asha Hartland, Beatrice Berendonk, Brandi Blackburn, Brooke Johnson, Cara Scheffler, Charlotte Taylor, Cheresse Burke, Courtney Havens, Creektaken, D. Franklin, d+tee, Dana Levy, Daniel Fishman, David Schwartz, Deb Horng, Deborah Dakin, Delia Sherman, Demet Charlotte Hoffmeyer-Zlotnik, Doreen Farrar, Edmond Hyland, Elisa Wiik, Elizabeth Chuter, Elizabeth Gentry, Eric Schneider, Fiona Morton, Francene Lewis, Gabe Krabbe, Gail Morse, H. Nieuwenhuijzen, Heather Holt, Holly Westlund, Intisar Khanani, Jacqueline Seamon, Jasmine Stairs, Jen Stiles, Jenn Greiving, Jenn Reese, Jenni, Jim Burke, Jim Dean, Joanna, Jody Myers, Julia Knowles, Julia Linthicum, Julia Rios, Kara Snow, Karen Keyte, Karen Kisner, Karen Riegle, Kate Proctor, Katharine, Kathleen Sheppard, Kathy Martin, Katrina Middelburg, Kayden Harper, Kimberly M. Lowe, Konstanze Tants, Kyna Foster, Lab, Laura B., Laura Watkins, Lauren, Leanne Rabesa, Leng M., Libby Gorman, Lillian Tschudi-Campbell, Linda Duvall, Lindsay

Eager, Lisa Moore, Liz, Llinos Cathryn Wynn-Jones, Lora Timonin, Lydia San Andres, Mariam Zama, Marissa Lingen, Mary Anne Anderson, Mary Grove, Mary Perthen, Mary-Anne Mitchell, Melita Kennedy, Melody, Michael Bernardi, Michele Wellck, Molly Van Ryn, Morgana Kay, Mynda Cruz, Nancy Glassman, Naomi Twery, Navessa Allen, Nicola, Nicole Hunter, Pamela, Patricia Anderson, Rachel Halpern, Rebecca, Rebecca Joseph French, Robert Tienken, Rosemary Claire Smith, Roxanne Baechler-Gill, Rupal Patel, S.P., Sadie Slater, Sam Karpierz, Sandstone, Sara Carmody, Sara Glassman, Sarah Cannon, Sarah Fleming, Sarah Fünke, Sarah Swarbrick, S.B. Beasley, Selina Lock, Sharon Corbet, Solomon Foster, Sorrel Jones, Stitchy Adri, Susan Franzblau, Susannah Cooke, Tahmi DeSchepper, Tamara Case, The SF Reader, Vickie R., Victoria Cook, Virginia Farris, and Vivian Behrman.

I appreciate every single one of you *so much,* and you all brightened 2021 for me.

ABOUT THE AUTHOR

Stephanie Burgis grew up in Michigan but now lives in Wales, surrounded by castles, mountains, and coffeeshops, with her husband (fellow writer Patrick Samphire), their two children, and their very vocal tabby cat, Pebbles. She writes wildly romantic historical fantasy novels and fun MG fantasy adventure novels, and has also published over forty short stories in various magazines and anthologies. Find out more and read excerpts from all of her novels and novellas on her website: **www.stephanieburgis.com**

www.ingramcontent.com/pod-product-compliance
Lightning Source LLC
Chambersburg PA
CBHW020528310726
48979CB00014B/2258/J

* 9 7 8 1 7 3 9 1 1 7 6 2 7 *